Praise for the nationally bestselling author Elizabeth Peters

"Elizabeth Peters really knows how to spin romance and adventure into a mystery."
Boston Herald American

"Elizabeth Peters is nothing less than a certified American treasure."
Clarion-Ledger (MS)

"Elizabeth Peters is a wickedly clever intellectual with a sharp sense of irony, whose women are smart, strong, bold, cunning and highly educated, just like herself."
San Diego Reader

"What's more fun than an Elizabeth Peters book? Not much that's legal!"
Salisbury Post (NC)

Books by Elizabeth Peters

THE FALCON AT THE PORTAL*
THE APE WHO GUARDS THE BALANCE*
SEEING A LARGE CAT*
THE HIPPOPOTAMUS POOL*
NIGHT TRAIN TO MEMPHIS
THE SNAKE, THE CROCODILE AND THE DOG*
THE LAST CAMEL DIED AT NOON* • NAKED ONCE MORE
THE DEEDS OF THE DISTURBER* • TROJAN GOLD
LION IN THE VALLEY* • THE MUMMY CASE*
DIE FOR LOVE • SILHOUETTE IN SCARLET
THE COPENHAGEN CONNECTION
THE CURSE OF THE PHARAOHS* • THE LOVE TALKER
SUMMER OF THE DRAGON • STREET OF THE FIVE MOONS
DEVIL-MAY-CARE • LEGEND IN GREEN VELVET
CROCODILE ON THE SANDBANK*
THE MURDERS OF RICHARD III
BORROWER OF THE NIGHT • THE SEVENTH SINNER
THE NIGHT OF FOUR HUNDRED RABBITS
THE DEAD SEA CIPHER • THE CAMELOT CAPER
THE JACKAL'S HEAD

Coming May 2, 2000 in Hardcover

HE SHALL THUNDER IN THE SKY*

*Amelia Peabody mysteries

ELIZABETH PETERS

STREET OF THE FIVE MOONS

A VICKY BLISS MYSTERY

AVON BOOKS, INC.
An Imprint of HarperCollins*Publishers*
10 East 53rd Street
New York, New York 10022-5299

Copyright © 1978 by Elizabeth Peters
Excerpt from *He Shall Thunder in the Sky* copyright © 2000 by MPM Manor, Inc.
Inside cover author photo by Osmund Geier
Published by arrangement with the author
ISBN: 0-380-73121-5
www.harpercollins.com

First Avon Books Printing: March 2000

AVON TRADEMARK REG. U.S. PAT. OFF. AND IN OTHER COUNTRIES, MARCA REGISTRADA, HECHO EN U.S.A.

Printed in the U.S.A.

WCD 10 9 8 7 6 5 4 3 2 1

*To Sara and Dave
and all the other Davidsons
with love*

One

I WAS SITTING AT MY DESK DOING MY NAILS when the door opened and the spy sneaked in. He was wearing one of those trench coats that have pockets and flaps and shoulder straps all over them. The collar was turned up so that it practically met the brim of the hat he had pulled down over his eyebrows. His right hand was in the coat pocket. The pocket bulged.

"*Guten Morgen*, Herr Professor," I said. "*Wie geht's?*"

Wie geht's is not elegant German. It has become an Americanism, like chop suey. I speak excellent German, but Herr Professor Doktor Schmidt was amused when I resorted to slang. He has a kooky sense of humor anyhow. Schmidt is my boss at the National Museum, and when he's in his right mind he is one of the foremost medieval historians in the world. Occasionally he isn't in what most people would call his right mind. He's a frustrated romantic. What he really wants to be is a musketeer, wearing boots and a sword as long as he is; or a pirate; or, as in this case, a spy.

He swept his hat off with a flourish and leered at me. It breaks me up to watch Schmidt leer. His face isn't designed for any expression except a broad Father Christmas grin. He keeps trying to raise one eyebrow, but he can't control the muscles, so they both go up, and his blue eyes twinkle, and his mouth puckers up like a cherub's.

"How goes it, babe?" he inquired, in an accent as thick as Goethe's would have been if he had spoken English—which he may have done, for all I know. That's not my field. My field is medieval Europe, with a minor in art history. I'm good at it, too. At this point it is safe to admit that I got my job at the museum in Munich through a certain amount of—well, call it polite pressure. Professor Schmidt and I had met while he was under the influence of one of his secondary personalities—a worldly, sophisticated crook, like Arsene Lupin. We had both been looking for a missing art object, and some of the good doctor's activities toward this end might not have struck his scholarly colleagues as precisely proper. No, it was not blackmail—not exactly—and anyway, now that I had been on the job for almost a year, Schmidt was the first to admit that I earned my keep. He didn't even mind my working on my novel during office hours, so long as I took care of pressing business first. And let's face it—there are few life-and-death issues in medieval history.

Professor Schmidt's eyes fell on the pile of typescript at my right elbow.

"How goes the book?" he inquired. "Did you get the heroine out of the brothel?"

"She isn't in a brothel," I explained, for the fifth or sixth time. Schmidt is mildly obsessed by brothels—the literary kind, I mean. "She's in a harem. A Turkish harem, in the Alhambra."

Professor Schmidt's eyes took on the familiar academic gleam.

"The Alhambra was not—"

"I know, I know. But the reader won't. You are too concerned with accuracy, Herr Professor. That's why you can't write a popular dirty book, like me. I'm stuck for the moment, though. There have been too many popular books about Turks and harems. I'm trying to think of an original example of lust. It isn't easy."

Professor Schmidt pondered the question. I didn't really want to hear his idea of what constituted original lust, so I said quickly, "But I distract you, sir. What did you want to see me about?"

"Ah." Schmidt leered again. He took his hand out of his pocket.

It didn't hold a gun, of course. I had not expected a gun. I had expected an apple or a fistful of candy; Schmidt's potbelly is the result of day-long munching. But at the sight of what emerged, clasped tenderly in his pudgy fingers, I gasped.

Don't be misled by the gasp. This is not going to be one of those books in which the heroine keeps shrieking and fainting and catching her breath. I'm not the fainting type, and not much surprises me. I'm not that old (still on the right side of thirty), but my unfortunate physical characteristics have exposed me to many educational experiences.

Let me make it perfectly clear that I am not kidding when I refer to my figure as unfortunate. I'm too tall, almost six feet; I inherited a healthy, rounded body, from my Scandinavian ancestors, along with dark-blue eyes and lots of blond hair; I don't gain weight, so the said body is slender in what are supposed to be the right places. As far as I'm concerned, they are the wrong places. All you Ugly Ducklings out there, take heart; you are better off than you realize. When people love you, they love the important things about you, the things that endure after wrinkles and middle-aged spread have set in—your brains and your personality and your sense of humor. When people look at me, all they see is a blown-up centerfold. Nobody takes me seriously. When I was younger, I wanted to be little and cuddly and cute. Now I'd settle for being flat-chested and myopic. It would save a lot of wear and tear on my nerves.

Sorry about the tirade. But it isn't easy to convince people that you've got a brain when all they can see are curves and flowing blond hair. Nor is it easy for a woman like me to get a job. Intellectual women mistrust me on sight. Intellectual men are just like all other men, they hire me—but for the wrong reasons. That was why meeting Professor Schmidt was such a break. Bless his heart, he's as innocent as he looks. He really thinks I am brilliant. If he were six feet four and thirty years younger, I'd marry him.

He beamed at me as he stood there in his spy costume, with his hand outstretched; and the object on his palm glowed and shimmered, almost as if it were smiling too.

It was a pendant, made of gold richly embellished with filigree volutes and leaf shapes. Two tiny gold figures of kneeling women supported the rigid loop through which a chain had once passed. All around the heavy gold rim were stones set in filigree frames—stones of green and red and pearly white. In the center was an enormous azure-blue stone, translucent as water contained in a crystal dome. There was a flaw in the central stone, a flaw that looked like a small rough-hewn cross.

A casual eye might have taken those stones for irregular, roughly polished chunks of glass. Mine is not a casual eye, however.

"The Charlemagne talisman," I said. "Schmidt, old buddy—put it back, okay? You can't get away with it; somebody is sure to notice it's gone."

"You think I have stolen it?" Schmidt grinned even more broadly. "But how do you suppose I have removed it from the case without setting off the alarms?"

It was a good question. The museum has a superb collection of antique jewelry, which is kept in a room built especially for it—a room that is one enormous vault. It is locked at night and watched continuously by three guards during the day. The alarm system is so delicate that breathing heavily on one of the cases will set bells ringing. And although Schmidt was one of the directors of the museum, neither he nor anyone else had authority to remove any of the historic gems from their cases unless he was accompanied by two other museum big shots and a whole battalion of security guards.

"I give up," I said. "I don't know how you got it out, but for heaven's sake, put it back. You've been in trouble before with your weird sense of humor, and if they find out—"

"Nein, nein." He shook his head regretfully, abandoning his joke in the face of my obvious concern. "It is not stolen from the case. I have not taken it from there. It was found last night in the pocket of a dead man, in an alley near the *Alter Peter.*"

My mind fumbled with this information for a few moments.

"This isn't the real brooch, then," I said.

"Aber nein. How could it be? I assure you, we would notice if the gem had been taken away. It is a copy. But, *liebe* Vicky, what a copy!"

I took it from his hand. Even though I knew it was not the real gem, my touch was tentative and respectful. The more closely I examined it, the more my amazement grew. I had to take Schmidt's word for it that this wasn't the real talisman, but it certainly looked good, even to my trained eye.

The goldwork was superb, each tiny filigree wire having been shaped and set with masterful skill. As for the jewels, even an expert gemologist would have had trouble deciding they were fakes without the use of the complex instruments of his trade. The original pendant had been made in the ninth century, long before modern techniques of faceting gem stones were developed. The rubies and emeralds and pearls on the golden frame were roughly polished and rounded—"cabochon" is the technical term. The only precious stones that are cut in that antique style today are star rubies and star sapphires; the rounded shape brings out the buried star refraction. The cabochon-cut sapphire in the center of this jewel shimmered softly, but did not glow with the buried fire of a faceted stone. I knew that it was not one sapphire, but two, placed back to back, and that the flaw in the center was not a "star" or a natural blemish, but a sliver of the "True Cross," which made the jewel into a very expensive reliquary, or talisman.

"You could fool me," I said, putting the pendant down on my desk blotter. "Come on, Schmidt, elucidate. Who was this character in whose pocket the pendant was found?"

"A boom," said Schmidt, with a wave of his hand.

"A what?"

"A boom, a vagabond, a drunkard," Schmidt repeated impatiently.

"Oh. A bum."

"Did I not say so? He had no money, no passport, no papers of any kind. Only this, sewn with care into a secret pocket in his suit."

"How did he die?"

"Not violently," Schmidt said, with obvious regret. "There was no wound. Of poison, perhaps, or drugs—horses, as they say. Or cheap hooch, or—"

"Never mind," I said. When Schmidt starts speculating, especially in what he fondly believes to be American slang, he can go on and on and on. "Really, Schmidt, this is fantastic. I suppose the police notified you. How did they know this was a copy of one of our pieces?"

"They thought it *was* our piece," Schmidt said. "They are men of culture, our *Polizisten*; one of them comes often to the museum and recognized the ornament. I was called in this morning."

"You must have had a fit when you saw it," I said sympathetically. "With your weak heart and all."

Schmidt rolled his eyes dramatically and clutched at his chest.

"It was a terrible moment! I knew of course that our pendant could not have disappeared; but was this the fake, or the one in our treasure room? Until our experts could examine both, I died a million deaths."

"It could still fool me," I admitted. "You're sure?"

"Do not say such things, even in jest! No, this is the imitation. But such an imitation! The gold is genuine. The stones are not glass, they are modern synthetics. You have no doubt heard of these imitation rubies, emeralds, sapphires? Some are such excellent copies that only the most sophisticated equipment can tell they are not real. And the workmanship of this . . ."

"I don't see why you're so upset," I said; for he was mopping his bald head, and his baby-blue eyes were narrowed in distress. "So some eccentric collector wanted a copy of the Charlemagne pendant. A good copy, not like the molds museums sell these days. The use of real gold is rather peculiar, perhaps, but the frame is hollow; I don't suppose there is more than a few hundred dollars' worth of precious metal involved here. What's the problem?"

"I thought you would understand!" Schmidt's eyes widened. "You are such a clever woman. But then jewelry is not your specialty. To go to such trouble, such expense, in order to imitate a piece like this. . . . There are only a few goldsmiths in the world capable of such work. They do not have to earn a living making copies. It is . . . too cheap and yet too costly, this copy. Do you see?"

When he put it that way, I did see. I nodded thoughtfully and looked more closely at the lovely thing on the desk.

Most women have a weakness for jewels. The only reason why men don't is because it is out of fashion. In earlier centuries men wore as many ornaments, with as much vanity, as women did. I could understand why someone might want a copy of the Charlemagne talisman for purely decorative reasons. I wouldn't have minded wearing one myself. But anyone who wanted a copy, just for fun, wouldn't go to the trouble of using such expensive materials, nor pay a jeweler of such skill the exorbitant sum necessary. There was another point that Schmidt had not mentioned. In order to copy the jewel with such fidelity, a designer would have to study the original in detail. Nobody had applied to the museum authorities for permission to do so, or Schmidt would have known about it. Therefore someone must have spent long hours studying photographs and descriptions, perhaps even visited the museum. Why do all this surreptitiously if his purpose was honest?

"You think some gang of thieves is planning a robbery," I said. "That there is a plot to substitute imitations for the real jewels."

"It is a possibility we must consider," said Schmidt. "You see that we cannot ignore such an idea."

"Yes, of course. You are quite right. I've seen movies about things like this—"

"Not only in fiction," Schmidt said gloomily, passing his handkerchief over his forehead. "The problem of skillful fakes has been with us since the beginning of time. As soon as man began collecting beautiful objects, for himself or in museums, the swindler and faker began their dastardly work. Vicky, we must find out about this. We must know for sure. If there is a harmless purpose—then, good. But if not, every museum, every collector in the world is vulnerable to a craftsman of such skill. Supposing that the substitution could be made, it might take us years to discover that ours was not the genuine object. A copy so good as this would defy more than a casual glance."

"Right." I touched the central sapphire of the pendant with my finger. It felt cool as water and smooth as ice. It was hard for me to believe the darned thing wasn't genuine. "So what are we going to do about it?"

"Not we. You." Schmidt's rosy face regained its normal good humor. "The police have investigated, naturally. But they have come to a—what is the English?—a dead stop."

"Dead end?" I suggested.

"Yes, yes. The man on whose body this was found had no identification. His description, his fingerprints, are not known to Interpol. Our police are magnificent, but there is a limit to what they can do. So I turn to the lady whose skill and imagination are like those of the great English Sherlock. I appeal to my Vicky! Find this man for me, this unknown creator of magnificent copies. You have done it before; you can do it now."

His blue eyes glowed like the cabochon stone in Charlemagne's talisman.

Modesty is not one of my virtues, but this naïve appeal made me feel uncharacteristically modest. It was true that once before I had had moderate success as a sort of historical detective, but I succeeded in that case because the solution to the problem depended on a body of specialized knowledge, which I happened to possess. I am a historian, not a criminologist, and if this was a case of art forgery on a grand scale, I rather suspected that the skills of the latter specialist would be more useful than those of the former.

However . . . Again my eye was drawn to the soft blue gleam of the great sapphire. Fake? It looked awfully real to me. There was something hypnotic about that stone, and about the appeal Schmidt had made. My work was pleasant but rather dull; even my pornographic novel had bogged down. And it was May, that month of all months when emotion overcomes good sense.

"Well," I said. I leaned back in my chair and put my fingertips together. (What fictional detective was it who did that? Sherlock Holmes? Schmidt made a wonderful Watson.) "Well,

Wat——I mean, Schmidt, I just might be willing to take this case."

II

The police official reminded me of Erich von Stroheim, whom I had seen on the Late, Late Show back in Cleveland, except that he didn't have a monocle. I guess they've gone out of style. He kissed my hand, however. I enjoy having my hand kissed. I can't imagine why American men haven't taken it up, it gets even us feminists.

I hadn't expected to have my hand kissed, but I had expected some interest. Bavarians like blondes. Bavaria, in case you didn't know, is one of the southern provinces of Germany; its people are members of the Alpine subrace, short and stocky and brunette, so they appreciate the Valkyrie type. I was wearing a tight sweater and skirt, and I let my hair hang down over my shoulders. I didn't care what Herr Feder thought of my brains, I just wanted to get all the information I could out of him.

After all, there wasn't much he could tell me. All the normal sources of inquiry had drawn a blank. The dead man simply wasn't known to the police.

"This does not mean he is not a criminal," Feder explained, rubbing his thick gray eyebrows. "It only means that he is not known to us or to Interpol. He may have been arrested in some other country."

"Have you checked in the States?" I asked, leaning back in my chair and taking a deep breath.

"What?" Feder's eyes moved reluctantly back to my face. "Ah—*verzeihen Sie, Fräulein Doktor.* . . . No, we have not. After all, the man committed no crime—except to die."

"The museum authorities are rather concerned."

"Yes, so I understand. And yet, Fräulein Doktor, is there really any cause for suspicion? Like all police departments these days, we are badly overworked. We have too much to do investigating crimes that have occurred; how are we to spend time and money inquiring into a vague theory? If the museum wishes to investigate on its own, we will extend the fullest cooperation, but I fail to see. . . . That is, I have no doubt of your intelligence, Fräulein Doktor, but—"

"Oh, I don't intend to pursue criminals into dark alleys, or anything like that," I said. We both laughed gaily at the very idea. Herr Feder had big, white, square teeth. "But," I continued, "I am curious about the case; I was about to take leave anyway, and Herr Professor Schmidt suggested I might pursue certain leads of our own, just to see what I could find out. I wonder . . . I guess I had better see the corpse."

I don't know why I made that suggestion. I'm not squeamish, but I'm not ghoulish, either. It was just that I couldn't think of anything else to do. I had no other lead.

I regretted my impulse when I stood in the neat, white antiseptic room that houses the morgue of Munich. It was the smell that got me: the stench of carbolic, which doesn't quite conceal another, more suggestive, odor. When they turned the sheet back and I saw the still, dead face, I didn't feel too good. Suggestion— the reminder of my own mortality. There was nothing particularly gruesome about the face itself.

It was that of a man in middle life, though the lines were smoothed out and negated by death. He had heavy black brows and thick, graying black hair; his complexion was tanned or naturally swarthy. The lips were unusually wide and full. The eyes were closed.

"Thank you," I muttered, turning away.

When we got back to his office, Feder offered me a little sip of brandy. I hadn't been that upset, but I didn't like to shatter his faith in female gentleness. Besides, I like brandy.

"He looks like a Latin," I said, sipping. It was good stuff.

"Yes, you are right." Feder leaned back in his chair, his glass held lightly between unexpectedly delicate fingers. "Spanish or Italian, perhaps. It is unfortunate that we found no identification."

"That seems suspicious."

"Perhaps not. The man was in the alley for hours, no one knows how long. It is possible that some casual thief robbed him. If he carried a wallet or pocketbook, it would have been stolen, for the money it contained. His papers, if any, would have been in that wallet. And a valid passport is always useful to the criminal element."

"Yes, of course," I agreed. "A thief would have overlooked the jewel, since it was sewn into his clothing."

"So we think. There were a few odds and ends in his pockets, the sort of thing a thief would not bother with. Handkerchief, keys—"

"Keys? Keys to what?"

Feder produced a positively Gallic shrug.

"But who can tell, Fräulein Doktor? They were not keys to an automobile. If he had an apartment, the good God alone knows where it might be. We inquired among the hotels of the city, but have had no luck. It is of course possible that he only arrived in Munich yesterday and had not registered at a hotel. Would you care to see the contents of his pockets?"

"I suppose I should," I said glumly.

I wasn't expecting anything. I just said that because I felt I shouldn't overlook any possible clue. Little did I know that in that pitiful collection lay the key that was to unlock the case.

It was a folded piece of paper. There were several other scraps like it, receipts from unidentified shops for small sums, none over ten marks. This particular scrap was not a receipt, just a page torn out of a cheap notebook. On it was written the number thirty-seven—the seven had the crossbar that is used by Europeans for writing that number, in order to distinguish it from their numeral one—and a curious little group of signs that resembled fingernail clippings. They looked like this:

I sat staring at these enigmatic hieroglyphs until Herr Feder's voice interrupted my futile theorizing.

"A puzzle of some sort," he said negligently. "I see no meaning in it. After all, the cryptic clue only occurs in *Kriminalromanen*, is that not correct?"

"How true," I said.

Herr Feder laughed. "It is, perhaps, the address of his manicurist."

"Were his nails manicured?" I asked eagerly.

"No, not at all." Herr Feder looked at me reproachfully. "I made a little joke, Fräulein Doktor."

"Oh." I giggled. "The address of his manicurist. . . . Very witty, Herr Feder."

I shouldn't have encouraged him. He asked me to dinner, and when I said I was busy, to lunch next day. So I told him I was leaving town. Usually I deal with such matters more subtly, but I didn't want to discourage him completely; who knows, I might need help from him if the case developed unexpected twists. Although at that point I didn't even have a case, much less a twist.

It was a gorgeous spring day, a little cool, but bright and blue-skied, with fat white clouds that echoed the shapes of Munich's onion-domed church spires. I should have gone back to work—I had a number of odds and ends to clear up if I was going to play Sherlock—but there was no point in clearing them up, if I didn't know where I was going. And I couldn't face Professor Schmidt. He would expect me to have deduced all kinds of brilliant things from my visit to the police.

I wandered toward the *Alter Peter*. I guess I should explain that this doesn't refer to an elderly gentleman, but to Munich's oldest church, dedicated to the Apostle. It was begun in 1181, which puts it into my period, but the redecorating of the eighteenth century converted it into a Baroque church, at least internally. Baroque sculpture and decoration take some getting used to; they look frivolous and overdone to modern tastes. But I like them. It seems to me a church ought to express the joy of religion as well as its majesty. The Zimmerman stuccowork at old St. Peter's always cheers me up. But I didn't go in. I walked through the neighboring streets for a while. It was a waste of time, actually. I didn't know which of the alleys in the vicinity had harbored my dead man, and if I had known, there was nothing to be gained from staring at the vacated space. The police would have searched the area thoroughly.

I passed through the Viktualenmarkt, with its booths of fresh fruits and vegetables and its glorious flower stalls. They were masses of flaming color that morning, all the spring flowers—yellow bunches of daffodils, great armfuls of lilac, fat blue and pink hyacinths perfuming the air. I ended up on Kaufingerstrasse, which was a favorite haunt of mine, because I adore window-shopping. It was just about the only kind of shopping I could afford. Some of the most delectable windows were those of the shops that sold the lovely peasant costumes of southern Germany and Austria. People still wear them, even in sophisticated Munich—loden cloaks of green or creamy-white wool, banded in red, with big silver buttons; blouses and aprons trimmed with handmade lace; and, of course, dirndls. They differ in style according to the area where they originated: the sexy Salzburger dirndl, with its lowcut bodice, artfully designed to make the most of a girl's secondary sex characteristics; the Tegernsee type, which has a separate skirt and jacket, the latter lengthened behind into a stiff, pleated peplum. I love those brilliant costumes, of bright cotton print or embroidered velvet; but I am not the dirndl type. However, I had my eye on an ivory wool cape with buttons made out of old silver coins, so I stopped by the shop to see if by any chance they were having a sale. They weren't. I turned away, and then something across the street caught my eye.

It was only an advertising sign for Lufthansa airlines. "Rome!" it exclaimed, above a huge photograph of the Spanish Steps lined with baskets of pink and white azaleas. "See Rome and live! Six flights daily."

All the pieces came together then, the way they do sometimes when you leave them alone and let them simmer. The swarthy skin and Latin look of the dead man; Herr Feder's joking suggestion that the cryptogram represented an address; the atmosphere of antiquities, treasure, and jewels that colored the whole affair.

I had been thinking vaguely of going to Rome on my holiday, and wondering where I was going to get the money. There was one particular area I longed to explore at leisure—a region near the Tiber, where Bernini's windblown angels guard the bridge that leads to the Castel Sant' Angelo. A region of narrow twisted streets and tall frowning houses. The

Via dei Coronari is the antique lovers' paradise. And not far from the Via dei Coronari is a street called the Via delle Cinque Lune—the Street of the Five Moons.

It was only a hunch. I couldn't even call it a theory. But the five curved signs might represent crescent moons; and surely it was more than a coincidence that that particular part of Rome specialized in antiques of a very expensive nature.

At any rate, it wouldn't do any harm to investigate number 37, Via delle Cinque Lune. I turned and walked toward the museum, planning some mild larceny.

I can be reasonably glib when I try. Tony, one of my former colleagues at the University, refers to me as Old Slippery Tongue. But I couldn't have put this deal across with anyone except Professor Schmidt. Goodness, but that man is gullible! I worry about him sometimes. Fortunately he is not quite as gullible about other swindlers as he is about me. He has a slightly exaggerated idea of my intelligence. I didn't even have to lie to him. He thought my interpretation of the cryptogram was absolutely super. "But of course," he shouted, when I had explained. "You have it! What else could it possibly mean?"

Well, I could think of about a dozen other possibilities. It's funny that Schmidt, who is so sharp in his own field, can't tell the difference between a fact and a feeble theory in any area other than medieval history. But I guess a lot of experts are like that. Heaven knows they fall for spiritualists and con men just as often as those of lesser brain power.

So I got my leave of absence, to start that very day, and a nice little expense account. How Schmidt planned to justify this expenditure to his colleagues I couldn't imagine, but that wasn't my problem. I cashed the check he gave me, called the airport and made a reservation, and rushed home to pack. My passport was in order, so the only thing left to do was figure out where I was going to stay in Rome.

It didn't take me long to decide. People on expense accounts don't stay in pensions or hostels. It wouldn't look good. I felt I owed it to my employer to check into the best hotel in town.

III

There may be more beautiful cities than Rome on a bright May morning, but I doubt that any of them will ever get to me in quite the same way. The Spanish Steps looked just like the picture on the billboard in Munich, with the massed flowers spilling down them like a pink-and-white waterfall. The tourists did spoil the scene slightly—the artist had thoughtfully omitted them from the billboard— but I didn't mind them; they added that note of nonchalant irreverence that is so typical of Rome. "Eclectic" is the word for that city; everything is all mixed in together: lush voluptuous Baroque fountains with sculptured columns from the time of the Caesars; a modern sports arena, all steel girders and molded concrete, next to a twisty dark street in which Raphael would feel right at home. Tying it all together, like a running ribbon of greenery, are the trees and plants—umbrella pines and cypresses, palm trees, ilex, and oleander; and salmon-pink geraniums and blue plumbago fringing balconies and roof gardens.

It was too early to dine, so I found a sidewalk café, ordered a Campari and soda, and watched the passing throng.

At least that was what I planned to do. I hadn't been seated for more than sixty seconds when a good-looking boy sat down next to me, smiled like a Fra Angelico angel, and made an extremely improper suggestion in Italian.

I smiled back at him and made an equally improper suggestion in Italian as fluent as his, but better accented. (The Roman dialect sounds atrocious; it is jeered at by other Italians, especially the Florentines, who speak lovely pure Tuscan.)

The boy's expression was ludicrous. He had expected me to understand only his sweet smile. I went on to explain that I was expecting my boyfriend, who was six feet six inches tall, and a star soccer player.

The boy left. I opened my guidebook and pretended to read. Actually, I was checking the map, and plotting.

Shops in southern Italy close between noon and four o'clock and then reopen until seven or eight. The streets are crowded during these lovely evening hours, when the heat of the day is passing and the light lingers. There was still plenty of time for me to visit the Via delle Cinque Lune and number 37 in a subtle and inconspicuous manner.

As I walked along, I began to realize that one of the elements in that plan wasn't going to be as easy as I had anticipated. I am not exactly inconspicuous. For one thing, I'm half a head taller than most Romans, male or female; I stood out like a perambulating obelisk in that throng of little dark people. It became increasingly evident to me that I was going to need some sort of disguise.

I felt even more conspicuous after I had crossed the Via del Corso and plunged into the twisting network of small streets around the Pantheon and the Piazza Navona. There are no sidewalks, except on the big main streets and corsos. The house facades front onto the pavement, which is so narrow in some places that pedestrians have to flatten themselves against a wall to let a Fiat go past. Every tiny piazza has a café or two, whose tables and chairs are insecurely protected from traffic by potted shrubs.

I walked slowly along the Via dei Coronari, peering into the windows of the shops. It wasn't easy to see the merchandise: there were no plate-glass show windows, brilliantly lighted, as in American stores. But the dark, dusty interiors of these shops held treasure. A worm-eaten but oddly compelling wooden saint, greater than life size, from some looted church: pairs of huge silver gilt candelabra; Meissen china, bodiless gilded Baroque cherubs, a dim, cracked triptych with scenes from the life of some virgin saint. . . .

I would have passed the entrance into the Via delle Cinque Lune if I hadn't been looking for it. You couldn't even get a Fiat into that passageway without squeezing, but it was lined with shops even darker and more expensive looking than the ones on the Via dei Coronari. One window had an embroidered Chinese robe that stopped me in my tracks. A concealed light brought out the shimmer of the gold threads, which outlined amber and citrine chrysanthemums and a peacock's tail of glowing blue-green. It must have been a high official's robe. I had seen one not nearly so lovely in the Victoria and Albert in London.

The number above the door of the shop was 37.

I went on slowly, looking in other windows and feeling absurdly pleased with myself. The odds were at least two to one that number 37 should be an antique shop; there were greengrocers and druggists on the street, plus private houses and apartment buildings. It was a small confirmation of my nebulous theory, but I was in a mood to appreciate any encouragement.

The street curved like the arc of a bow and

ended in another equally narrow passageway called the Via della Stellata. At the far end of this latter street I could see a patch of sunlight and a piece of a fountain. It was Bernini's "Fountain of the Rivers," in the Piazza Navona.

I don't often read mystery stories. For light reading I prefer bad historical novels with voluptuous heroines and swashbuckling heroes, and lots of swordplay and seduction. But in some of the mysteries I had read, the heroes—and villains—used to break into places quite a lot. They usually burgled the back entrance through an alley that was conveniently located behind the place they wanted to search.

There was no alley behind the Via delle Cinque Lune.

The street didn't even form one side of a square. As I have said, it was curved. Maybe there was only one entrance to the shop. From the garbage piled by the door that seemed a likely hypothesis.

I turned and went back along the Street of the Five Moons. I didn't stop to look at the mandarin's robe this time, but I took careful note of number 37 itself. There was nothing distinctive about it except for a name painted in discreet black lettering above the door—

A. Fergamo. It meant nothing to me. But I saw something else I had not noticed before—a slitlike opening on one side of the building, so narrow that the sun did not penetrate the gloom within.

On my way back to the hotel I stopped to make several purchases. I took them to my room and freshened up; then I went to the hotel dining room and ordered the specialty of the house, with a bottle of Frascati. It was all on Professor Schmidt, and I toasted him as I drank my wine.

I left the hotel about ten. It was too early for breaking and entering, but I didn't want to wait any later for fear of attracting attention. Even in Rome, nice girls don't go out alone at 2 A.M. The streets were still crowded with people. They all seemed to be paired off like Siamese twins, even the middle-aged tourists. The elderly ladies arm in arm with their paunchy, balding escorts looked rather sweet. There is something about Rome on a spring evening. . . . I had to remind myself that I had more important matters to deal with.

I ducked into the first dark doorway and put on my disguise. It wasn't very complex, just a dark raincoat, a pair of glasses, and a navy-blue scarf tied closely over my hair. I was wearing sneakers and brown slacks. That was all I needed—that, and a stooped, shuffling walk and a sour look that curved the corners of my mouth down. Nobody bothered me after that.

I prowled the streets of Rome for almost three hours. Lights went out as I wandered. Shops closed, windows darkened. When midnight struck from the countless church towers, I was on the Lungotevere Sangello, one of the broad boulevards that follow the winding course of the Tiber. I stood for a long time with my elbows on the stone parapet, looking down at the river where the reflected shapes of St. Peter's and the Castel Sant' Angelo shimmered in the dark waters. The lights of the Via della Conciliazione led straight as a ruler toward the circular piazza of St. Peter's, and the great dome blocked out a circular section of the sky.

Rome is a swinging city; it doesn't roll up the sidewalks at midnight. But some areas are more lively than others, and the antique area had gone to bed at ten o'clock. When I tore myself away from the magnificent view, I found most of the streets deserted.

It was a good thing I had visited that part

of town by day: I had a hard time finding my way. Once I had left the busy boulevards by the Tiber, I might have been in another world, for this part of Rome hasn't changed in externals for hundreds of years, and it doesn't go in for streetlights. I had a flashlight—one of my purchases earlier that day—but I didn't want to use it. So I shuffled along, head bowed, through the darkened streets. Occasionally I passed another form as dark and shadowy as my own. At the far end of a curving street I would sometimes catch a glimpse of bright lights and hear a ghostly echo of revelry from the Piazza Navona. It is one of the tourist centers, and some of the cafés and restaurants stay open far into the night. It was only a few blocks away, but it might as well have been a few miles. The lights didn't penetrate into the gloomy passageways where I wandered. I hoped the constabulary of the city kept itself busy watching over exuberant tourists.

Finally I found number 37 and the passageway alongside the shop. Lord, was it dark in there! The street was dark enough; this slit looked like the mouth of a big animal. I groped into it, sliding my feet so as not to stumble over something I could not see. My hands felt gritty as they trailed along the crumbling brick of the wall.

There may have been windows in the wall, though I doubt it; why construct windows that open onto a two-foot-wide alley? I was looking for a door, and I soon found it. Then I used my flashlight, shielding it with the ample folds of my raincoat. The door was solid and the lock was a big, old-fashioned type.

Any adolescent with a grain of initiative learns how to pick locks. I learned in tenth grade from Piggy Wilson. He used to steal bikes—not for filthy gain, just to ride around on. He had a thing about bicycles. . . . Anyhow, all you need for an ordinary lock—not the combination, or Yale, types—are a couple of long, stiff steel probes and another long metal gadget with a hook on the end. Remember buttonhooks? They were before my time, too, like the high-buttoned shoes on which they were once used. But I had read about them, and I had found one in an antique shop of the cheaper sort, on the fringes of the Via dei Coronari area.

With the buttonhook and a thin steel probe it was no problem to force the lock. I had expected there might be chains and bolts as well, and had planned to worry about them when I found them. To my surprise and pleasure the door gave to the pressure of my hand as soon as I had unlocked it. I should have been suspicious, instead of pleased. I should have known there was a reason why the door wasn't bolted.

I heard the reason before I saw it. It was a growl that sounded as if it came from the throat of a grizzly bear—a low bass rumble, with lots of teeth behind it.

I switched on the flashlight. In its beam I saw the source of the growl. Not a grizzly bear, nothing so harmless—but a dog the size of a small horse, black as Satan except for a mouthful of white fangs. Talk about the Hound of the Baskervilles. There it was, except for the phosphorescent slaver—a Doberman pinscher, the fiercest guard dog in the world.

Two

NO WONDER THEY HADN'T BOLTED THE BACK door. I wondered why they had bothered to lock it.

I could have slammed the door and taken to my heels. I had time. It wasn't courage, but the reverse, that prevented me from taking flight. I was paralyzed. After a long second or two I saw something I hadn't noticed before. The dog's lips were curled back, its low growl never stopped; but its tail lifted and gave a tentative wag.

The room into which the door opened wasn't large; it was an entryway rather than a room. The floor was cement, the walls and ceiling were festooned with dirty cobwebs, and the canine amenities were not luxurious— only a pile of filthy sacks in one corner and a couple of battered tin plates, both empty. On one plate was a shriveled scrap of pasta, obviously the remains of the dog's dinner. The other dish, the water dish, was bone dry.

People say southern Europeans aren't as sentimental about animals as Americans are. But I had seen scraps left by kindhearted Romans for the stray dogs and cats that infest the ancient ruins, and once I had watched a gruff, tough-looking laborer feed half a dozen cats in the Roman Forum, producing cans of food and a can opener from his pants pocket. It was undoubtedly a daily ritual, since the half-wild felines came running at his call and preened, purring, under his touch. The man who tended the Doberman wasn't that kind of Roman. He hadn't even bothered to give the animal fresh water.

I walked into the room, crooning in the voice I use to Duke, my retriever back home in Cleveland.

"Poor old boy, *poverino*, did the bad mans forget to feedums? Here, *carissimo*, sweetheart, mama will get you some water."

The dog leaped.

He would have knocked me flat on my back if Duke hadn't taught me how to brace myself against that kind of rush. The Doberman was a big fake—a sheep in wolf's clothing. Dogs are like people, there are good ones and bad ones; but although even a nice dog may be soured by bad treatment, most of them are much more forgiving than humans.

I managed to get the door closed, and then I sat down and played with the dog for a while, letting him drool happily all over my hands. I finally persuaded him to let me stand up, and then, before I did anything else, I went looking for a source of water.

I found it in a tiny room that contained a sink and a toilet and a lot of cockroaches. I filled the dog's water bowl and watched him gulp it up with growing indignation. He was awfully thin. I suppose they kept him underfed on the assumption that he would be all the more ready to munch up an intruder. So I thought I would just see if I could find something to eat. The most I expected was a coffeepot and a box of crackers, the sort of thing a clerk might have on hand for snacks. But I hit pay dirt. Another little cubbyhole next to the lavatory contained a hot plate and a surprising collection of goodies—cans of pâté and smoked oysters, and a tin of expensive English tea, plus another tin of cookies. "Fancy Biscuits," it said on the lid.

The Doberman adored the pâté, but he liked the smoked oysters best of all. I gave him a handful of cookies to finish off with, and I promised myself that if this place turned out to be the den of the master criminal, as I hoped it would be, I would see that the custodian of the dog got an extra-heavy sentence.

With the dog right behind me, breathing noisily on the back of my raincoat, I explored the shop.

Heavy metal shutters had been pulled across the front windows, so I was able to use my flashlight. I didn't spend much time in the front of the shop, though I would happily have lingered over some of the treasures it contained. All the objects were beautiful and expensive. Most of the furniture was of the ornate, heavily gilded Baroque type that is still popular in Italy. There was a Venetian glass chandelier that might have graced a ducal palace in the seventeenth century, plus shelf after shelf of crystal, silver, and rare china. One case held jewelry, and I examined it eagerly. A single glance told me there was nothing for me here. Most of the pieces were nineteenth century—handsome and expensive, but not rare like Charlemagne's unique gem. So I returned to the back of the shop.

It was fitted up as an office, with a desk and a couple of straight chairs, and a big rusty filing cabinet. The dog lay down and started chewing absentmindedly on the end of the tattered rug while I looked through the desk drawers.

They held the things one might expect to find—paper, carbons, pencils, and the like. I turned to the filing cabinet.

I was handicapped by not knowing what I was looking for. I didn't expect to find a detailed plan of some larcenous plot, complete with the names of the conspirators and floor plans of museums. But I hoped I would run across something that would prime the pump—if you will excuse a homely metaphor dating back to my days on the farm—some name or phrase that would have a sinister meaning to my suspicious mind.

The surprising thing was that I found it, but not in the filing cabinet. Like the desk, that article of furniture contained only the things normal to a business establishment like this one. There were folders full of receipts from the craftsmen with whom an antique dealer ordinarily deals—furniture restorers, weavers, and so on. Several jewelry firms were mentioned. I jotted down the names, but I didn't expect much from that source. A dealer in antique jewelry sometimes has to have a piece cleaned or restored. I recognized one of the firms, an old, prestigious establishment on the Via Sistina. These transactions appeared to be open and aboveboard.

One of the folders was interesting, but I don't suppose I would have noticed it if I hadn't been groping desperately for some clue. It was a thin folder, with only a dozen pieces of paper inside, and unlike the other things in the file drawer it was comparatively new and clean. The papers consisted of a list of names—very distinguished names. Practically all of them had titles, and a few of them were familiar to me.

For reasons which will become evident as this narrative proceeds, I am going to change those names—to protect the innocent, as they say. "The innocent" is me. I have enough trouble getting along in life; I don't need lawsuits. The point is that the names I recognized were those of men who owned rare and beautiful art objects. The title of the Graf von——, to select just one example, went back to the tenth century, and so did some of the contents of his castle in the Bavarian Alps. One of his possessions, a saltcellar that was attributed to Cellini, had been reproduced in a dozen art books.

I looked over the names with considerable interest. Were these men potential victims of a master thief? The prizes would be well worth the effort, and a private home, however grand, is a lot easier to rob than a museum. But it was only a theory. I could hardly call on these ladies and gentlemen and ask to look over their collections. I had no proof of anything yet. Besides, if the Charlemagne talisman was a representative example of the forger's work, I wouldn't be able to identify a fake.

The dog had become bored with the rug, although, from the stains on it, I imagine it had an interesting variety of flavors. He was lying with his head on my foot, which had gone numb from his weight. I was feeling ridiculously relaxed by that time—there is nothing more soothing than a dog at one's feet—and I began to get a little peckish. So I went to the cubbyhole-pantry to get some cookies. I was tempted to make myself a cup of tea, and went so far as to take the lid off the tin. The box was almost full.

The box of cookies had been almost full too. That probably proved something, but I couldn't believe it was anything important. I decided not to bother with the tea, but I ate the rest of the cookies, with considerable help from the dog. What the hell, there was no way I could conceal the fact that someone had broken into the shop. Whatever else the dog might have done, he could not have opened the cans of smoked oysters.

I dusted the crumbs off my hands and returned to the office for a final look around. There was nothing in the wastebasket, nothing behind the file cabinet. I decided I might as well go. I hated to leave the dog, but I could hardly take him to my hotel. When I bent down to pat his massive head and apologize for deserting him, I saw he had found something else to nibble. The design on the paper caught my eye, and I pulled it out of the dog's jaws.

He had eaten one corner of the paper, but enough remained. It was a drawing—a detailed, scale drawing—of a crown. Not one of those big, fat, plushy crowns modern monarchs wear when they are opening Parliament; this was a diadem of twisted gold wire and tiny enameled flowers. The flower petals were made of turquoise and lapis lazuli and carnelian. The colors weren't indicated on the drawing; but I knew that crown. Talk about antique jewelry—this piece was four thousand years old. It had come from the tomb of an Egyptian princess. The Metropolitan Museum has one like it. This one had been found early in the nineteenth century, before governments established regulations about removing antiquities from the country in which they were discovered. Like the Elgin Marbles, it had been taken to England by the wealthy excavator. Unlike the Marbles, it was still in a private collection.

I put the drawing in my pocket and headed for the back door. I had to talk to the dog for quite a while before he would let me out. I had refilled his water dish, but I still felt guilty; the last thing I saw before I switched off my flashlight was his mournful look. I didn't bother locking the door. Why should I protect the premises of a gang of crooks?

The shop was one of the hangouts of the people I was after. I was sure of that now. The drawing might not be proof for a court of law, but it was good enough for me. The detailed measurements and scale sketch were precisely what a craftsman would need in order to copy a piece, and this particular piece of jewelry was made to order for the man who had produced the copy of the Charlemagne talisman. The value of the crown lay in the design and the workmanship and the rarity. It could be duplicated at a fairly reasonable cost.

I got back to the hotel about 3 A.M having divested myself of my coat and scarf along the way. The desk clerk smiled slyly as I went through the lobby, and I thanked God for dirty minds. It never would have occurred to that man that I was late because I had been breaking into an antique shop.

II

I had breakfast in bed next morning, and very good it was, too, except for the coffee. I cannot imagine why the people who invented espresso have never learned to produce decent coffee of any other variety.

It was a gorgeous morning, like practically every morning in Rome. The fountains in the Piazza d'Esedra sparkled in the sunlight. I was wearing my brightest tourist costume, all red-and-white stripes and big sunglasses. I wanted to be noticed. There was no way the shop people could know I was their nocturnal visitor. I strolled along the Via dei Coronari in a leisurely fashion, and went into a couple of the shops. It was almost noon before I reached number 37.

There were two German tourists in the shop. At least they were speaking that language, in loud, forceful voices. They had the solid look of prosperous merchants, and the woman was wearing slacks, which was a mistake on her part. I listened for a while, my back turned, pretending to examine the objects in a glass case near the door. The lady was a collector of Chinese snuff bottles, and her comments on the one that had been shown to her were not flattering. The price was too high, the carving was poor. . . . The usual comments made by a buyer who hopes to knock the price down.

The proprietor responded in a voice so soft I could scarcely make out the words. It was obvious from his tone that he didn't give a damn whether the *gnädige Frau* bought the bottle or not. After a while this became obvious to the *Frau* as well; with an irritated exclamation she stamped out of the shop, followed by her husband.

I turned and stared interestedly at a Baroque lamp, dripping with gilded bobbles and bangles. I didn't expect the clerk to approach me; he did not impress me as a supersalesman. My assumption was correct. He sat perfectly still, behind a desk at the back, and I wended my way toward him, looking at the merchandise like any casual shopper. Then I looked at him and smiled.

"Buon giorno," I said.

"Good morning," he answered.

I waited for him to add something, like "May I help you?" but he didn't. He just sat there, leaning back in his chair and studying me with a supercilious smile.

I didn't need the clipped, characteristic accent to tell me he was English. The tea and biscuits I had found the night before had led me to expect that the present manager of the shop was of that nation, and his appearance was unmistakable. He reminded me of Lord Peter Wimsey—not only the fair hair and the skin scarcely darkened by the Roman sun, but the air of mild contempt. You couldn't say his nose was big, but it seemed to dominate his face, and although he was sitting down and I was standing, he gave the impression of looking down his nose at me.

"Goodness gracious," I said, opening my eyes very wide. "How did you know I was American?"

The smile broadened.

"My dear girl!" said the Englishman, and said no more.

I was seized by a sudden desire to say something that would shock that irritating smile off his face—to ask whether he had any ancient Egyptian jewelry for sale, perhaps. But I thought better of it. There was something about the man, casual and overbred though he appeared to be, that made me suspect I had better deal carefully with him. His hands, clasped negligently on his knee, were as well tended as a woman's. He had long, thin fingers—musicians' fingers, people say, though most of the musicians I have known have hands like truck drivers.

I started to babble, explaining that I wanted a present for my fiancé, who loved old things. The man's cool blue eyes narrowed with amusement as I went on. He waved one of his beautiful, manicured hands.

"Browse, then, love. Take your time. If you see anything you like, fetch it over and I'll tell you about it."

"Thanks. Don't get up," I said.

"I hadn't intended to."

I didn't seem to be getting anywhere. I was wondering what to do next when an outrageous explosion of noise erupted in the back of the shop. The Colosseum was only a few blocks away; I was irresistibly reminded of the Christians and the lions. Crashes, screams, growls. . . .

Growls. That was all the warning I had before the dog burst through the curtains at the back of the shop and launched himself at me.

I hadn't forgotten him, but I had assumed he would be tied up or removed to more rural surroundings during the day. I certainly had not counted on his memory, or his hearing, being so good.

Some obscure impulse made me grab the Baroque lamp as I fell. It was a heavy thing, but it went over with a satisfying crash. The manager leaped to his feet with a profane remark. Flat on my back, with the dog rapturously licking my face, I writhed and shrieked.

"Help, help, get him off, he's gnawing at my jugular!"

The Englishman came trotting toward me. He didn't trot fast, and I was infuriated to observe that instead of flying to my rescue he stopped to pick up the lamp and examine it, scowling, before he twisted his hand in the dog's collar and yanked him off me. He did it effortlessly, although the animal must have weighed almost a hundred pounds.

"Jugular indeed," he said contemptuously. "Get up, young woman, and wipe your face. You have damaged a very valuable lamp. Bruno!"

I thought he was talking to the dog, for the poor creature immediately lay down at his feet, cringing. But Bruno was a man—a swarthy, heavy-set, villainous-looking fellow who came rushing in from the back of the shop brandishing a heavy stick. The Englishman caught this weapon as Bruno was about to bring it down on the dog's back.

"Stop it, you fool," he said in Italian.

"But he is a killer," snarled Bruno. "See, he has attacked me, ripped my shirt—"

"Intelligent dog. Good taste—sartorial and otherwise. . . . Leave the animal alone, cretin. Americans are foolish about animals; she'll have the police on us if you aren't careful."

The word *cretino* is a particularly nasty insult in Italian. Bruno's unshaven jowls darkened and his eyes narrowed; but after a moment he shrugged, lowered the stick, and snapped his fingers.

"Come, Caesar."

The dog followed him, belly down on the floor. It made me sick to watch. The Englishman's face was quite impassive throughout this exchange—which, naturally, I pretended not to understand—and my initial dislike for him took a great leap forward. Usually the English are fond of dogs. Obviously this one was a degenerate specimen. It confirmed my conviction that he was a crook.

I scrambled to my feet, unaided by any gentleman, and brushed my dusty skirt.

"The lamp," said the Englishman, eyeing me coldly.

"My ribs," I said, just as coldly. "Now don't give me any nonsense about paying for the lamp. You're lucky I don't sue you. What do you mean, keeping a dangerous animal like that around?"

He didn't speak for a moment, he just stood there with his hands in the pockets of his beautifully tailored jacket. His face was superbly controlled, but as the seconds ticked away I had an uncomfortable impression that all sorts of ideas were burgeoning behind the bland facade.

"You are quite right," he said finally. "I must apologize. In fact, we owe you more than an apology. Perhaps you had better consult a doctor, to make sure you are not injured."

"Oh, that's all right," I said. "I'm not hurt, just shaken."

"But your dress." He was all charm now, smiling, showing even white teeth. "At the very least it will need to be cleaned. You must let us pay for it. Do give me your name and the name of your hotel, so we can make good the damage."

I wanted to swear. There was a good mind

behind that handsome face of his, and now he had me neatly boxed in. He knew enough about animals to draw the proper conclusion from the dog's behavior. He couldn't be positive that I was the midnight intruder, but he was damned suspicious, and if I refused to give him my name, his suspicions would be strengthened. Furthermore, he was quite capable of having me followed; that's what I would have done if I had been in his shoes. So whether I refused to answer, or gave him a false name, he could check up on me. I wasn't a professional, there was no way I could hope to shake off an anonymous follower who would probably look exactly like half a million other Roman men. The only possible course now was to tell the truth and hope that my candor would disarm his suspicion.

So I told him who I was and where I was staying, and fluttered my eyelashes and wriggled my hips at him, as if I hoped there was a more personal motive behind his interest. He responded, in an outrageous parody of male ego that would have been funny if I had not lost my sense of humor. If he had had a mustache he would have twirled it.

My vanity was somewhat wilted as I retraced my steps toward the Piazza Navona;

but as I walked on I began to hope that perhaps the incident hadn't been so disastrous after all. I was at an impasse in my investigations; now the gang might be forced to make the next move.

How right I was! I was only wrong about one thing. I expected it would take them a day or two to check up on me, so I didn't anticipate trouble right away. Certainly not before nightfall. Instead they snatched me out of the Roman Forum, right under the noses of a thousand tourists.

Three

I DREAMED ABOUT SPAGHETTI. WHEN I WOKE up I could still taste the garlic. I soon discovered that the taste came from the cloth that was wound over my mouth. I was blindfolded, too, and my wrists and ankles were tied. I was lying on a flat, fairly soft surface. That was the extent of my knowledge. I couldn't move, I couldn't see, and breathing wasn't awfully easy either. I like garlic, but not on rough cotton cloth.

I had a beast of a headache and a funny feeling in my stomach, which was mostly terror, but might also have been a reaction to the drug I had been given.

It was the blindfold that made me panic. Once, when I was about twelve, I ran away from home and crept into a cave in the hills when night fell. I woke up in total darkness, and for a minute I couldn't remember where I was. It was horrible. I still have nightmares, about it. This was even worse—this time I *knew* the unseen surroundings held danger, and not being able to see what form it would take made it harder to endure. I squirmed and strained at the ropes for some time—I don't know how long, it seemed like an eternity. Then I got a grip on myself. I was only making things worse and my best hope was to get my wits about me and try to think. Though I had no doubt what had happened to me, I couldn't imagine how they had managed it. The last thing I remembered was the sunlight on the weathered white columns of the Forum—the single column of Phocas, near the Rostrum, and the magnificent triad of the Temple of the Dioscuri. The dark pines and cypresses of the Palatine Hill made a fitting backdrop for that ruined splendor. The Palatine . . . Yes. I had been on the hill, later; I had climbed the paved slope toward the ruins of the imperial palaces. After that it was a complete blank. I forced myself to go back to the events I did remember.

After leaving the antique shop I had had lunch at one of the open-air restaurants on the Piazza Navona. I could have sworn no one followed me there. The people at the nearby tables were all tourists: a young French couple, arguing angrily about money; a German family; a group of American Midwesterners gobbling down spaghetti as if they were all underweight, which they weren't. The piazza was crowded, as it always is. Bernini's great sculptured figures of the rivers poured out the flowing water, and some ragged little Roman urchins splashed in it, giggling, till a policeman came and chased them away. Across the piazza the facade of St. Agnese in Agone raised twisted towers into the sky. Cars and motorcycles roared around the oval track; just as the Roman chariots had raced around Domitian's stadium in the bad old days. The piazza had replaced the stadium, but the spirit of speed lingered on.

I looked suspiciously at the other pedestrians when I left the restaurant, but, as I had anticipated, it was impossible for me to tell whether anyone was after me—for purposes of violence, I mean. One little man, who barely reached my shoulder, trotted after me for half a mile, flashing his teeth in what he mistakenly believed to be an irresistible smile. This swain had a rival—a boy on a Vespa, who trailed me for blocks, shouting things like "What ya say, baby?" until he ran into a large policeman. But surely neither of them. . . .

Come to think of it, the famed Roman ardor would make a super excuse for following a female suspect. But neither of my boyfriends had stuck with me after I bought my ticket to the Foro Romano.

I went to the Forum because it's practically the only place in town that is open in the afternoon, and because I thought I might find a quiet place to plan somewhere in the ruins. A lot of other people had had similar ideas. The Forum was crowded, and baking in the afternoon sun. So I had climbed the Palatine Hill looking for shade and privacy. It's a maze up there, with ruined walls crossing and crisscrossing each other. The first primitive settlement of Rome had been on that hill, and occupation continued without a break for centuries. I got lost. Everybody does. I don't know where I was when they caught up with me. There were low walls of crumbling brick, and a lot of scraggly bushes. . . . And that was my last coherent memory, except for a nightmare flash of a dark, scowling face and a needle pricking my arm. They could have walked right out with my unconscious body draped over a shoulder, if they did it brazenly enough. Spectators would assume I had fainted.

Having figured out *how* I got where I was, I tried to find out *where* I was. The only senses left to me were smell and hearing. I sniffed vigorously. No use; the only thing I could smell was garlic. At first my ears were no more useful. Then I heard the rattle of a lock.

I lay still, on my left side, as they had originally placed me. Thanks to the echo, I knew I was facing the door of the room—closet—hall . . . wherever it was, I heard the door open, then a man's voice.

"She still sleeps," he said in Italian. I didn't recognize the accent; it resembled the harsh Roman dialect, but was more rustic.

There was a laugh—a nasty laugh; and another voice said something I can't repeat because I didn't recognize the key word—some variety of local slang, probably. The gist of the suggestion was unfortunately only too clear.

"No," the first voice said regretfully. "It is not allowed. She must be questioned."

"I would like to question her," said Villain Number Two, with another merry chuckle. I had a clear picture of him in my mind, from that horrid, high-pitched laugh. He would be short and squat, with greasy black hair and a mouth like that of a toad—wide and lipless and wet.

"After all," he added, "who would know or care? It would not harm her voice, eh, Antonio?"

They went on talking about it for a while. I followed the debate with considerable interest. Finally they left; I heard the door open and close. I was relieved, but not much. Antonio had been steadily losing the argument, perhaps because his heart wasn't in it. For some idiotic reason I was more worried about Villain Number Two than I was about the anonymous characters who were going to question me. I had every intention of squealing, without shame or reserve, if the questioning involved physical violence. Why should I be a heroine? But that greasy, leering voice, when I was blind and helpless. . . .

When the door opened again, I tried my best to scream. Nothing came past the gag except a gurgle. Footsteps ran toward me. I started to thrash around. Someone scooped me up as easily as if I had been a hundred-pound weakling, one arm under my knees, the other under my shoulders; and off we went, at the same rapid pace. We hadn't gone far before my struggles made him lose his grip. Instead of picking me up again, he shoved me up against a flat surface, one arm squeezing my arms against my sides, the length of his body pressed against mine so I couldn't move. His other hand was on the back of my head, squashing my face against his shoulder.

"Stop squirming," muttered a voice into my ear. "Or shall I give you back to Antonio and Giorgio?"

I think I knew who he was even before I heard his voice, from the general aura of him— the scent of soap, starched cotton, expensive tobacco. Contrary to orders, I continued to squirm, because I couldn't breathe. He caught on; the fingers at the back of my head relaxed, allowing air to reach my nose, while he plucked at the knot that held the gag in place. As soon as it came off I sucked in my breath. I had about a million questions, but I never got to ask them. His lips and tongue blocked my mouth just as effectively as the gag had done—and a lot more distractingly.

In its inception, it was a purely practical kiss; he had to shut me up, without a second's delay, for Antonio and Giorgio burst into the room we had just left. Their voices sounded as if they were only a few feet away, but it was clear from my companion's behavior that they could not see us, though they could hear us as easily as I could hear them. My eyes were still blindfolded, remember, and as that crazy embrace continued, I became less able to concentrate on essentials.

As kisses go, it was memorable. After I started to cooperate—which, I am ashamed to admit, occurred almost immediately—his participation became less practical and more enthusiastic. It was a ridiculous performance, as leisurely and thorough and effective as if he had all day and nothing else on his mind. Without wishing to sound immodest, I believe my own contribution was not negligible.

He stopped what he was doing, though, as soon as the agitated steps of Antonio and Giorgio had retreated. I noticed that his whisper was a little breathy, but if anything he sounded more amused than passionate.

"Thank you, that was very nice. . . . No, don't talk. I don't intend to answer any of your questions, so it would be a waste of time. I'm going to get you out of here. Giorgio is not a nice man; I'd hate to think of wasting talents like yours on him. Besides, my boss may have plans. . . . Don't talk! You won't be out of danger until we leave the house, and you must do everything I tell you and keep utterly quiet, or you will be recaptured; and then Giorgio will have an excuse to work his dastardly will. *Capisce, signorina dottoressa?*"

"How did you know?" I began. Again his lips brushed mine. This time they did not linger.

"I said, shut up. I shan't answer questions. Will you do as I say, or shall I raise the view halloo for Giorgio?"

I didn't think he would actually carry out the threat, but I was not about to take chances. There was a hint of ruthlessness in that suave voice, even when it whispered.

"Okay," I said meekly.

"Good. I am going to untie you, but you must leave the blindfold on. You owe me that for saving your life, or at least your . . . can one say 'virtue,' these days? I doubt it. And 'virginity,' surely—"

"Oh, stop it," I hissed irritably. "I agree. I suppose you are going to tell me to drop this case and leave well enough alone."

"Precisely. You don't know anything vital, that's obvious, or you wouldn't have done anything so idiotic as come round to the shop. I don't intend that you shall learn anything from tonight's adventure. If you know what is good for you, you will go home, like a nice little doctor of philosophy, and stop meddling in matters that don't concern you. Now come along, and for God's sake, keep quiet."

During the last speech—he was a long-winded devil—he had cut the ropes on my ankles and wrists, and rubbed the former till the numbness had worn off.

While he spoke I had been devoting my operative senses to learning all I could about the place where we were standing. It wasn't too difficult to figure out where we were. The sense of enclosure and the smell of dust, plus the feel of draperies brushing me when I moved. . . . We were behind some heavy curtains, velvet or plush, in the same room where I had been held prisoner. I understood why Giorgio and Antonio had not seen us, and why it was imperative for me to be utterly still while they were in the room.

There were several witty, debonair comments I might have made, but to tell the truth I wasn't feeling particularly debonair. This was not the first time I had been in danger. In fact, I had been in worse spots. I had not become blasé about it, though. I don't think I ever will. I was willing to do anything to get out of—wherever I was—alive. Afterwards . . .

well, I would cross that bridge when I got to
it.

So I let him put his arm around my shoulders in order to guide me, and I minced along
in meek silence. It was surprising how much
I was able to deduce about my surroundings
even without my sight. The floor, for instance.
It was smooth and slightly slippery—highly
polished wood, probably. When the surface
changed to carpeting, my feet knew the difference right away. I could even tell that the material wasn't the thick synthetic wall-to-wall
stuff that is so popular back home. This floor
covering was thinner, and once I tripped over
what must have been fringe. Oriental rugs?

At any rate, before we had gone far, I was
sure I was not in a cheap apartment or tene-
ment. The smells of wax and polish, the general feeling of echoing spaciousness, suggested
a large house—something rather grand, actually. We walked on marble for a while; at least
it was hard and cool underfoot. And we
walked for a long time, indoors. The place
seemed as big as a museum.

My companion didn't speak. The arm
around my shoulders was stiff with taut muscle; his fingers curved over my upper arm
with a tension that was more effective than

any verbal warning. Once I heard voices off in the distance; another time he stopped and pulled me into a small, closed-in space until footsteps passed and faded.

As the flight proceeded I recovered some of my courage, and my curiosity revived. What sort of place was this? Could it be a museum after all?

I got the chance I was waiting for when we reached the top of a flight of stairs. I didn't know they were stairs at first, not until he picked me up and began to descend them. I suppose it was easier for him to carry me than guide each step I took, but I had a feeling he rather enjoyed it. I put my arms around his neck and rubbed my face against his shoulder.

He laughed—if you could call it that—just a puff of air into my left ear. I tickled the back of his neck. It was all pretty corny. But he loved it—he can deny it all he wants to, but he did. When we reached the bottom of the stairs he didn't put me down but continued to carry me along a marble-floored corridor lined with long mirrors. I knew the mirrors were there because I saw them. I had managed to shift the blindfold just enough to see out from under it with one eye.

The corridor went on for a long way. From

time to time the mirrors were interspersed with oil paintings in long, heavy frames. I had never had that precise view of great paintings before; all I could see were feet, the hems of flowing robes, and the grass and rocks of painted backgrounds.

That gallery was long. Before we reached the end of it my gallant rescuer was pretty well out of breath. To do him justice, it wasn't only exertion that made him gasp; my hands and mouth were free, and I was using them nicely. In the process I got the blindfold back in place. I had seen all I needed to see.

We passed through a swinging door—I heard the sound as it swung back into place—and into a narrower corridor that smelled faintly of cooking. Then he put me down. My arms were still around his neck and my blind face was lifted, trustingly. . . . The position was ideal for what he had in mind. His fist landed neatly on the point of my upturned chin.

I woke up in the taxi, with my head on his shoulder. At first I didn't know it was a taxi; all I could see were lights flashing by, like long streamers of fire.

"Wake up, darling," said a voice. "Arise, fair moon, and dim the envious sun. . . . That's the girl."

I turned my head and saw the face I had expected to see grinning down at me. The end of his nose was about half an inch from mine, and as my senses came back to me and I remembered what had happened, I was so angry I snapped at him, like a mad dog. He just laughed and kissed me. I didn't struggle. It would have been undignified.

When he had finished, he held me out at arms' length and looked at me critically.

"Not too bad. A young lady who has been out on the town must expect to show some signs of wear and tear. I can't tell you how I've enjoyed this."

"No," I said. "I wouldn't try, if I were you . . . Where are we?"

"Almost at your hotel. Can you walk, do you think?"

I flexed my legs. He shifted position hastily, and I smiled—or rather, I bared my teeth.

"Don't worry, I won't kick you. Although it would give me immense satisfaction to do so. Yes, I can walk. Demoralizing as your embraces are, they are not totally incapacitating."

"What a vocabulary," the Englishman said admiringly. "Brains *and* beauty . . . All right, love, you should do well enough tonight, but

I advise you to get out of Rome first thing tomorrow morning."

The taxi stopped. He had the door open and was out before I could think of a suitable retort. Reaching into the car, he pulled me out onto the sidewalk.

We were dead smack in front of the hotel, one of those high-class establishments which looks like, and perhaps was, a Renaissance palace. The doormen have more gold on their uniforms than any other doormen in Rome. One of them—the same man who had seen me come in at 3 A.M. the night before—was a few feet away, staring.

I had been drugged, tied up for who knows how many hours, and then punched on the jaw. I knew what I looked like—not a poor, defenseless, abused heroine—just another drunk.

"*Buona notte, carissima,*" caroled my blond bête noire in dulcet tones. "*Grazie—per tutto. . . .*" He put out his arms.

I sidestepped the embrace, wobbled, staggered, and fell back against a convenient lamppost. The taxi driver chuckled. The Englishman grinned more broadly. I turned on my heel and, with what dignity I could muster, went reeling up the magnificent marble stairs of the Hotel Belvedere, under the concentrated stares of the doorman, two bellboys, a concierge, three taxi drivers, and a few dozen assorted tourists.

I should have felt humiliated and defeated. But I was hiding a grin of my own—a lopsided grin; my jaw hurt. The hectic hours had been worth it. I had a clue. The first genuine honest-to-God clue I had found yet.

Four

THERE WAS A DIFFERENT STAFF ON DUTY next morning, but they had clearly heard about me. The precocious lad who brought my breakfast lingered until I gave him the evilest look I could manage. He retreated hastily, and I hung out the "Do not disturb" sign.

I drank about a pint of coffee to begin with, and then tackled the food. By the time I got through I felt my old self again, except for a slight tenderness around the chin. I didn't need that to remind me of what I owed a certain smart-aleck Englishman.

I should have been grateful to him, and I was—the way I was grateful to my dentist after he had filled a big cavity without anesthesia. The man had saved me from an undefined but unpleasant fate. And yet that grinning devil had somehow turned the whole affair into a farce. I simply couldn't take seriously any plot that involved a weirdo

71

like . . . I didn't even know his name. He had reduced my case into a personal duel. My greatest desire now was not to catch the crooks, but to get even with . . . I didn't even know his name!

But I would find out. I needn't say, I am sure, that I had no intention of taking his advice and clearing out. If he had planned it deliberately, he couldn't have chosen a better way of making me stay on. And thanks to his male vanity, I now had the clue I needed.

My knowledge of antique jewelry is not that of an expert. I had recognized the Charlemagne talisman because the original was in my own museum, and the Egyptian princess's crown was an art object, rare and unforgettable. But I do know paintings. I had seen only the bottom half, sometimes less than that, of the paintings in the long gallery, but that was enough. I had recognized not one, but three of them. Murillo's "Madonna of the Hills" is barefoot, like any pretty, dark-eyed peasant girl. I would have known those dainty arched feet anywhere, just as I would have recognized the landscape that forms the setting for Raphael's "Saint Cecilia." The third painting particularly was a giveaway. According to the legend, Saint Peter was crucified upside down. Solario had painted him in traditional position, and I had gotten an excellent view of the poor saint's trailing white hair and beard. He looked a lot more peaceful than I would have looked in that position.

The only question remaining was: Who owned these pictures? It's impossible to remember the location of every great work of art in the world; the "Pietà" in St. Peter's, the "Mona Lisa" in the Louvre, yes; but Raphael painted a lot of pictures, most of them saints or madonnas. It was no problem. All I needed was a library or a museum. I was feeling disgustingly pleased with myself as I leaped out of bed and headed for the shower.

The sun was high when I emerged from the hotel. I knew I had to get moving, because many of the museums are closed in the afternoon. But I lingered to admire the view, a rugged landscape of tiled roofs and twisted towers, with the dome of St. Peter's off in the distance floating like a giant balloon against the blue sky.

There are a lot of museums in Rome, but I had no problem deciding which one to visit. The Galleria Concini has a particularly fine collection of jewelry. I had meant to check it out in case my other lead didn't work, because it struck me as being the sort of place a gang of thieves would find enticing. The Vatican has a more valuable collection of treasures, but a small, private museum like the Concini would be considerably more vulnerable.

I trotted down the Spanish Steps, between the great tubs of flowering azaleas and the gawking tourists. The younger ones were sprawled all over the steps, drinking Cokes and soda. People were hawking cheap jewelry and leather goods, and offering their services as guides. Down at the bottom the charming little fountain was almost hidden by loungers, some of whom, in defiance of authority, were surreptitiously soaking their hot feet. It was all very cheerful and noisy, and it was only by chance that I spotted a face that looked familiar.

After a near stumble, I decided the man wasn't Bruno, the dog handler. He looked enough like him to be his brother, but so did a lot of other men in the crowd. Bruno was a typical southern Italian—swarthy, stocky, dark haired. The man wasn't paying any attention to me, and by the time I turned into the Via del Babuino I had lost sight of him. My euphoria had received a slight check, however. The incident had reminded me that I was all the more vulnerable to attack because I knew only a couple of the members of the gang by sight. It was silly to assume that they were all sinister, dark men; a pursuer could be disguised as a housewife, a nun, or a tourist. Just then a tourist did approach me. The poor guy only wanted to know how to find the Colosseum, but I shied like a nervous mare when he thrust his map at me.

The Galleria Concini is near the Pincian Hill. I prefer not to be any more specific about its location, and that isn't its right name, either. The reason for my reticence will become apparent as I proceed.

I reached it without further incident, as a novelist might say, except for a narrow escape from a Volkswagen as I circumnavigated the Piazza del Popolo. The Galleria was open. Its handsome Renaissance facade was approached by a long flight of curving stairs. My calves, already suffering from the long climb up from the piazza, ached at the very sight of them, but I struggled up and plunged into the cool, dark cave of the entrance hall. The little old lady behind the barred cage told me the library was on the second floor, and extracted five hundred lire from me.

I had to go through several of the exhibition

halls to reach the elevator. Only my stern sense of duty kept me moving. The museum had a superb collection of Quattrocento paintings, including a Masaccio polyptych I had admired for years.

The librarian's frosty eye softened when I showed her my card. At Schmidt's insistence I had had a batch of them printed up when I started work; they contained my full name and titles, which sound rather impressive in German. The mention of the National Museum gave me free access to the library shelves.

The room was quite handsome. It had been a grand *salone* at one time, when the Palazzo Concini was still a private residence. There was only one other researcher, a little old man with no hair, and glasses so thick they looked opaque. He did not glance up when I tiptoed past him with the book I had selected. I took a seat at a neighboring table. It took me about a minute and a half to find what I wanted. I checked all three paintings, just to be sure, but the first one I looked up, the Murillo, provided the necessary information. It was in the private collection of the Conte del Caravaggio, Rome.

In my exultation I slammed the book shut. It made more of a noise than that hallowed chamber had heard in years. The little old man at the next table wobbled feebly, like those bottom-heavy toys that sway when you nudge them. For a minute I thought he was going to topple over, flat on his face on the table, a la Hitchcock. You could die in that place and nobody would notice for hours. But finally he stopped swaying, and I made my way back to the desk with exaggerated care.

When I asked if I could see the director, the librarian's face looked shocked. I think I could have gotten in to see the Pope with far less argument. But finally she consented to telephone, and after a muttered conversation she turned back to me looking even more surprised.

"You will be received," she murmured, in the whisper demanded by that dim vault with its frescoed ceiling and statued niches. I felt as if I ought to genuflect.

The director's office was another flight up. I was allowed to take the private elevator, which opened directly into an anteroom presided over by a stately-looking man with a beard. I was about to greet him with the humility his exalted position demanded, and then I found out he wasn't the director after all, only a secretary. He offered me a chair, and I cooled my heels for a good twenty minutes before a buzzer on his desk purred and he beckoned to me. The carved mahogany door behind him was an objet d'art in its own right. He opened it with a bow, and I went in. By then I was slightly annoyed at all the pomp and circumstance. I marched in with my chin in the air, prepared to be very cool and haughty, but the sight of the woman behind the desk took the starch right out of me.

Yes, woman. This is a man's world, and nowhere in the world is male chauvinism more rampant than in Italy, but I never thought for a moment that this female was a secretary. She would be the boss of any establishment she chose to honor with her presence.

Being something of a female chauvinist myself, I should have warmed to her. Her male secretary was a particularly nice touch. Instead I took an instant dislike to the creature. I was about to say "unreasoning dislike," but there was good reason for my reaction. She looked at me as if I were a bedbug.

The room was arranged to provide a setting that would awe most visitors. Its high windows, draped in gold swags and festoons, opened onto a terrace so thickly planted with shrubs and flowers that it looked like a descendant of one of the Hanging Gardens. The Persian carpet on the floor was fifty feet long by twenty-five wide—a glorious, time-faded blend of cream and salmon, aquamarine and topaz. The desk should have been in the museum downstairs, and the paintings on the walls were the greatest of the great masters.

But the woman didn't need that setting. She would have been impressive in a soup kitchen. Her black hair surely owed something to art, for the lines in her face betrayed the decades— at least four of them, if I was any judge. She had one of those splendid profiles you see on Roman coins, and I got a good look at it, because her head was turned sideways when I came in. She was looking out the window.

The secretary's discreet murmur made several things clearer. It was loaded with long, hissing feminine endings. "Principessa, Direttoressa. . . ." and then the name. What else? The last of the Concinis was still hanging on in the family mansion.

She meant to make me feel like a great overgrown clod from some barbarian country, and she succeeded. I went clumping across the floor—my feet looked and sounded like size fourteens—hating that Roman profile more every second. I reached the desk and looked in vain for a chair. She gave me thirty seconds—I counted them to myself—and then turned, very slowly. A faint smile curved her full lips. It was a closed smile, with no teeth showing, and I was reminded of the enigmatic smiles of early Greek and Etruscan statues—an expression that some critics find more sinister than gracious.

"Doctor Bliss? It is a pleasure to welcome a young colleague. Your superior, Herr Professor Schmidt, is an old acquaintance. I hope he is well?"

"Crazy as ever," I said.

I hate being tall. I had a feeling she knew that, and was deliberately forcing me to stand and tower over her. So I looked around for a chair. I spotted a delicate eighteenth-century example, with priceless needlepoint on the seat, yanked it into position beside the desk, and sat down.

She stared at me for a moment. Then her lips parted and she laughed. It was a charming laugh, low pitched like her speaking voice, but vibrant with genuine amusement.

"It *is* a pleasure," she repeated. "You are correct; Professor Schmidt is crazy, that is why he endears himself to his friends. May I serve you in any way, my dear, or is this purely a social call?"

I was disarmed, I admit. She had accepted my response to her challenge like a lady.

"I wouldn't take up your time with a purely social call, pleasant though it is," I said. "I have a rather peculiar story to tell you, Principessa—"

"But we are colleagues—you must call me Bianca. And you are . . . ?"

"Vicky. Thank you. . . . This is going to sound as crazy as Professor Schmidt, Prin— Bianca. But it's the honest truth."

I told her the whole story—almost the whole story. She listened intently, her chin propped on one slender ringed hand, her black eyes never leaving my face. The eyes began to sparkle before I had gotten well under way, and when I had finished, her lips were twitching with amusement.

"My dear," she began.

"I said it would sound crazy."

"It does. If your credentials were not so excellent. . . . But I know Professor Schmidt; I know his weakness. Confess, Vicky, is this not a story that is just to his taste?"

I laughed ruefully. "Yes, it is. But—"

"What real evidence have you, after all? A

dead man—but dead of natural causes, you said—with a copy of one of your museum pieces. Have you any proof that criminal acts were intended? Forgive me, but it seems to me that you and Professor Schmidt have postulated a plot on very slim evidence."

"That might have been true two days ago," I said. "But what about the antique shop on the Via delle Cinque Lune?"

"A sketch, however detailed, is not evidence, my dear. I am glad, by the way, that I do not have to take official notice of your activities. I know the shop, Vicky. Signor Fergamo, the owner, is a most respected man."

"He might not know that the shop is being used for criminal purposes," I argued. "That damn—I mean, that English manager—"

"I don't know him." Her delicate brows drew together as she pondered. "He must be new. The former manager of the establishment was Fergamo's son-in-law. Even so . . ."

She paused politely, waiting for me to answer.

She had me over a barrel. The single piece of conclusive, damning evidence I had was the story of my kidnapping, and that was the one thing I had omitted from my narrative. I'm not sure why I hadn't told her about that; I guess

I felt it sounded so demented that it would cast an air of incredibility over an already unbelievable story. After all, she was a member of the old Roman nobility, and so was the man I suspected of being part of the gang. Would she believe an accusation against Count Caravaggio? She was more likely to conclude that I was some kind of escaped lunatic.

All this went through my head in a flash of thought. I couldn't see any way out of the dilemma.

"You're sure you haven't lost any jewels?" I asked feebly.

Her eyes twinkled, but she managed to keep a straight face.

"I will check. Does that please you?"

"Thank you."

"Not at all. It was gracious of you to warn me. As you say, it does no harm to take precautions. But while I am looking over our collection, is there any way in which I can make your holiday in Rome more enjoyable? Introductions, suggestions?"

That gave me an opening.

"There are some private collections I'd like to see," I said innocently. "I had intended to telephone, but it would certainly make things easier if you could vouch for me."

"It would be a pleasure. Which collections?"

"Count Caravaggio's."

"Caravaggio?" Her eyebrows soared. "My dear is that wise?"

"Why wouldn't it be?"

She studied me thoughtfully, her chin in her cupped hand, her eyes shining.

"Very well," she said, after a moment. "You may find him amusing. I will telephone immediately."

Like every object in the room, even the utilitarian telephone was a work of art—a gilded mother-of-pearl set that might have stood on the desk of a French President. She got through right away, but it took the count's butler some time to locate him. While she waited, Bianca put a cigarette in a long jade holder. She looked like a cross between the Dragon Lady and an ad for expensive, custom-made cigarettes.

Finally the count came on the wire. She addressed him by his first name.

"Pietro? . . . I am well, thank you, and you? . . . Excellent. I have a treat for you, my dear; a charming young lady from America who is a distinguished art scholar. She wishes to view your collection. . . . Yes, yes, indeed she is. . . . One moment, I will ask."

Her hand over the mouthpiece, she smiled at me.

"Have you lunched yet, Vicky? Pietro would like you to join him if you have no other engagement. In half an hour's time."

Knowing what I know now, I probably should have declined that invitation. Even knowing what I knew then, I should have taken time to think it over. Being me—impetuous and not always too bright—I was delighted, and said so. The principessa returned to the telephone.

"She accepts with pleasure, Pietro. *Bene;* in half an hour, then. Yes, my dear, we must dine one day soon. . . . Good-bye."

"I can't thank you enough," I said, as she replaced the instrument. "I guess I won't have time to go back to the hotel first."

"I think not. Please make use of my private quarters if you wish to freshen up. My secretary will show you."

I thanked her again, and rose. She leaned back in her leather executive's chair, her hand toying idly with a magnificent diamond brooch. Like her rings, it glittered expensively. Obviously she was not gainfully employed because she needed the money.

"Don't thank me yet," she said. "I warn you,

Pietro can be rather . . . But I feel sure you can cope."

I thanked her for the third time. She was smiling quite broadly as I left; in a lady less elegant, I might have been tempted to call it a grin.

II

The minute I met the count I knew why she had given me that funny, cat-and-canary smile.

I had never met a man who wore a corset before. It was so obvious, not only from the rigidity of his tummy, but from his slightly apoplectic expression and the stiff way he walked.

He was beautifully dressed. Roman tailors are superb, and he patronized the best. His suit was of dazzling white linen with a cummerbund of scarlet silk. He had a red carnation in his buttonhole. His hair had been brushed across his head and lacquered into place, but it didn't quite cover the bald spot. I wondered why he didn't buy a toupee. Maybe he hadn't quite faced the extent of the disaster; people don't see what they don't want to see. His face was as round as his uncorseted stomach would have been, and if I hadn't been prejudiced I would have thought it a pleasant face. His little black mustache was an obvious imitation of Clark Gable's. He had a habit of stroking it with one finger while he talked—when his hands weren't otherwise occupied.

He was gorgeously turned out, but his hands were the pièce de résistance—soft and white and plump, the nails polished to a mirror surface. I had a good opportunity to judge, because they were all over me from the minute I walked into his library.

I had taken a taxi, for fear of being late, but the count was in no hurry to get to his food. He kept pressing sherry on me. Poor man, I suppose he thought I'd get drunk. I let him pat me and stroke my arm for a while. Then I decided he had had enough fun for the day, so I pushed my chair back and stood up.

"Your home is magnificent, Count," I cooed. "This is the first time I have ever seen an Italian palace—one that is still lived in, I mean, not a museum."

"Ah, this." With one eloquent gesture the count waved away marble floor, gold-and-crystal chandeliers, rosewood paneling set with malachite and lapis lazuli, thousands of rare leather-bound volumes. . . . "The place is falling apart. It is no longer possible to live with any elegance, thanks to the oppressive, reactionary, revolutionary government. I keep my finest treasures in my country house at Tivoli. There I have managed to keep up a decent style of living. My best collections are there. You must see them. You are a scholar—though I cannot believe so beautiful a woman can be also a scholar. . . ."

He heaved himself up off the couch, his face turning an alarming shade of purple as he made the effort, and trailed after me.

"You like books?" he inquired. "See this—one of my favorites. It has plates done especially for one of my ancestors by Raphael himself."

He managed to get both arms around me as he reached for the book. My eyes literally popped when I looked at the first drawing. I had always thought of Raphael as specializing in madonnas.

"It's amazing," I said honestly, and then closed the book, in some alarm, as the count began wheezing. "Maybe you shouldn't look at these pictures, Count, if they get you so—"

"You must call me Pietro," he interrupted, catching at my shoulder. I let him hold on; I thought he needed the support.

Well, this went on for quite a while. We finished the sherry and the book—some of the plates were really extraordinary—and by then we were old friends. He was a harmless old guy, all he wanted to do was touch. I kept moving, not because he worried me, but because I thought evasion amused him. At the end of the conversation he invited me to be his house guest.

"Not here," he said, waving a disparaging hand at the oriental rugs, the ormolu desk, the Donatello statues. . . . "It is unbearable here when the weather is hot. Tomorrow I move to my house at Tivoli. You will join me there. You will appreciate my collections, since you are an expert, although I cannot believe a woman so beautiful, so voluptuous. . . ."

At that interesting moment the butler opened the door and announced lunch. Pietro's fat pink face lengthened.

"We must go, I suppose. Helena will be rude if I do not come at once."

"Helena?" I took the arm he offered me. He squeezed my hand against his side. "Is she your wife?"

"No, no, my mistress. A very unpleasant woman. A beautiful face and body, you understand—though not so beautiful as yours—"

"I guess you should know," I said resignedly.

"But very jealous," said Pietro. "Very rude. Do not let her intimidate you, Vicky, I beg."

"I won't. But if you find her so obnoxious, why don't you get rid of her?"

"It is not so easy, that," said Pietro sadly. "Wait till you meet her."

Believe it or not, I had almost forgotten my motive for looking up Count Caravaggio. He was such a silly little man. It was almost impossible to picture him as a master criminal. We were crossing the huge hall, with its original Greek statues set in shell-shaped niches, when I was brought back to reality with a rude thump. A door opened, and a familiar form emerged.

"You," I gasped, like a good Gothic heroine.

The Englishman raised one eyebrow. Not both, just one. I hate people who can do that.

"I fear you have the advantage of me," he said, in an offensive public-school drawl. "Your Excellency?"

"Yes, yes. I introduce you," said Pietro, without enthusiasm. "It is my secretary, Miss Bliss. Sir John Symthe."

"Sir?" I said. "Smith?"

"With a *y* and an *e* on the end," said John Smythe suavely. "An obscure title, but an old one, and not without honor."

"Oh, yeah?" I replied uncouthly. "What about those stories about your ancestor and Pocahantas?"

"A cadet branch of the family," said the Englishman, without cracking a smile.

Pietro, who had not understood any of this, interrupted in a petulant voice.

"We are late for lunch. It is well we meet you, John; you must make arrangements for tomorrow. Miss Bliss—she is Doctor Bliss, in fact, a learned lady—she will accompany us to Tivoli. You will have one of the cars pick her up at her hotel. The car I will travel in, you understand?"

"I do understand, your Excellency," said Mr. Symthe. "Believe me, I understand."

"Come, then, we are late for lunch," said Pietro. Towing me with him, he trotted across the hall, with Mr. Smythe trailing behind.

I didn't believe in that title of Symthe's for a minute. Actually, I didn't believe in his name either. At least it gave him an identity, a name at which I could direct all the epithets I had been thinking up.

My first lunch at the Palazzo Caravaggio was an experience I won't soon forget. I don't know which was more memorable, the food, the furnishings, or the people. Pietro did not stint himself. He was a gourmet as well as a gourmand; the food was marvelous, from the pasta in a delicate cream sauce to the towering meringue laced with rum, and he ate most of it. The quality of the food told me something interesting about the man, something that was confirmed by the contents of the long, formal dining room. He had superb taste. Every piece of furniture was an antique, lovingly tended. The plates were eighteenth-century Chinese, the tablecloth was one of those heavy damask things that take three days to iron. I could go on, but that gives you a rough idea. Pietro was a much more interesting character than he appeared to be at first. He might be a fat, self-indulgent little lecher, but he was also a fat, self-indulgent, cultivated little lecher.

I can't say his taste in women was complimentary to me, however. In this area he seemed to prefer quantity to quality.

Helena was already at the table when we entered the dining room. I could have identified her without Pietro's preliminary statement. I mean, I never saw a woman who looked more like a mistress. If she continued to stow away spaghetti at that rate, in another year she would no longer be voluptuous, she would be fat. But she was still young—not more than twenty—and her ripe, quivering masses of flesh had the gloss of fine ivory. A good deal of it (the flesh) was displayed by her strapless, practically topless, green satin dress. Masses of blond hair tumbled over her shoulders, in the careless style made popular by an American television actress. She had a pursed little mouth and big brown eyes as expressionless as rocks. She took one look at me, and the rocks started to melt, like lava.

Another woman was seated at the foot of the table. Pietro led me toward her and introduced his mother, the dowager countess. Unlike her son, she was painfully thin. Her face was a map of fine wrinkles, surmounted by beautifully coiffured white hair. She bowed her head graciously when Pietro presented me as a learned lady who had come to study his collections. She looked very fragile and sweet in her black dress trimmed with cobwebby lace, but I suspected it would not do to underestimate her. The dark eyes that peered out of her sunken sockets were as bright and cynical as a mockingbird's.

Pietro led me back to the head of the table and indicated the chair on his right. Helena was already seated at his left. She barely acknowledged Pietro's gabbled introduction, and after a pained, expressive look at me he seated himself, while one of the dozen footmen who were standing around pulled out my chair.

The Englishman seated himself. There was still one vacant place. Pietro glared at it.

"Late again. Where is the wretched boy? We will not wait. The food will be cold."

The first course was a cold soup that resembled Vichyssoise, made with cream and leeks and other ingredients I couldn't identify. Pietro had finished his bowl before the door was opened by a servant and the missing person appeared.

He was absolutely beautiful. I have to use that word, though there was nothing feminine about his features. The tanned chest displayed by his open shirt was as neatly modeled as that of Verrocchio's young David. He was beautiful as young creatures are before their features harden. Thick dark hair tumbled over his high forehead. His costume was casual: slacks, a rumpled shirt open to the navel, espadrilles on his feet.

Pietro let out a roar.

"So there you are! What do you mean by being late? Pay your respects to your grandmother. And do you not see that we have a guest? *Per Dio*, you are a sight! Could you not at least wash your hands before appearing?"

I was amused—which shows you I am not as smart as I think I am. But Pietro sounded like so many of the exasperated parents of teenagers whom I had known in America and in Germany. The boy was obviously his son. Only a father could be so annoyed.

The boy, who had been wandering slowly toward his chair, stopped and looked blankly at his father. Then he turned toward the dowager and bowed.

"Grandmother, excuse me. I have been working. I lost track of the time."

"That is all right, my darling," said the old lady fondly.

"It is not all right," snarled Pietro. "Vicky, this ill-bred young boor is, for my sins, my only son. Luigi, greet the distinguished lady doctor Miss Bliss, a scholar of art history. No, do not offer your hand, *idiota*, it is too dirty. Go and wash!"

Luigi had obediently advanced toward me, his hand extended. It resembled a sculpture by someone like Dali—perfectly shaped, with long, spatulate fingers; but it was blue and pink and green and red.

"Of course," I said, smiling. "You are a painter."

"He is a bad painter," said Pietro. "He dabbles in oils. He makes messes."

The boy gave his father a look of naked loathing. I really couldn't blame him.

"I'd like to see your work someday," I said tactfully.

"You will hate it," Pietro said. "Go Luigi, and wash yourself."

"Never mind, never mind," snapped his grandmother. "You make too much of a small thing, my son. Sit down, Luigi. Eat. You are too thin. Eat, dear boy."

Pietro shut up. With a triumphant look at his father, Luigi took his seat.

"She spoils him," Pietro muttered out of the corner of his mouth. "How can I maintain discipline when she contradicts everything I say?"

I had no intention of getting involved in a family argument. So I just smiled and ate my soup.

The conversation did not scintillate. The dowager addressed a few courteous remarks to me, but she spoke mostly to Luigi, urging him to eat more, asking how he had slept, and so on. He was faultlessly sweet to her, and I decided that Pietro was too hard on the boy. He had lovely manners. So what if he was untidy and absentminded? There are worse faults.

Pietro was too busy gobbling to talk much, though he and Smythe exchanged a few words on business matters—all Greek to me. Helena didn't say a word. She was seated directly across from me, and her unblinking stare would have gotten on my nerves if I hadn't been so fascinated by the way she was eating. Her hair kept getting in the spaghetti. I kept expecting her to fork up a strand of it, but she never did.

There was plenty of wine with the meal, and by the time the servants removed the last plates I was, to say the least, replete. Pietro was in far worse condition. When he stood up, I feared for the cummerbund. It was strained to the utmost.

The dowager was helped out of her chair by one of the footmen. She limped toward the door, leaning heavily on a handsome ivory-headed stick, pausing only long enough to thank me for coming and to apologize for the infirmity that made it necessary for her to retire.

Pietro tried to bow to his mother. He managed to incline his head a couple of inches, but he didn't bend well. The look he turned on me was fond, but glazed.

"He will make the arrangements," he wheezed, waving a pudgy hand in Smythe's general direction. "Tell him when you will be ready, dear lady; the car will be there. I anticipate that moment. You will doubtless wish to return to the hotel now to pack. Sir John will have the car brought round."

Helena came up out of her chair as if she had been stung.

"Car?" she repeated, in a voice as shrill and toneless as an old phonograph record. "Tomorrow? What is this, Pietro?"

Pietro was already halfway to the door.

"Later, my treasure, later. I must retire now. You will excuse me—my old war wound—"

He went scuttling out. Helena turned furious eyes on me.

"What is this? The car, tomorrow—"

Smythe came around the table and stood beside me.

"Car, tomorrow," he agreed. "The lady is

joining us at Tivoli. Ah"—as she started to speak—"don't lose your temper, Helena. Think it over. It won't do you any good to make scenes, his Excellency hates them. In fact, I think he is getting weary of your scenes."

"Ah, you think so?" Helena had no gift of repartee. "You think so, do you?"

"Yes, I think so. Have another piece of cake, my dear, and calm yourself. You will excuse us? I felt sure you would. . . ."

To my amusement, Helena took his advice, sinking back into her chair and beckoning to one of the servants. John Smythe took my arm and led me out.

"Don't bother ordering the car for me," I said. "I need a walk. I feel like a stuffed cabbage."

"You'll soon lose your girlish figure if you visit the count," Smythe said. "And that isn't all you might lose. . . . Don't you ever listen to advice?"

"Not from people named Smythe," I said. "Couldn't you think up a better name than that?"

"Why bother? Most people aren't as critical as you. Stop trying to change the subject. If you hurry, you can catch the evening express to Munich."

I stared across the hall, putting my feet down hard.

"I will be ready tomorrow morning," I said. "Nine o'clock?"

"Pietro doesn't get up till noon. Did you hear what—"

"I heard. I'll be ready at nine; tell Pietro that. I don't think," I added thoughtfully, "that he would appreciate your attempts to interfere with his private arrangements."

"If that were all you had in mind, I wouldn't interfere," said this deplorable man. "Helena is about due to be retired; the position will be open."

I saw no reason to dignify this suggestion with a reply. As I approached the front door, the butler slid out of an alcove and opened it for me. I turned and waved gaily at Smythe. He was standing with his arms folded, and if looks could kill. . . .

"Until tomorrow," I said. "*Arrivederla*, Sir John."

III

Michelangelo's "Pietà" is behind glass now, ever since that maniac tried to hack it up a few years ago. There are no words to describe it, although a lot of people have tried. As I stood looking up at it I wondered, as I have so often, what flaw of the flesh or the soul impels vandals to want to destroy beautiful things. Even religious sanctions couldn't save works of art; the followers of one god use "faith" as an excuse for mutilating the images of another. The two strains run through the human race, from the earliest time: dark and bright, foul and fair—the destroyers and the creators. Sometimes I get the feeling that the former type is winning.

I had walked across to St. Peter's from the Aventine, and a darned long walk it was, too. I needed it, not only for the physical exercise. I had some thinking to do, and I think best when I'm moving. Besides—not to be morbid about it—I thought I might not have a chance to do much more sightseeing in Rome.

I wasn't worried about being followed. Why should they follow me when I was about to walk into the lions' den like a good little Christian? I did not doubt that the palazzo was the lions' den, but I wasn't at all sure who the lions were. Pietro couldn't be the mastermind. He just couldn't be. It was possible that there were things going on in the palace that he didn't know about; it was a huge pile, a city block square, three or four stories high; there was room enough there to train a guerrilla army without his noticing.

Nor could I believe that Smythe was the head crook. A crook he was, undoubtedly, but not the boss. Of the other inhabitants of the palazzo only one seemed to me to be a likely possibility—the dowager. Helena was classically stupid, the boy was too young. On the face of it, it might seem silly to suspect a bent old woman, but the mastermind needn't be actively engaged; all he (she) had to do was plot. And I suspected there was an active mind behind the contessa's wrinkled face.

However, there might be other people in the family whom I had not yet met. Or Pietro might be a subordinate conspirator under the direction of a smarter crook who lived elsewhere. Certainly someone in the palace was involved in the plot. It was the only lead I had, and I had been presented with a unique opportunity to follow it.

I managed to put the whole business out of my mind when I reached the basilica, feeling I was entitled to a few hours off duty. I had bought a guidebook from one of the shops along the Via della Conciliazione, and I wandered around the vast body of the church reading and looking like any other tourist. My mind kept wandering, though. The monument to the exiled Stuart kings reminded me of Smythe. The little statue of St. Peter, whose bronze foot has been worn smooth by the kisses of generations of pilgrims, recalled his less saintly namesake. The porphyry disk on the paving near the main altar marked the spot in the old basilica where Charlemagne had received the imperial crown, and I thought of the sapphire talisman that had started me on my quest.

It was a pleasant interlude, though. I sat for a long time on the rim of one of the fountains in the piazza, drinking a warm (and outrageously expensive) Coke I had bought from a vendor, and admiring the sweeping curves of the great colonnades.

After I had gotten back to the hotel I wrote a long letter and made a telephone call. I gave the letter to the concierge when I went down to dinner. He swore he would see to its dispatch personally. He looked like a nice, honest man, but I figured a ten-thousand-lira tip wouldn't hurt. It was a legitimate business deduction, after all.

Five

PIETRO'S CAR WAS A ROLLS, NATURALLY. I was sitting in the lobby when it arrived. I had been there for almost two hours. I had become bored with my room, and, to tell the truth, I had also become a little nervous. It had occurred to me that my complacent analysis of the situation might not be completely accurate. The invitation might have been a bluff, to get me off guard so I wouldn't be expecting violence. If the gang wanted to put me out of the way, it would be safer for them to do it in the anonymity of a large hotel rather than wait till I was Pietro's house guest. I had taken precautions, of course. But until the gang knew I had taken them, they wouldn't do me any good. So I hied myself and my suitcases down to the lobby and sat there reading my guidebook and watching the guests come and go.

Money is a great thing. When the Count Caravaggio's car was announced, the staff of the hotel ran around like little beetles. I marched to the door escorted by two bellboys and the doorman, feeling like the queen; everybody was bowing and scraping and smiling obsequiously. The car was incredible—about a block and a half long, painted silver. I do not jest. The chauffeur and the hotel staff dealt with my two scruffy suitcases and I climbed into what is, I believe, referred to as the tonneau.

There was room back there for a small dance band, but the only occupants were Pietro and his secretary and Helena. From Pietro's expression—and Italians have the most expressive faces of any nationality—I deduced that he had tried to get rid of Helena, but had failed, and therefore had permitted "Sir John" to ride along. I got to sit next to Sir John. Everybody except Helena kissed my hand.

Pietro was resplendent in a linen suit and silk cravat. Helena wore silk slacks and a T-shirt with the insignia of a Roman yacht club. She was not wearing a bra. Her exuberant hair, and a pair of big sunglasses, covered most of her face, but the part that was visible did not look happy.

I have never seen anything like that car. It had a bar and a color TV (they had just been introduced into Italy) and a telephone and brocade curtains that swished into place at the touch of a button. I kept expecting a topless dancer to pop out of the upholstery. By the time Pietro had finished displaying its marvels, we were out in the suburbs.

"I hope we did not keep you waiting," he said. "It was Helena's fault. She is very slow."

Helena glared at him and he glared back. I had to agree with Smythe's assessment. It looked as if Helena was on her way out. A sensible woman would have seen this and modified her behavior accordingly, but Helena didn't have much sense.

"That's all right," I said cheerfully. "As long as we arrive by five o'clock. I have to make a phone call then."

As I had hoped, this announcement created a stir. Pietro stared. Smythe, beside me, shifted position slightly.

"Telephone call," he repeated. "Dare I hope . . ."

"It's my Uncle Karl," I said. "Such an old fussbudget. I promised I would telephone him every day. You know how these Germans are."

Smythe, damn him, began to chuckle. Pietro looked surprised.

"You have a German uncle? I thought you were American."

"He's only an adopted uncle," I explained. "Good old Uncle Karl Schmidt. He gets absolutely hysterical if he doesn't hear from me every single day. I don't know what he would do if he didn't hear from me. I'll pay for the calls, of course."

"That is not important," said Pietro. He looked very thoughtful.

"Oh, I think it is," I said. "I feel the rich are apt to be imposed on, don't you? Just because you have a lot of money doesn't mean you are obliged to pay for my telephone calls."

"Mmph," said Pietro.

Smythe was still shaking with amusement.

"I suppose you've got some document or other in the hands of your solicitors, to be opened in case you are not heard from," he said.

"I mailed it off last night."

Smythe let out a whoop of laughter. Pietro glowered at him. Helena shifted position, wobbling like a molded-jello salad.

"You make no sense," she said. "I do not understand."

"That's probably just as well," said Smythe.

"All right, Vicky. . . . I may call you Vicky, mayn't I?"

"No," I said.

"And you must call me John. You have made your point, my dear Vicky, so let's forget business for a while. Enjoy the scenery. We will not pass this way again, as some poet has expressed it."

Pietro's face had been an absolute blank during this exchange. Either he was an excellent actor, or he really had no idea what we were talking about. At least I was sure about Smythe. That man's effrontery was unbelievable.

According to legend, the founders of Tivoli were Catallus of Arcadia, who fled from his country with Evander during the war between Eteocles and Polyneices, and his son Tibertus. Sounds like a soap opera, doesn't it? All those names. Smythe told me this, and more, as the big car rolled smoothly along the road. He absolutely babbled. Nobody else got a word in.

I already knew that Tivoli, not far from Rome, was a favorite location for the country villas of Roman nobles. The ancient Romans went there to escape the heat of the city; the most famous of their country estates was the one built by the emperor Hadrian, the ruins of whose palace complex still stand. The Villa d'Este is the best known of the Renaissance villas. The villa and its magnificent gardens are the property of the Italian government now, but the Villa Caravaggio is still inhabited. It is like the Villa d'Este, but on a smaller scale. That means it is only as big as a medium-sized hotel. The villa itself has the usual painted and gilded reception rooms and large, drafty bedchambers, three floors of them, built around an arcaded courtyard. But the glory of the place is its gardens. There are fountains all over the place—fountains with groups of monumental statuary, fountains set in fake grottoes, fountains flowing over rocks and down stairs, fountains that suddenly explode out of nowhere and drench the unwary pedestrian. There were long avenues of cypresses and hedges higher than my head, walled gardens and covered arcades. I got a bird's eye survey as we drove through the grounds.

When we approached the villa, Helena, seated across from me, started squirming uneasily. I couldn't see much of her face, and it was not, at best, the most expressive of human countenances, but I realized that she was in the grip of some strong emotion—not a pleasant emotion. There were beads of sweat on her upper lip, although the air conditioning had produced a near-Arctic temperature inside the car.

The car stopped. The chauffeur leaped out and opened the door. Pietro was the first one out. He extended his hand to help me, and Smythe followed. Helena didn't move.

"Hurry," Pietro snapped. "Luncheon will be served shortly. The food will be cold."

Helena pushed herself back into the corner of the seat. She shook her head violently. Bleached hair filled the interior of the car.

"Very well, then," Pietro said angrily. "Antonio will drive you back to Rome. I told you not to come."

Helena let out a low moaning sound and shook her head again.

"Sit in the car, then," Pietro shouted. "Sit and melt. Sit all day, all night. *Dio*, what a nuisance this woman is!"

He stormed up the stairs, leaving us standing there. I looked at Smythe. He was smiling. He was always smiling, curse him. He winked at me and then bent to look into the car.

"Come along, Helena, don't be foolish."

I realized then what was wrong with the girl. She was absolutely terrified. Her lower lip was trembling, and so was the hand she hesitantly extended. Smythe took hold of her and yanked her out of the car, handling her ample poundage with ease. He was a lot stronger than he looked. Even after he had set her on her feet she clung to his hand.

"You will protect me?" she whispered, staring up at him. "You will not let it hurt me?"

"Of course not," Smythe said. "Now hurry, do. You know how angry his Excellency gets when he is kept from his food."

Helena tottered along, clinging to his arm. She was not my type, but I couldn't help feeling sorry for her; I would have pitied anyone who was in such a blue funk of fear.

"What are you so afraid of?" I asked.

"That's a good question," Smythe agreed. "Perhaps I ought to know what I have naïvely promised to protect you from. My talents, though enormous, are limited; anything along the lines of King Kong or the Loch Ness monster—"

"It is a monster," Helena muttered. "A phantom. The ghost of the Caravaggios."

"A ghost," I said. "Ha, ha. Very funny."

"No, it is not funny," Helena said. "It is terrible! All in black, hooded like a monk, but the face. . . . The face is . . ."

She made a gurgling sound, like a stopped-up sink. It was a very effective performance. I could feel my flesh creep, even in the warm noontide.

"The face," I said impatiently. "What about it? No, let me guess. A melting, dissolving, phosphorescent horror . . ."

"A rotting, mummified, withered, brown, noseless horror," Smythe contributed.

"A skull!" Helena shrieked. I heard a thud behind us, and turned. The chauffeur, following with the baggage, had dropped a suitcase. He was staring at Helena with horrified eyes.

"Oh, a skull," Smythe said, yawning. "That's a bit old hat, don't you think? I liked my rotting mummy better."

"You laugh? It will laugh with you—a great soundless laugh, like a scream of horror. I saw its teeth, two rows of blackened teeth. . . . It walks the gardens by night, but who knows whether it will not soon enter the house? I have seen it once, a face of silver bone shining in the moonlight, laughing. . . ."

She wasn't pretending. The plump arm that brushed mine was icy cold.

Of course that didn't mean that the phantom was real. It only meant that somebody had scared poor old Helena out of her socks. If something walked the grounds of the villa by night, disguised from casual strollers, there must be a reason for concealment.

Smythe seemed to be as surprised and impressed by the story as I was. I had to remind myself that the man was an accomplished actor, and as untrustworthy as a polecat.

"It sounds perfectly dreadful," he said sympathetically. "But I shouldn't worry, Helena; specters of that type never come inside a building."

"*É vero?*" Helena asked hopefully.

"*Assolutamente,*" Smythe said firmly. "I know something about ghosts. My ancestral home is absolutely littered with the creatures. Frightful nuisances; rattling chains all night, spotting up the floor with bloodstains that can't be removed. . . . Furthermore, you're in luck, Helena, old thing. I'll wager you didn't know that Doctor Bliss here is a real expert on spooks. You tell her all about it and she'll tell you how to deal with it. Right, Vicky?"

"Oh, yes," I said, glowering at him. That might have been a hit in the dark, but I didn't think so.

"There, you see?" Smythe patted Helena on one of the more rounded portions of her anatomy. She revived enough to wriggle and giggle at him.

The villa was a beautiful place, magnificently furnished with antiques, but I was too preoccupied to appreciate its wonders. I passed through the great hall with scarcely a glance and followed one of the maids up the stairs to my room. Smythe left us on the second floor, with a murmured apology, but Helena stuck to me like a burr. My room was a grandiose chamber, like the throne room of a doge's palace, with a balcony overlooking the gardens and the "Fountain of the Baboons." Helena threw herself down on the bed and peered at me through her sunglasses.

"Do you really know all about ghosts?" she demanded.

"Oh, sure," I said.

"Then you must tell me what to do, to be safe."

"First you had better tell me what you saw," I said, sitting down beside her.

She hadn't much to add to her original description. She had only seen the apparition once—one night in April, the last time they had visited the villa. She had had a fight with Pietro and had gone for a walk, in order to calm herself, as she put it. The vision had sent her screaming back to Pietro's willing arms, and at her insistence they had returned to Rome the following day. She had not wanted to come back to the villa.

"But he no longer cares for my feelings," she whined. "He forced me to come. I think he does not believe me, about the phantom. I swear to you—"

"Oh, I believe you. But I'm surprised at Pietro. Isn't there a family tradition about the ghost? Many old families have such stories."

"He says not. But he lies, perhaps; he is a great liar, Pietro. Now tell me what to do to be safe. And," she added firmly, "do not tell me to leave this place. If I go, I will lose him. And that I cannot afford to do just yet."

I thought she meant "afford" in the most literal sense. Well, that was her business, and I do mean business. It didn't concern me. On the whole, I preferred to have her stick around; she would distract Pietro, and I didn't want him following me everywhere I went. I dipped into my childhood memories of horror movies.

"You ought to have a crucifix," I said.

"But I have them—many of them." She plucked at a chain that hung around her neck and drew out a cross. It was a handsome thing, made of platinum set with diamonds.

"Ah, but has it been blessed by the Pope?" I inquired seriously.

"No. . . ." Helena took off her sunglasses, frowning. "But I have some that were."

"Wear one of them, then, all the time. You should be perfectly safe then."

"That is all?" She sounded disappointed.

"You weren't wearing it when you saw the ghost, were you?" I assumed she hadn't been wearing it, or much else; the quarrel had occurred late at night. "Oh, well. To be perfectly sure, what you should do is hang some garlic at every window and door. And over the fireplace, if there is one. Iron is good, too. Something made of iron over each opening—door, windows—"

"What else?" She sat up, hands on her knees, eyes bright.

"Well," I said, getting into my stride, "holy water. Can you get some?"

"*Sì, sì.* I sprinkle it on me, eh? That is good. And perhaps garlic too, on a chain with the crucifix?"

I was about to agree when I realized that Pietro might balk at embracing the lady if she were reeking of garlic. I didn't want to break up that romance; it would keep him out of my hair.

"No," I said firmly. "The crucifix and the garlic don't go together. They cancel each other, *capisce*?"

"Ah, *sì*. It is sensible."

"That should do it. Stay in at night, of course. Ghosts do not walk by day. And," I added cunningly, "you are perfectly safe when you are with Pietro. He is the lord of the manor. It is his ghost; it won't bother him."

"*Sì, sì*; how clever you are, Vicky!" She beamed at me. Like most simple souls, she was easily convinced. She hoisted herself to her feet. "I will dress now. It is time for lunch."

I had suspected it might be. Somewhere in the depths of the villa someone was banging on a gong, and had been doing so for some time.

I ran a comb through my hair and followed the sound of the gong, which had assumed a slightly hysterical resonance. The closer I got, the more outrageous the noise became; I had my hands over my ears when I came upon it—a mammoth structure as big as the one that is banged in old Arthur Rank movies. Pietro was swatting it with a huge mallet. His tie was up under his left ear and his face was bright red with anger and exertion. When he saw me he dropped the mallet. The gong shivered and echoed and died, and I took my fingers out of my ears.

"It is too maddening," Pietro exclaimed. "The boy is always late; never is he on time; and now Helena too. And Sir John, where is he? They all conspire to keep me from my lunch. I suffer from a rare disease of the stomach, my doctor tells me I must eat at regular hours."

"I was late too," I said. "I'm sorry. I didn't know about your rare disease."

Pietro straightened his tie, mopped his face, smoothed his hair, and smirked at me.

"But for you it is different. You are a guest. I should have given you more time. Come, we will go in. We will not wait for them."

We didn't have to wait long for Helena and Smythe. She gave me a big grin as she entered; her crucifix, of gold and pearls, was prominently displayed. Smythe followed her in and took a seat next to me.

The meal was a pattern of the others I was to eat in that house. The boy never appeared at all, nor did the dowager. Pietro explained that his mother often dined in her rooms. That was almost all he said. Smythe didn't contribute much either. He seemed preoccupied. As soon as we had devoured the vast quantities of food, Pietro went staggering out to take a nap. Helena followed him, and I caught Smythe's arm as he passed me on his way to the door.

"Don't you think it's time we had a talk?" I asked.

I forget whether I've mentioned that he was just about my height—an inch or so taller, maybe, but the heels on my sandals made up the difference. We were eyeball to eyeball as we stood there, but by some alchemy he managed to give the impression that he was looking down at me—down the full length of his nose.

"I suspect it will be wasted effort on my part," he drawled. "But I'm willing to give it another try. Let's stroll in the gardens, shall we?"

"How romantic," I said.

It might have been, if someone other than Smythe had been my escort. The cool tinkle of the fountains followed us through shady walks and avenues lined with flowering shrubs. When I tried to talk, Smythe shushed me.

"May as well find a quiet spot," he said.

We rounded a corner, and I jumped six feet off the ground. Straight ahead was a giant monster's head carved of stone. It was so big that the open mouth was taller than I am. Its snarling expression and horned, serpent-entwined head would have been startling even in miniature.

"I suppose that's your idea of a joke," I said, getting my breath back.

"Sorry. I forgot the damned thing was there. It's not a bad place for a private chat, actually. Come on in."

He walked through the mouth, stooping slightly to avoid the stone fangs that fringed it.

I followed him. The stone of which the atrocity was carved was a rough, dark substance, pumicelike in texture, but much harder. Lichen and moss had grown over the surface like peeling skin. It was a singularly unappealing piece of work.

The hollow head had been fitted up as a summer house. Light came in through the eyes and mouth and nose slits, but it was still pretty dark. Smythe sat down on a bamboo chair and waved me toward another.

"Are there any more little charmers like this around?" I asked.

"Several. The ninth count got the idea from a friend—Prince Vicino Orsini—back in the sixteenth century."

"I've read about the Orsini estate," I said. "Bomarzo—isn't that the name of it?"

"I don't remember. It's about fifty miles north of Rome. Quite a tourist attraction, I understand."

"Never mind the guidebook excerpts," I said. "I want—"

"My dear girl, you introduced the subject."

"Consider it finished, then."

"Did you really leave a letter with your solicitor?"

"I left a letter, but not with my solicitor. I don't have a solicitor. I admit that the evidence I've collected so far isn't conclusive. If it were, I'd go to the police. But I'm sure you will agree that my demise or disappearance would confirm my suspicions in a particularly inconvenient fashion."

"Inconvenient for us, certainly. We don't want publicity."

"Then what do you intend doing about it?"

"About what?" His left eyebrow lifted.

"Why, this—the plot—the. . . ."

He leaned back in his chair, his hands folded on his flat stomach, and smiled at me. "Really, Victoria, you're being unreasonable. I don't see why I should do anything. It's up to you to take action, I should think. What are *you* going to do?"

"Find out all about the plot," I said. "Then go to the police and have you all put in jail."

"How very unkind of you. I do think you are jumping to conclusions. What makes you suppose this is a police matter?"

I got a grip on myself. His nonchalant, oblique style of conversation was affecting mine; we were talking around the subject and not saying anything.

"You seem to know all about me," I said. "I suppose you checked up on me after I gave you my name. You know where I work; you also know that your man in Munich—"

"Lovely title for a thriller," he interrupted.

"It's been done. Stop interrupting. Your man in Munich is dead, and you know he had the Charlemagne talisman—"

Smythe sat upright. His smile had faded, and his eyes were bright and speculative.

"So that was it. No, I didn't know what had stimulated an employee of the National Museum to burglary, but the mere fact was enough to make us suspicious of you. Even so, my dear, the existence of the talisman is irrelevant. What a nasty suspicious mind you must have, to leap to the conclusion that our pretty little copy meant larceny."

"Where you made your mistake was having me kidnapped," I retorted.

"You don't suppose I would do anything so stupid?" Smythe demanded scornfully.

"Who did, then?"

"None of your business. Good Lord, girl, you didn't really imagine I was going to blurt out a detailed confession as soon as you had me to yourself? You can't prove a bloody thing. You can sit here till moss grows on you, and you still won't be able to prove anything."

"Oh, really?"

"Yes, really. We have our tracks very nicely covered, I assure you. You won't learn anything here, but it is possible that you may get into trouble. My colleagues are harmless souls, on the whole, but one or two of them. . . . I spoke quite sharply to them about kidnapping you, and I hope it won't happen again. But I can't promise, and I'm damned if I'm going to make a habit of rescuing you. Why the hell don't you go away?"

"You wouldn't be so anxious for me to leave

if there were nothing to be learned here," I said.

"Rudimentary Logic One. How to Construct a Syllogism. That doesn't follow, you know. I told you, I am not completely certain of my colleagues' reliability." His tone changed. He leaned forward, his blue eyes softening. "Look here, Vicky, it's really quite a harmless little plot. Why can't you drop it?"

"If I knew all about it, I might agree with you," I said sweetly.

Smythe opened his mouth as if to speak. Then he fell back in his chair and started to laugh.

"No, no," he said, between chuckles. "I was tempted to spin you a pleasing yarn. I could do it, you know. But you have a mind that is almost as twisty as mine. You'd never believe me, would you?"

"Frankly," I said, throwing tact to the winds, "I wouldn't believe you if you told me the sun rises in the east. Why don't *you* give it up? If the plot is that harmless, it can't be worth much. I'm very persistent, and my friends already know quite a lot about you."

Gravely Smythe removed a white handkerchief from his pocket, waved it in the air, and then returned it to its place.

"The parley is over," he said. "We don't seem to be getting anywhere. I am going back to the house; I have work to do. Coming?"

"I'm beginning to like this place," I said. "I think I shall stay awhile."

Smythe walked to the mouth—the door, that is. He turned. Against the sunlight he was a dark paper shape, a silhouetted shadow. I couldn't see his features, but when he spoke his voice had lost its humorous tone.

"I admire your bravado, Vicky. But don't push it too far. There are things that walk in the garden here—and not only by night."

Which was a nice thought to leave with a girl who was sitting inside a monster's head.

II

I fell asleep out there in the monster's head, lying on a nice soft chaise longue. It was very unusual for me to do that. I never sleep in the daytime. I don't usually eat lunches like that one either, with almost half a bottle of very potent wine.

Things started to liven up about four o'clock, when Pietro rose from his nap—if that's what he was doing up there in his room. As I was to learn, he was usually somnolent and lazy in the morning, but he revived, like a night-blooming cereus, as twilight approached, and by midnight he was going strong.

He was a rather engaging little man. Unlike many blasé millionaires, he really enjoyed life. Not that I've known that many millionaires; I base that statement on what I read in the magazines. Wine may have contributed to his joie de vivre. He started drinking as soon as he got up, and continued until he collapsed. He drank fairly slowly, just a little bit faster than his body could absorb the stuff, so it took him quite a while to get loaded. He passed through several distinct stages along the way. The first sign of inebriation was a profound intellectuality. He would talk about history and politics and philosophy, using a lot of long words and quotations from Greek philosophers I had never heard of. He invented them, I think.

As the dinner hour approached, sensuality replaced the lure of the intellect. If I was alone with him during that period I had to keep moving, but eating used up most of his libidinous urges, and after dinner he became soft and sentimental. That was when he played old Nelson Eddy-Jeanette MacDonald records on his huge hi-fi and tried to do Viennese waltzes.

The belligerent mood succeeded this one, but being a noble Italian, Pietro wanted to fight with swords instead of fists. During these hours he often challenged people to duels. At about midnight he became quite vivacious and told a lot of old jokes and did vaudeville routines. He fancied himself as an amateur magician. He had all the paraphernalia, including one of those trick boxes for sawing a lady in half, but by that time his hands were getting unsteady, and even the housemaids refused to be sawed. Sometime in the early hours of the morning he collapsed and was carried off to bed by his valet and Mr. Smythe. I don't know what he needed a mistress for, unless it was during the pre-dinner hour.

It was during the intellectual stage that first evening that he decided to show me his collections. He warned me that it would take days to study them properly; this was just a quick run-through, to give me a chance to decide what I wanted to concentrate on.

I've seen a lot of beautiful things. Museums are my favorite hobby, as well as my profession. But that was a unique experience. The objects he showed me were not museum pieces, they were part of the furniture.

"But what about thieves?" I said, midway through the tour. "This place is wide open, Pietro; anybody could get in."

"But how would they get out? Carrying that . . ." And he gestured at a greater-than-life-size marble torso of Hercules that stood on a pedestal in the *salone*. "You would need a truck, would you not, and a block and tackle. It is not easy to put such an apparatus into my drawing room."

"That's right, I guess." The little man wasn't as foolish as he looked. "But what about the smaller objects?"

"There are many servants, even when I am not in residence. My housekeeper checks the inventory daily. As for the very small, very valuable objects, naturally I keep them in my safe."

"Things like jewelry?" I said.

"Ah, you like jewelry?" Pietro patted my arm, and for a minute I thought the sensual phase was arriving a little early. But he went on. "That I keep in the vault. You would care to see it?"

"Oh, yes," I said, wide-eyed. "I just love jewelry."

"Ah, women," sighed Pietro. "You are all

alike—even you clever ladies are like all the others where jewels are concerned."

The safe was a small room, right next to his sitting room upstairs, and he had sense enough to stand between me and the combination lock as he opened it.

"It is changed yearly," he explained, twirling knobs. "A little person comes from the bank."

At his suggestion I sat down on a velvet divan and he brought out boxes, which he piled on a low table in front of me. Then he started opening the boxes.

For half an hour or so I forgot I was a well-educated, cynical specialist, gainfully employed in a museum. I wallowed in jewels.

The pieces that really got to me were the Renaissance jewels. There was a pendant of gold and enamel, with a mermaid made out of a Baroque pearl. Its contours formed the mermaid's torso; her raised arms and flowing hair were gold. The scales of her fishtail were made of roughly polished emeralds. And there was a necklace two feet long, made of stones as big as the end of a man's thumb—emeralds and rubies and amethysts and topazes. Another necklace was of square-cut rubies framed in gold, with a cabochon ruby the size of a bantam hen's egg dangling from the center. There was a headdress like one I had seen in a Botticelli painting—fine bands of gold supporting a star sapphire with stylized flower petals all around it. A star-shaped brooch set with pearls and rubies and emeralds framed in twisted gold wire. Rings. . . .

I tried to look at these jewels with a critical eye, but it wasn't easy, because Pietro insisted that I try them on. Rings on my fingers, bells on my toes. . . . He was getting to the amorous stage. I was absolutely clanking with jewels when the door burst open and Helena stormed in.

Alas, it appeared that we were no longer buddies. She glared at me and burst into impassioned speech.

"So this is where you are! You give this to her—never have you let me have so much as a miserable little ring, and you shower this—this—"

What followed was a fascinating excursion into Roman gutter slang. I had never known there were so many different words for a lady of ill repute. Pietro stood it for a while, and then he let out a roar.

"*Silenzio!* How dare you come here and use such vulgar language to a lady? A learned lady, who comes to study my collection! She is—she is writing a book, which will make me famous, is that not so, Vicky?"

"Oh, yes," I said. "I surely am. You surely will be."

Helena started to speak again, but Pietro shouted her down.

"Go! Go and learn manners. I do not give you so much as a ring, no! These jewels have been in my family for centuries. They belong to the Contessa Caravaggio, not to a—a—"

"That's all right," I said, as he glanced apologetically at me. "I know what you mean. You had better put the jewels away, Pietro."

And—I hate to admit it, but I must—as I started to remove the ornaments from my fingers and throat and breast, my hands were stiff and reluctant. That was when I first began to understand the lure of precious jewels—a violent emotion that has prompted a good deal of bloodshed over the centuries.

It wasn't until I got back to my own room and began getting ready for cocktails that I could think sympathetically of Helena.

If those damned pieces of crystallized carbon affected me as they had done, what must they do to Helena? I will do myself some justice; it wasn't only the value of the stones that fascinated me, it was the beauty of the workmanship. The Renaissance jewelers weren't simply craftsmen, they were the great artists of the period. Cellini was a sculptor as well as a goldsmith; Ghirlandaio, Verrocchio, and Michelozzo worked as jewelers. The "Doors of Paradise," those matchless bas-reliefs at the Baptistery in Florence, were designed by a goldsmith named Ghiberti.

The unknown workman who had copied the Charlemagne talisman was in good company. I wondered if any of the jewels I had seen that day were fakes.

I guess this is as good a time as any to talk about fakes. It isn't a single subject, it is a dozen subjects, because the techniques used in imitating jewelry, for instance, obviously differ from the methods used for porcelain or paintings. But all imitations have one thing in common, and that is this: if they are well done, it is practically impossible to tell them from the real thing.

The stuffier connoisseurs and art critics like to think they can spot a fake masterpiece by its stylistic failings alone. After all, if Rembrandt was so great, he should not be easy to imitate. This is a nice theory, but it is wrong. Every single museum in the world, including the snootiest, has objects tucked away in the basement that their experts would like to forget about—forged paintings and sculptures that they paid through the nose to get because they thought the pieces were genuine. Oh, sure, once a piece of art is known to be a fake—because the forger confessed, or chemical tests exposed it—then it's easy to pick the thing apart. "The drapery in the imitation Greek bas-relief is not as crisp and sure as in the original. . . ." Bah, humbug. The best of the experts have been fooled.

Take the case of Van Meegeren, who was probably the most famous and most successful art forger the world has ever known. If he hadn't confessed, his fake Vermeers would still be featured in museums. His was a rare and lovely case of poetic justice, because he had to confess in order to save himself from a far more serious charge. During the German occupation of Holland, Van Meegeren sold one of his paintings to that clod Goering, who thought he was a connoisseur. Goering believed he was buying a genuine Vermeer, of course. Unfortunately, so did the Dutch government, and after the war, when they were catching up with traitors and quislings, they arrested Van Meegeren on a charge of collaborating with the Nazis—specifically, for selling national art treasures. The really amusing thing about the case was that when Van Meegeren confessed to faking dozens of Vermeers, the art world refused to believe him. What—the great "Supper at Emmaus" a fraud? Nonsense. It was obviously by Vermeer; in fact, it was his masterpiece! Not until Van Meegeren painted a new Vermeer, in his cell in the city jail, were the skeptics convinced. Then—such is human nature—they all started picking flaws in the paintings they had once hailed as treasures.

I knew something about how paintings are faked. I also knew that the only sure way of detecting a good forgery is by means of chemical and physical tests. For instance, a careless modern forger might use paints such as synthetic cobalts, ultramarine, or zinc white, which weren't manufactured until the nineteenth century. But a good forger would avoid such sloppy errors. Van Meegeren was careful to use only the pigments obtainable in Vermeer's day. They are still available; there are no "mystery pigments" or unknown techniques. Most forgers know enough to use old canvases, and they are skilled at imitating things like cracks and wormholes and patinas.

There are all kinds of tricks, I'm sure—and any honest art historian will admit it, after a drink or two—that there are still lots of forgeries adorning the sacred halls of the world's great museums. As for private collectors, they are hopelessly outclassed, especially if they buy things of questionable origin. They daren't consult appraisers or scholars if they suspect the objects are stolen.

I felt sure that a great deal of antique jewelry had been faked, too, but the only piece I could remember reading about was the Saitaphernes tiara. A tiara is not necessarily a delicate half crown like the ones worn by fairy princesses. This piece was shaped like a tall pointed hat made of thin gold and covered with embossed scenes and inscriptions. The inscriptions had been copied from genuine Greek texts, so they sounded authentic, and the workmanship was good enough to fool the boys at the Louvre, who bought it for that great collection! The jeweler was a Russian named Rouchomowsky. Like Van Meegeren, he had a hard time making the art world accept his confession when he finally broke down. Again let me repeat—there are no lost techniques. Rouchomowsky had learned how to perform the ancient art of granulation—designs formed by tiny beads of gold, no bigger than grains of coarse sand, each one of which is individually welded into its place. Some of his forgeries were excellent copies of ancient Etruscan goldwork.

If Rouchomowsky could do it, so could someone else. The more I thought about it, the more I realized that this gang had an undetectable racket. The only certain method of detecting fakes is by scientific tests, and if you use authentic materials, there is no way in the world they can test wrong. Gold is gold. It varies in purity, of course, but a careful faker would make sure he used the same type normally employed by the Greek or Renaissance craftsmen he was copying. Imitation jewels used to be easy to spot, but nowadays, since the discovery of synthetic jewels, a well-made piece can virtually defy laboratory tests. I wondered why Schmidt was so sure he had the genuine Charlemagne talisman. If I had been in his shoes, I would have taken good care of both of them.

I put on my one long dress—black jersey, very slinky—and took out my own personal jewelry collection. I must say it looked rather tacky.

Six

THE MEN WERE WEARING DINNER JACKETS; and if I had not felt less than kindly toward "Sir John Smythe," I would have had to admit that formal wear suited his slim build and fair hair. His cummerbund was nice and flat. Poor Pietro looked like a melon with a purple ribbon tied around it.

The dowager was sitting by the drawing-room windows, in a tall carved chair like a throne. Her presence subdued her son slightly. He had to confine his amorous proclivities to Helena, since the old countess beckoned me to her side and kept me engaged in conversation.

She was cute. She reminded me of my grandmother. Not that they looked alike; Granny Andersen was a typical Swede, big-boned and blond even in her seventies, with eyes like blue steel chisels. But they were both matriarchs. The dowager had a passion for fashionable scandal. She wanted to know all the latest about Elizabeth Taylor's new husband, and what Jacqueline and Princess Grace were doing. I wasn't up to date on that subject, but I was a good listener. We both agreed, regretfully, that while recent American presidential wives might be very nice ladies, they had not contributed much to the world of glamour.

Before long, young Luigi wandered in. He looked vaguely around the room, as if he had forgotten what he came for; then he caught his grandmother's eye and ambled over to her. She put out her thin, veined hand and drew him down to a seat on a low stool at her side. They made a pretty picture sitting there— sweet old age and attentive youth.

"My darling, you have not greeted Doctor Bliss," said the dowager fondly.

Luigi looked up at me. I felt a slight shock. He might look dreamy and disconnected, but his eyes were furiously alive—black, blazing, intent.

"*Buona sera, Dottoressa,*" he said obediently.

I returned the greeting, and then silence fell. Luigi continued to fondle his grandmother's hand, running a delicate thumb over her bony fingers, almost in the manner of a lover.

"You look tired, my treasure," she said.

"What have you been doing? You must conserve your strength, you are growing."

"I am well, Grandmother." He smiled at her. "You know that to work is for me the highest pleasure."

She shook her head anxiously.

"You work too hard, my angel."

He didn't look overworked to me. He'd have been a howling success as a pop-music star, setting the little girls shrieking, if he hadn't been so clean.

"What sort of work do you do, Luigi?" I asked. Then, as he held out those expressive, stained young hands, I said, "I'm sorry, I forgot. What sort of painting do you do?"

It was badly phrased. Most young painters imitate one style or another, but none of them like to be reminded of that; they all think they are innovators. Before I could repair my blunder, Pietro let out a sneering laugh.

"His style, do you mean? It is of the most modern school, Vicky. Totally without form or sense. Blobs of color smeared on a canvas."

The boy's eyes flashed.

"I am still experimenting." He spoke directly to me, ignoring his father. "To me art is a very personal experience; it must flow directly from the unconscious onto the canvas, do you not agree, *signoria*?"

"How could she agree?" Pietro demanded. "She is a scholar, a student of art. Did Raphael allow his unconscious to overflow onto the canvas?"

"Well, now," I said, remembering the etchings, "that might not be so far off as—"

"No," shouted Pietro. "Form, technique, the most meticulous study of anatomy. . . . Vicky, do you not agree with me?"

I was about to give some light, joking answer when the tension in the room caught me. They all stared at me with fierce, hungry eyes—the boy, his father, the old woman. I realized that we weren't talking about art at all. This was an old feud, a basic struggle between father and son. I also realized that I would be an idiot to commit myself to one side or the other. Looking around for help, I caught John Smythe's ironical eye. Get yourself out of this one, he seemed to be saying.

"I'm not a critic," I said modestly. "As a medieval scholar I appreciate form, naturally, but I do feel that one's approach to art must be basically visceral. I couldn't comment on your work without seeing it, Luigi."

It wasn't a bad answer; it could be interpreted according to the predilections of the hearer. Luigi's face lit up. Goodness, but he was a handsome boy!

"I will show you," he said, starting to rise. "Come now and we will—"

"Luigi!" The dowager tugged him back onto the stool. "You forget yourself, my child. It is almost time for dinner."

"Tomorrow, then." The boy stared at me.

"It will be a pleasure," I said.

"It will be a great pain," said Pietro rudely.

II

I am probably the only person in the whole world under thirty who knows all the words to "Lover, Come Back to Me." It isn't my fault, it's the fault of my idiot memory, which retains all the meaningless facts it has ever encountered. Granny Andersen used to play the songs from the old Romberg and Victor Herbert operettas on the piano. God help me, I know them all.

On this occasion the knack proved to be useful. After dinner, when we returned to the drawing room, Pietro and I sang along with Nelson and Jeanette, and by that time I had drunk enough wine to ignore Smythe's hilarity in the background.

After we had listened to "The New Moon," Pietro passed into the belligerent stage and challenged Smythe to a duel. I forget what brought on the challenge; some fancied insult or other. As I might have expected, Smythe accepted, and the two of them pranced up and down the *salone* whacking at each other. There weren't any swords handy, so they used umbrellas, and even the dowager was reduced to helpless laughter as she watched them. She went to bed then, and Pietro showed us card tricks and produced a very fat, very indignant white rabbit from a top hat. Apparently the rabbit had been asleep—in the hat or elsewhere—and was annoyed at being disturbed; it bit Pietro, and was carried off by the butler while Helena fussed over her wounded lover and bound his wounded thumb up in a long gauzy hankie. I enjoy slapstick, but by then I had had enough; I said good night and went to bed.

A long cold shower shook some of the wine fumes out of my head, and instead of retiring I went out onto the balcony.

It was the kind of night you wouldn't believe. Full moon—a big silvery globe caught in the black spires of the cypresses, like a Christmas ornament. The bright patina of star points made me homesick for a minute; you only see stars like that out in the country, away from the city lights. In the pale moonlight the gardens looked like something out of a romantic novel, all black and silver; the fountains were sprays of diamonds, the roses ivory and jade. My knees got rubbery. It might have been the wine, but I don't think so. I slid down to a sitting position among the potted plants, my arms resting on the low balustrade, and stared dreamily out into the night. I wanted. . . . Well, I'll give you three guesses.

Then a figure came drifting out of the shadows, across the silver-gray stone of the terrace. It was tall and slim, with hair like a white-gold helmet molding its beautifully shaped head. It stopped under my balcony, flung up its arms, threw back its head, and declaimed, in the bell-like tones common to Shakespeare festivals and the BBC:

"*Sweet she was and like a fairy.*
And her shoes were number nine. . . ."

I picked up a flower pot and let it fall. It missed him, but not by much; he had to leap aside to avoid the spattering fragments. I could hear him laughing as I ran inside.

III

Like rats and hamsters, Pietro was a nocturnal animal. Knowing he seldom arose before noon, I figured that morning was the best time to explore. So I was up at eight, bright and shining and ready for action.

What was I looking for? Well, I had no idea. Smythe had been a little too anxious to assure me I wouldn't find anything at the villa. Ordinarily you would assume that a gang of crooks wouldn't bring a suspicious investigator to the scene of the action, but Smythe was just weird enough to be trying the double fake. It's an old adage, that if you are trying to hide from the law you go to a police station. Maybe the criminals were carrying on their nefarious activities under my very nose. There was one activity that would damn them for sure—the workshop of the craftsman who was manufacturing the fake jewelry.

Breakfast was set out in the small dining salon, on silver salvers and hot plates in the English fashion. I ate alone, and then started to explore.

I got lost several times. The villa was a huge place, and I couldn't be sure I had seen it all even after I had been poking around for some time. The cellars were the most confusing part. Some of the rooms were carved out of the limestone of the hillside itself. It seemed to me that this would be a good place for a hidden workshop, so I explored the underground regions as thoroughly as I could without a plan of the place, but I didn't find anything except a lot of spiders and cobwebs, plus a wine cellar with hundreds of bottles.

It was with considerable relief that I left the dank darkness of the cellars for the sunny warmth of the gardens. Faint music accompanied me as I wandered—the splashing of fountains, the singing of birds, the rustle of leaves in the breeze. But after I had walked for a while I began to get an itchy feeling between my shoulder blades—the feeling you get when someone is watching you.

There were plenty of places to hide—shrubs and hedges and ornamental stonework all over the place. But there was no sign of a human being. I suppose that got on my nerves. We city types aren't used to solitude. We are like rats breeding and biting each other in overcrowded spaces. I was suffering from an insane combination of agraphobia and claustrophobia. I was out of doors, with nothing around me but trees and bushes and the sky above, and yet I felt closed in. The weathered statues seemed to eye me cynically from their broken eye sockets, and the carved fauns and satyrs laughed as if they knew some nasty secret I didn't know.

The gardens had been laid out with a view to the comfort of the stroller. There were benches all over the place, seats of marble and wrought iron, carved and decorated with mosaic. I discovered no less than four summer houses fitted out with cushioned chairs and low tables. One was shaped like a miniature circular temple, with the prettiest little Corinthian columns all around. Eventually I found the grotesque giant head where Smythe and I had had our dialogue the day before. I had been too preoccupied on that occasion to get more than a generalized impression of horribleness; when I examined the head more closely I found it even more awful. I went around it, following a paved path of dark stone, and discovered that the head was the guardian of another garden filled with even more repulsive statues.

They were strategically placed so that I

came on them suddenly, without warning, increasing the shock of their grotesque contours. One of them was an elephant—at least I guess that is what it was supposed to be, although it had horns as well as tusks, and claws on its forepaws. The trunk was wound around the torso of a man whom it was trying, quite successfully, to tear in two. The sculptor had succeeded in capturing the victim's expression very well. He looked just the way you would expect a man to look when he is being ripped apart.

The other statues were even worse. There were few atrocities, animal or human, the sculptor had missed. I went on in a daze of fascinated disgust. The lovely flower beds and tinkly little fountains scattered around only made the sculpture worse.

I was halfway along a terrace rimmed with bas-reliefs of a particularly obscene nature when a sound behind me made me spin around. One of the statues was moving.

It was a life-sized male figure with a demon's face, a head of curling snakes, and a fanged mouth. The gritting, grinding noise that accompanied its movement sounded like its version of a laugh. It was coming straight at me, and I don't mind admitting I jumped back. Something jabbed me on the shoulder, something hard and cold. I whirled just in time to avoid the stony embrace of another figure, which had moved out of the azaleas that shrouded its hoofed feet. The place was alive with movement and sound, a cacophonous chorus of grating laughter. Stony arms lifted, heads turned to glare at me with empty eyes.

I tripped over my own heels and sat down hard, right in the path of a dragonlike beast that was grinding remorselessly toward me.

My scream was not a calculated appeal for help; it was an outraged rejection of what was happening. I was quite surprised when it produced results. The dragon figure let out a squawk and jerked to a stop. The other figures also stopped moving. In the silence a bird let out a long, melodious trill.

He came over the carved parapet like Nijinsky in *Le Spectre de la Rose*, in one long, smooth leap, landing lightly on his feet. He stood still, hands on his hips, looking at me severely. But his first swift movement had given him away, and the rapid rise and fall of his chest showed he wasn't as calm as he was trying to appear. His fair hair stood up in agitated tufts.

Making the other guy speak first is an old ploy in diplomacy. The Indians knew the psychological advantages of it, and modern business executives use the same trick when they tell their secretaries to get the other person on the line before they pick up the phone. Smythe and I might have stayed there for days trying to outstare one another if I hadn't realized that my hand was smarting. I sucked at the cut, and then glanced down at the rough metal track, almost hidden in the grass, on which I had scraped it.

"You're not hurt," Smythe said; and then, realizing he had lost that round, he went on angrily, "Serve you right if you were. People who poke their noses into other people's business often get hurt."

"You aren't trying to tell me these things go off automatically," I said.

He hesitated for a moment—wondering if he could get away with that claim—and then shrugged.

"No. The mechanisms are operated from the grotto behind this wall. There is a series of switches. Someone must have turned all of them on."

"Someone?" I inspected my bleeding hand.

"I turned them off," Smythe said indignantly. "Why should—"

"I can think of several reasons." Since he

didn't offer to assist me, I stood up all by myself. "But if you think a silly stunt like this one is going to scare me away . . ."

"Are you sure it was only meant to frighten you?"

"I cannot imagine why we continually converse in questions," I said irritably. "Like one of those abstract modern plays. . . . These sick stone nightmares couldn't hurt anybody, unless they toppled over on him. They look stable enough."

I reached out and pushed at the stone dragon. I didn't have to reach far.

"Of course they aren't stable," Smythe snapped. "They are mounted on wheels. And, although they are bottom heavy and unlikely to fall over, I don't know what would have happened if you had fainted, or hit your head in falling, with that thing bearing down on you."

"The heroine tied to the railroad track?" I produced a fairly convincing laugh. "Nonsense. It was just a joke. Somebody has a weird sense of humor. Who? Pietro?"

"I shouldn't think so." His hands in his pockets, the picture of nonchalance, Smythe strolled toward the entrance to the garden of grotesques. I followed him.

"Pietro has no sense of humor," Smythe went on. "He never operates these monstrosities. You must have noticed how rusty they are."

"Then who wired them for electricity?" I asked, walking wide around a groping, man-sized lizard. "That wasn't done in the sixteenth century."

"No, but they moved then, by an ingenious system of weights and compressed air, pulleys and iron rods. The sixteenth-century sense of humor was rather brutal, and the Count Caravaggio of that era was definitely a man of his time. Pietro's grandfather was the one who wired the monsters. Cute, aren't they?"

He patted the protruding rear end of a saber-toothed tiger that had its head buried in the throat of a screaming peasant.

"Adorable," I agreed. "How did you happen to come on the scene at such an appropriate moment?"

"The count sent me to look for you. It's almost lunchtime. One of the gardeners saw you heading in this direction."

"Oh. Well, thanks for rescuing me."

"Pure accident," Symthe said coldly. "Don't count on its happening again."

IV

After lunch Pietro went back to bed and I continued my inquiries. The morning had been entertaining but unproductive. What I needed to find were the service areas of the villa. I had not seen many of the staff who worked out of doors, only an occasional gardener, and I had a hunch that I might recognize a familiar face or voice among that group. I also wanted to investigate the outbuildings. If the mystery goldsmith's workshop was somewhere on the estate, it wouldn't be open to the public, but at least I could scout out possible places and search them later, after the workmen had gone home. I was beginning to get an odd feeling of urgency about that search. I suppose I had come to think of the unknown master as a potential victim rather than a member of the gang. I saw him as a sweet little old gray-haired man with spectacles on the end of his nose, like the shoemaker in Grimm. Maybe the gang was holding him prisoner, forcing him to turn out masterpieces. . . .

It was a fantasy worthy of Professor Schmidt at his most maudlin. I had been working for that man too long. I was beginning to think the way he did.

First I found the garage—or perhaps I should use the plural. The building held five cars and had room for half a dozen more. The silver Rolls Royce shone in lordly splendor, looming over a low-slung red sports car. There was also a dark-green Mercedes, a station wagon, and a tan Fiat.

I did a double take on the Fiat, and then decided it must be Luigi's. Maybe he was going through the same sort of reverse snobbism that affects well-to-do American teenagers. That's why they dress so sloppily, in torn T-shirts and faded jeans; they are being one with the oppressed masses. It's rather sweet, I think. Silly, but sweet. Or maybe Luigi's daddy was teaching him how the rest of the world lives. Parents are funny. The poor ones sweat and strain to give their kids all the advantages they lacked, and the rich ones preach the virtues of adversity and tell long, lying stories about how they had to walk ten miles to school every day.

In addition to the garage I found stables, a greenhouse, dozens of assorted sheds and cottages, and a carpenter's shop. This last establishment kept me occupied for some time, but the tools were the usual saws and hammers and things. I found lots of buildings, but no people except for an elderly gardener asleep under a tree. I had picked the wrong time of day to check up on the employees. Like their master, they were all sleeping off their lunches. So I gave up and returned to the house, and put through my call to Schmidt. It was early, but I figured he would be waiting, all agog and full of questions, which he was.

He hadn't received my letter yet. That wasn't surprising, since the Italian mail service is erratic at best, so I gave him a brief rundown on the latest developments, which didn't take long, unfortunately. I had plenty of time to dress and get ready to go down for cocktails, anticipating another tedious evening with Romberg and Rudolf Friml and the Great Pietro, master of illusion.

The evening started innocently enough. As I approached the door of the drawing room I was greeted by a rippling cascade of notes. Someone was playing Chopin, and playing quite well.

The ivory drawing room was Pietro's favorite. It was a lovely room, done in white and gold, with a great crystal chandelier and gilded stucco cherubs chasing one another around the ceiling. The furniture was upholstered in ivory brocade. The grand piano was gold too, but it was a Bechstein, and the paint hadn't affected its tone.

When I entered the room Smythe cocked an impudent blue eye at me and switched from the ballade he had been playing to a more romantic étude. The footman on duty offered a tray. I took a glass of champagne, and went to the piano.

"Not bad," I said. "Why don't you take up music as a profession, and stop leading a life of crime?"

"Not good enough," Smythe said briefly. His hands chased one another up and down the keyboard. "I do better with a harpsichord, but I'm not professional at that either."

"I'd like to hear you. Surely Pietro has a few harpsichords scattered around."

"The harpsichord is in the green *salone*," Smythe said.

"At least play something sensible," I insisted. He had switched to one of the more syrupy themes from a Tchaikovsky symphony.

"I play mood music," Smythe said, nodding his shining golden head toward a sofa in the corner of the room.

The light of early evening suffused the room, leaving the corners in blue shadow. I hadn't noticed Pietro and his lady; they were sitting side by side, holding hands and whispering sweet nothings.

"What happened?" I asked in a low voice. "I thought they were about to break up."

"So did I. Someone must have given the lady good advice. I thought it was you."

"I gave her some advice, yes. But I didn't think she'd apply it so literally. By the way, I know you checked up on me, but I didn't realize you had done such a thorough job. That crack about my experience with ghosts—"

"I'd love to hear the details of that story sometime," said Smythe, energetically pounding out chords.

"I doubt that you ever will. How did you—"

"My dear girl, your friend Schmidt has told half Munich about his brilliant assistant."

"And you have friends in Munich?"

"I have friends in all sorts of places. And I make new friends very easily."

"I'll bet you do."

I turned away from the piano. Pietro detached himself from Helena and sat up.

"So there you are, Vicky. I have been telling

Helena about the architecture of ancient Greek temples."

"Oh, really," I said. "Fascinating subject, isn't it, Helena?"

Helena giggled. She sounded as if she were in a very pleasant mood. She stirred lazily, and as she did so I caught a flash of light that dazzled me. Pietro had gone to the table, where a tray of hors d'oeuvres was set out, so I sat down next to Helena.

No wonder she was in a good mood. Pinned to the sweeping contours of her breast was the source of the dazzle—a brooch as big as a bread-and-butter plate. It was a Baroque piece, white gold and diamonds and pearls, set with plaques of antique cameos. Eighteenth century taste, like Helena's, was inclined to be gaudy. But she was obviously very happy with her prize; her round face beamed as she contemplated the jewel over her double chin.

"Wow," I said. "It must be love."

Helena giggled again.

"It is only a loan," she whispered, in a conspiratorial tone. "So he says. But I think I will forget to give it back to him, eh?"

"Mmmm," I said.

"Come to the window, so you can see it better."

I was happy to do so, since I wanted a closer look at the brooch. Helena didn't take it off; she probably thought I would grab it and run, as she would have been tempted to do if the situation had been reversed. But I could see it quite well. It was prominently displayed.

I could have sworn it was genuine. No, take that back; I wouldn't have staked my reputation on any piece in Pietro's collection, knowing what I knew. But this didn't seem like the sort of thing my jeweler friend would copy. The laboratory boys haven't succeeded in making a synthetic diamond that can be mass-produced cheaply. Besides, though this brooch was worth more money than I was, it wasn't unique. Pietro had other jewels in his collection that were worth much more.

I admired the effect, while Helena preened herself and simpered. We were still standing there by the window when the door opened and the dowager entered, leaning on her grandson's arm.

Helena must have known there would be trouble over that brooch, but she was ready to brazen it out. She stuck out her chin and her chest; the diamonds caught the sunlight in a scintillant flash, and the dowager, whose eyes were as keen as her old limbs were feeble, stopped short. She didn't speak, but I heard her breath come out in a hiss like that of an angry snake. Her beady black eyes narrowed, reminding me of the zoological fact that birds were reptilian in origin.

Pietro hastily turned his back and began eating hors d'oeuvres. Luigi dropped the old lady's arm. She made no attempt to stop him, although she must have anticipated what he would do. She limped to a chair and sat down.

Then Luigi exploded.

There is no point in repeating what he said, even if I could remember all the words. He had an excellent command of vulgar invective, as do most kids his age, but the tirade was rendered pathetic by the fact that he couldn't quite keep his voice under control. Finally it broke altogether—with sheer rage, I'm sure—and he ran out of the room. The footman held the door for him.

If I don't mention the footman or the butler or the maid more often, it is because I would have to mention them too often. Servants were all over the house, like fleas, jumping out at you when you didn't expect them. Many of the more personal family encounters I was to witness took place in front of this audience; none of the Caravaggios seemed to mind them, but I couldn't be sure whether it was because they were regarded as members of the family or as pieces of furniture.

Pietro sputtered helplessly during his son's outburst. When the boy ran out, he would have shouted, had he not caught his mother's eye. The dowager said nothing. She didn't have to. It was quite clear what she thought of the whole thing, and with whom her sympathy lay. Obviously both she and Luigi assumed Pietro had given his girl friend the brooch to keep.

The remainder of the cocktail hour passed uncomfortably. At least I was uncomfortable, and so was Pietro. Helena, never sensitive to other people's feelings, basked in the reflected glitter of diamonds. The dowager sat like a stiff black effigy, her wrinkled white hands folded over the top of her stick. She never took her eyes off the swaggering, self-conscious figure of her son.

The only thing that made the situation bearable was Smythe's playing. He went from Tchaikovsky to Bach to Vivaldi and finally lapsed into Rudolf Friml, which he performed with a swooping, saccharine sweetness that made the melodies sound like satires of themselves. I don't think he was playing to be helpful, he was only amusing himself; but music does soothe the savage breast, and it pleased Pietro.

It was a long evening, though. The dowager stuck with us till long after dinner—in order to punish Pietro—and it was almost ten o'clock before the four of us returned to the drawing room for coffee. Like a naughty little boy, Pietro relaxed as soon as his mother left. He had drunk quite a bit, and was well into his aggressive mood; the fact that he had had to repress it in front of the old lady made him even more belligerent. He turned on Smythe, who was drifting toward the piano, and snarled.

"A fine performance, I must say. So this is how you carry out your duties!"

Smythe raised an eyebrow and did not reply. Pietro looked at me.

"He has been here less than a week, and you see how he behaves! Like a guest in the house. I take him in, employ him, because he is well recommended; he does no work, he sits by laughing when my own son insults and defames me. What do you say to that?"

"Terrible," I said. The complaint was totally unreasonable, of course, but I was not inclined to defend Sir John Smythe. If Pietro had proposed stringing him up for horse stealing, I'd have lent a hand on the rope.

"Don't be so silly, Pietro," Helena said, fingering her diamonds. "What do you expect Sir John to do? It is your problem if your son misbehaves."

The old saying, that it takes two to make a fight, is a lie. One person can start a fight all by himself if he is determined to, and Pietro was. Helena's defense of Smythe only gave Pietro a convenient handle. By the time he was through, he had accused his secretary and his mistress of carrying on an affair right under his nose. I think he was looking for an excuse to take the brooch back, and Helena, never too bright, fell right into the trap.

Smythe fell into another kind of trap. When Pietro started slapping his chest and shouting about his family honor, Smythe put his coffee cup carefully down on a table and stood up.

"Oh, all right," he said in a bored voice. "Let's get it over with. Fetch the umbrellas."

"Ah, you mock me," screamed Pietro. "Umbrellas, you say? You wish to make me a laughingstock. You do not take me seriously. You will see if a Caravaggio is to be insulted." And he rushed out of the room.

He was back in less time than I would have

supposed possible, brandishing—yes, you guessed it—only it wasn't one sword, it was two, one in each hand. He flung one of them down on the floor in front of Smythe. Gold shone. I remembered those rapiers; they were a matched pair, part of the jewel collection, because they had gorgeous decorated hilts. They were court swords, meant to be worn with a fancy uniform; but the blades were of Toledo steel, and quite sharp.

Smythe contemplated the weapon blankly as Pietro tried to struggle out of his coat. The footman had to come and help him. Then he took up his sword and fell into what he fondly believed was an attitude of defense, flexing his knees and waving his arms.

"Come," he shouted. "Defend your honor, if you have any!"

"Wait a minute," I said uneasily, as Smythe bent to pick up his weapon. "Those points look pretty sharp. He could hurt himself."

"He could also hurt me," said Smythe indignantly. "After all, I didn't start this nonsense."

Pietro ran at him, roaring. He slid neatly to one side, and the point of the sword punctured the back of the chair in which he had been sitting. Pietro tugged at it, cursing luridly, and Smythe moved discreetly back a few feet. He looked at his sword and then at Pietro's plump posterior, temptingly tilted as he tried to free his sword from the sofa.

"Don't do it," I said. "You'll just make him mad."

"He's mad already," was the reply. "Stark, staring mad. Why don't you soothe him? Say something calming."

I glanced at Helena, thinking she might try to control her outraged lover, but she was giggling happily as she watched. Two men were dueling over her; what more could a girl ask of life? I looked at the footman, and realized I wasn't going to get any help from that quarter. Before I could think what to say, Pietro had tugged his sword free, bringing a little cloud of stuffing with it, and had turned back to his secretary. He took a wild swipe at Smythe, who brought his blade up just in time. Steel rang on steel, and I sat up a little straighter. Pietro was beside himself. That blow would have split Smythe's skull if it had connected.

The duel with the umbrellas had been pure farce, but only because the weapons were harmless. Pietro hadn't pulled his punches that time, and he wasn't doing it now; I couldn't tell whether he was so drunk he did not realize he was holding a sharp blade, or whether he didn't care. There was a streak of violence in that little fat man after all. And he knew how to fence. Luckily Smythe seemed to have had some experience too. Pietro was no Olympic gold medalist, but Smythe's defense was complicated by the fact that he didn't want to injure his infuriated employer, or even allow him to injure himself. Smythe had to defend two people, and refrain from attacking. He wasn't smiling as he retreated, with careful consideration for the rugs scattered hither and yon on the dangerously slippery polished floor. Once Pietro tripped on a fringe; if Smythe's blade hadn't knocked his aside, he would have stabbed himself in the calf.

I decided the affair had gone on long enough. If Pietro didn't cut somebody, he would have a stroke; he was purple in the face and streaming with perspiration. I slid in behind him, and as his arm went forward I grabbed his biceps with both hands, and squeezed.

That hurts. Pietro shrieked. The sword dropped clattering to the floor, digging a long gouge in the parquetry.

Smythe stepped back and lowered his point. I could see that he was about to make some rude remark, so I dropped to my knees and wound my arms around Pietro's legs. It made a pretty picture, I must say, and it also kept Pietro from falling over.

"I couldn't let you kill him," I choked. "Pietro—it would be murder! Your skill is too great. It would be like fighting an unarmed man."

Pietro's fiery color subsided.

"Yes," he said grudgingly. "Yes, you are right. It would not be honorable."

He was still angry, though. He turned on Helena, whose face mirrored her disappointment at the tame ending. She had wanted to see some blood.

"No thanks to you that my honor is not tarnished," he snarled. "You hoped I would be killed, eh? Then you and your lover would steal away with my jewels. Give them to me!"

Clutching the brooch, Helena backed away. Pietro followed her, waving his arms, and elaborating on his theme. Smythe sat down. He had collected both swords and was holding them firmly.

"Leave them alone," he said, as I started after Pietro and Helena. "He'll pass out soon, and then we can all go to bed."

Pietro did not pass out. The exercise had

used up some of the alcohol he had consumed, and he was quite lively and looking for trouble. He pursued Helena in their ludicrous game of tag, and she retreated. The French doors onto the terrace were wide open, and I wondered why she didn't go out; she could get clean away from him in the gardens. But she avoided the windows, and finally he got her backed into a corner. I didn't see exactly what happened, only a scuffle of flailing arms and agitated movements. Then Pietro toppled over and hit the floor.

"The winner and new champion," Smythe chanted. "A knockout in the first round."

Helena tugged her dress back into decency.

"He was trying to strangle me," she muttered. "I had to hit him. Do you think he is—"

"Out like a light," said Smythe, bending over his employer. "We had better carry him to bed. I wouldn't go near him tonight, Helena. He will have cooled off by morning, but . . ."

"I don't go near him again," snapped Helena. "He is a beast, a monster. I leave him."

She went puffing out of the room, her long skirts swinging. Her fingers were still clamped over the brooch.

Smythe and the footman carried Pietro upstairs. My room was beyond his, Helena's was on the other side. Her door was closed when I passed it, but I thought I heard the sounds of agitated activity within. It sounded as if she were moving the furniture.

I got ready for bed, although I wasn't tired. When I had put on a robe and slippers, I went out onto the balcony.

No capering comedian waved at me from the terrace tonight. The grounds were dark and still, with only a few pinpoints of light visible from the cottages of the employees who lived on the estate. To the left the lights of the town of Tivoli made a bright splash on the dark horizon.

It looked very quiet and peaceful down there. I thought of getting dressed and doing some exploring, but somehow the idea didn't arouse my girlish enthusiasm. I tried to find rational reasons for my reluctance, and had no difficulty in doing so; it was early yet by Italian standards, many of the workers would still be awake, and I had no particular goal in mind, since nothing I had seen had suggested the need for further investigation. There was no sense in wandering around in the dark through unfamiliar terrain. But that wasn't the real reason why I hesitated. I didn't like the look of that dark garden.

I had been thinking of the Caravaggios as a comic family, something out of a TV serial, or one of those silly French farces. Now I realized that there were undercurrents of tragedy and unhappiness among them. A man may smile and smile and be a villain. He may make a damn fool of himself and be a villain too.

However, I didn't think Pietro was the master criminal I was after. It was possible that he was a victim instead of a crook. Smythe was certainly one of the conspirators, he had admitted as much. He had only come to work for Pietro recently. I had suspected that from the fact that the tidbits I found in the antique shop had barely been touched. Pietro was one of the names in that new file in the shop. If these men, all wealthy collectors, were the potential prey of the swindlers, then Smythe was the means by which the gang gained entry to the houses they meant to rob. He probably had impeccable credentials. They are much easier to forge than antique jewelry. Using such references, he could gain entry to the villas of his victims as a secretary, or even as a guest. He could use one victim as a reference to the next sucker in line, since the substitutions would never be suspected.

Yet one thing didn't fit this theory. I had been kidnapped and imprisoned in the Caravaggio palace. Smythe had not been responsible for that job—or so he claimed. This implied some member of the family was involved in the plot.

The unknown I was looking for was the master criminal, the chief crook, and somehow I couldn't believe that any of the people I had met fit that role. They weren't smart enough. Luigi was a mixed-up, unhappy boy whose relations with his father were bad; he might explode and act in anger, but he didn't have the experience to invent a plot as complicated as this one. The dowager was a possibility. I had known several sweet white-haired old ladies who wouldn't balk at a spot of larceny, and although she was physically frail, there was an intelligent sparkle in her eyes.

I couldn't see Smythe as the mastermind either. He was smart enough, but he lacked something—energy, perhaps. Yet I couldn't eliminate him. The kidnapping might have been a trick to frighten me off. All that talk about a fate worse than death, all the implications of torture and mayhem—an act, to make me think I was in deadly danger, from which he had rescued me. A combination of gratitude and fear might have persuaded some women to give up the case. And Smythe had never intended me to identify the palazzo; only luck and my own expertise had given me that bit of information.

A soft breeze from the garden lifted my hair. It was perfumed with a nameless flower scent, infinitely seductive. It was interfering with my thinking. I went back into my room and climbed into bed with a book.

The book was one of a selection that had been thoughtfully placed on my bedside table, along with a bottle of Perrier water and a few crackers. I had no doubt that Pietro had selected the books. I chose *Tom Jones* because it was the most innocent of the lot. I had never read it before. It was rather interesting, but there were long dull sections between the sexy passages. I was plowing through one of these parts, not paying much attention, when I heard a sound in the corridor. It was the sound of a door softly opening and closing. Then there was a muffled thud.

I couldn't ignore that. Pietro was out cold, so the nocturnal wanderer had to be Helena or Smythe. Luigi's room was farther along the corridor, and the dowager's suite was in another wing. Each room had its own bath, so there was no reason for anyone to leave his room for that purpose.

I turned out the light before I opened my door. There were dim bulbs set in silver wall sconces along the hall, with long stretches of gloom between them. As I stood there peering out through the slit in the door, a figure came out of a dark area into the light, with an eerie effect of materializing out of thin air. It was Helena.

She had not gotten far from her room, because she was towing two enormous suitcases. It wasn't difficult to understand what she was doing. She must have realized that she and Pietro were just about through, so she was making her getaway, with the brooch. But she was so greedy she couldn't bear to abandon any of her clothes.

I watched her for a while. She couldn't carry both suitcases; she dragged one for a few feet and then went back for the other one. She was panting so hard I could hear her from where I stood, twenty feet away. I found the sight mildly amusing, till I saw her face.

I had never realized how strong an emotion greed can be. It was tough enough to overcome even the fear that distorted her face.

I stepped out into the hall. She would have screamed if she had had breath enough. She made a strained squawking sound and dropped to her knees—clutching the suitcases.

"What the hell are you doing?" I asked.

"*Dio mio!* Is it you? You have frightened me! I think I am having a heart attack."

"No wonder, carrying those heavy bags. Why sneak out in the middle of the night?"

I knew the answer, but I was curious to hear what she would say.

"I must leave here," she whispered, rolling her eyes. "I am afraid. There is something wrong, can't you feel it?"

"But why not wait till morning?"

She hesitated, trying to think of some convincing lie. The expression on her sly, stupid little face annoyed me, and I went on, deliberately cruel. "What about the ghost? I thought you were afraid to go out at night."

"You said it would not come in the house! I have called the garage, the chauffeur is waiting with the car. . . ."

Her face was shining wet with perspiration. It was not a warm night. I still didn't like her much, but her unmasked terror and her plump

175

little hands, clutching at my skirts made me feel guilty.

"I was joking," I muttered. "Would you like me to help you? You can't carry those suitcases alone."

"Would you? Would you help? I am so afraid, and yet it is worse to stay than to go. . . . If I wait, Pietro will convince me to stay. I am never so afraid in the daylight," she added naïvely.

I lifted one of the suitcases, and staggered. Helena giggled feebly. I gave her a hard stare. That suitcase was too heavy. I wondered if she had some silverware in there, as well as the brooch.

I started down the hall. Helena puffed after me, half dragging, half pushing the other suitcase. We reached the top of the grand staircase, and by a combination of muscle and persistence I managed to get one suitcase down to the hall. Then I went back to help Helena.

"Hurry, hurry," she muttered. "We are too slow."

It *had* taken us a long time to traverse that long corridor. We had made a certain amount of noise, too, banging the suitcases around. But I couldn't understand why I felt so edgy, unless the girl's terror had infected me. The household was sound asleep. No one would bother us. She said she had called the garage, so presumably the car was waiting outside even now.

The entrance hall was a ghostly place, lighted by a single lamp suspended on a long chain. It swayed slightly on an unseen, unfelt current of air, and shadows slid across the painted ceiling so that the gods and goddesses of Mount Olympus seemed to shift naked limbs and wink as they looked down on us struggling mortals.

The swaying of the lamp should have alerted me. Air doesn't move in an enclosed space unless something displaces it. But my back was toward the library door, and it was not until I saw Helena's face freeze that I realized something was wrong. Her mouth was wide open, but she was too petrified to scream.

I whirled around. If I hadn't heard her description, I probably would not have made out details at first; it stood in the dark doorway, blending with the shadows. Yet I sensed its shape—the trailing folds of the long robe, the hands hidden in full sleeves, the cowled head.

Then it glided out into the hall, under the light of the lamp.

Helena got her breath back and let out a scream that sounded like an air-raid siren. It hurt my ears, but it didn't faze the phantom, who took another step toward us. Helen's scream faded out. She collapsed into an ungainly heap, half over the suitcases.

The light fell on the austere bone within the cowl. The fleshless skull shone, not with the pale glimmer of ivory, but with a wild glitter. It had an odd, incredible beauty; but its immobility was more terrifying than any menacing gesture might have been. Then someone started pounding on the door. The cloaked figure turned. With the shining skull face hidden, it became a thing of darkness that seemed to melt into the shadows and disappear.

Helena woke up and started screaming again. The pounding on the door continued. Doors opened upstairs. I thought of slapping Helena—and a tempting thought it was, too—but decided I had better get some help first. So I went to the door. It took me a while to get it open, but finally I admitted a man in a chauffeur's uniform—not the same man who had driven us out to the villa originally, someone else. He shied back when he saw me, rolling his eyes.

"*Avanti, avanti*," I said, somewhat impatiently. I am not accustomed to having men recoil when they look at me. "The signorina has fainted—no, I guess she hasn't, she's just hysterical. Help me with her."

Her screams had subsided into loud gulping sobs. I looked up. The stair railing was fringed with staring faces, most of them female. The maids, who slept on the top floor, had been awakened by the hubbub. Then two male figures pushed bravely through the throng and came down the stairs.

Luigi had pulled on a pair of jeans. His feet and his beautiful torso were bare. Smythe was still wearing evening trousers and white shirt.

The suitcases and Helena's huddled form told their own story. It wasn't until Luigi's inimical eye fell on me that I realized my own position was somewhat ambiguous.

If those suitcases were filled with loot, as I suspected they were, then I was an accessory after the fact to grand theft. It behooved me to get them back upstairs unopened, and make sure Pietro's possessions were restored to him.

"We met the ghost," I said, in a lame effort to distract attention from the bulging bags.

"You don't say so," Smythe said. "Did it fit the description?"

"The description didn't do it justice," I said. "Let's get Helena back to bed."

"And what was she doing creeping out of the house in the middle of the night?" Luigi demanded. "No, don't answer. It is only too obvious. Antonio, what do you mean, helping this woman to run away?"

The chauffeur burst into an animated *apologia*, his hands flying. His excuse was reasonable; he had never been told he was not to obey Helena's orders. But Luigi's frown seemed to intimidate him. He was practically groveling when the boy cut him off with a curt, "*Basta*. Go back to your house."

"It must be nice to be one of the upper classes in a region where feudal loyalties still linger," Smythe murmured. "Our peasants are too damn liberated."

He smiled affably at me, and I smiled back. His attempt to divert my attention hadn't worked. Even if Luigi had not used the man's name, I would have recognized his voice. He was one of my kidnappers.

That wasn't the only thing I learned from the evening's adventure. The servants hauled Helena and her suitcases back to her room and

Luigi stamped off, radiating aristocratic hauteur. I returned to my own room, leaving Smythe standing alone in the hall.

There was no lock on my door. I shoved a chair under the knob and then bolted the doors giving onto the balcony. It would be a little stuffy for sleeping, but I preferred it that way.

I didn't know who had played the spectral monk. It could have been anybody. Smythe, Luigi, Pietro—if he was faking his drunken stupor—or the dowager—if she was pretending to be more crippled than she really was. The elderly masterminds in mystery stories often do that—pretend to be paralyzed so they will have an alibi. Or it could have been one of the servants. I was inclined toward Smythe, partly because he had that kind of sense of humor, and partly because it had taken him a little too long to get downstairs after Helena started screaming. Luigi had had to find his pants—he probably slept in the buff—but Smythe had been fully dressed, and therefore awake. However, Smythe was a cautious soul, not the sort of man to rush headlong into danger without reinforcements.

The important thing about the ghost was that I had recognized, not its animator, but its face. Those stylized bones and sculptured cheekbones were unmistakable.

I was reminded of something my father had said once, when in my younger and more supercilious days I had complained that my college courses weren't relevant to modern life. "Relevant?" he had bellowed, with the snort he used when he was particularly exasperated. "How the hell do you know what is going to be relevant?" He was right—though I would probably never tell him so. An art history course should be just about as esoteric and unrelated to the stresses of modern life as anything could be, but it had already proved useful to me in several life-and-death situations. This evening it had helped again.

The skull face was Aztec—a mask like the ones worn by priests of that macabre theology, in which skulls, skeletons, and flayed human skins played a large part. The Aztecs made skulls out of all sorts of material; sometimes they covered real bone with shell and turquoise mosaic. In a museum in London there was a small crystal skull carved by a long-dead master. The one I had seen tonight had been modeled on that one, though it was much larger and I was willing to bet it wasn't made of rock crystal. It was one of the little old goldsmith's creations, and a super job. Somehow I felt sure that the workshop where that skull had been made wasn't far away.

Seven

FIRST THING NEXT MORNING I WENT TO HE-
lena's room. She had insisted that one of the
maids sit up with her, and the poor girl was
glad to be relieved. I started investigating the
suitcases. Helena woke up while I was doing
it.

"Shut up," I said, when she complained.
"Do you want the police after you? Pietro
might let you get away with the brooch, but
he won't stand for this." I held up a T'ang fig-
urine of a horse, which she had lifted from the
drawing room. I wondered how she had
known its value.

"I was angry," she muttered. "Do you blame
me?"

"Not for being angry. I do blame you for
being stupid. For God's sake, no wonder this
suitcase was so heavy!"

The weight had come from a solid silver
candelabrum, almost three feet high.

I stood up, dusting my hands ostentatiously.

"You put this stuff back," I ordered. "If you still want to leave, I'll help you. But you can't take all this along."

She hadn't removed her makeup the night before. It looked awful in the cold light of day, all smeared and streaked by the bedclothes. She blinked sticky lashes at me.

"I am staying. He cannot cast me off."

"Aren't you afraid of the ghost?" I inquired.

"You are not."

"No, but I wish I knew who . . ." Helena had pulled the sheet up to her chin, but there was a gleam in those shallow dark eyes of hers that made me demand, "Helena, do you know who it was?"

"No."

"And if you did, you wouldn't tell me. That's what I get for trying to be nice. Get up out of that bed and put your loot back, or I'll tell Pietro myself."

When I got down to the breakfast room I was surprised to see Pietro seated at the table gobbling eggs. He greeted me with a cry of pleasure.

"You're up early," I said.

Pietro handed his empty plate to the footman, who refilled it, and looked inquiringly at me.

"*Caffè*," I said. "Just coffee, please."

"I have much to do today," Pietro explained. "We were so early to bed last night. . . ."

He hesitated, looking warily at me.

"You weren't feeling well," I said. "I hope you are better this morning."

"My old war wound," Pietro said, sighing.

I wondered how much he remembered of what had happened the previous night. I didn't wonder about the war wound; it was as apocryphal as a lot of other things about my charming host.

"Your wound must be a sore trial to you," I said, watching with awe as Pietro devoured his ham and eggs and then accepted a bowl of cereal. He was international in his food tastes—Italian dinners, English breakfasts. In that way he got the absolute maximum of calories.

"Yes, I must keep up my strength," said Pietro. "I have business today—business and pleasure. My old friend, the Principessa Concini, comes today. She will stay to dine, but first we have business to transact. A publication she is preparing, about my collections. Perhaps you will be able to advise us."

"I will be honored."

"Sir John will also help. That is why he is here, to assist in arranging the collections."

"How long have you known Sir John?" I asked casually.

"Not long. But he comes most highly recommended. However..." Pietro put down the sausage he had been munching and looked at me soberly. "However, I do not completely trust him."

"Why?" I asked, breathlessly.

"No, I do not trust him. You are a young lady guest in my house; I feel I must warn you."

"Please do."

Pietro leaned toward me and lowered his voice.

"I fear he is not altogether honorable in his dealings with women."

"Oh," I said, deflated.

"Yes," Pietro nodded portentously. "Yes, I have reasons to suspect this. A man of my experience... Be on your guard, my dear Vicky. Not that you would be susceptible. I cannot imagine that any women would find him attractive, but my observation tells me otherwise."

The door behind Pietro opened noiselessly.

I caught a glimpse of blond hair, at a level that strongly suggested the owner was bending over with his ear to the door.

"Oh, Mr. Smythe has a certain crude charm," I said. "Some unsophisticated women, with no taste and limited experience, might be temporarily attracted to him."

The door closed rather sharply. Pietro turned his head.

"What was that?"

"Nothing important," I said. I pushed my coffee cup away and stood up. "I think I'll go for a walk. Your gardens are so beautiful."

"You should see them at night, when they are illuminated. They are bright as day. We will have the illumination tonight, perhaps."

"That would be nice."

"Yes, we will stroll among the blossoms and the gentle fountains in the summer night," said Pietro, looking as soulful as a little fat man can look. "Wait for your walk until then, when I can accompany you and point out beauties in hidden corners that you might otherwise miss."

"I'll just take a short stroll now," I said. "It won't spoil the beauties you can point out to me, I'm sure."

189

I left him wheezing with amusement at my sly wit.

Smythe joined me as I walked across the terrace.

"Beautiful day," he said. "Mind if I join you?"

"Oh, are you my watchdog today?" I inquired. "Yes, I do mind. Lurking in the shrubbery suits you better."

Smythe fell into step with me.

"Of course you *could* run," he said. "Then I would run after you. We'd look pretty silly, wouldn't we, pelting along the cypress avenues?"

We walked on in a silence that I hoped was repressive. It didn't repress Smythe for long.

"Where are you going?" he asked.

"Oh, everywhere . . . anywhere. I haven't explored half the grounds yet."

"You won't find it."

"What?"

"Whatever it is you are looking for."

"What do you want to bet?" I inquired.

We entered the courtyard next to the garage. The Rolls was out, being washed by two men with hoses and buckets. One of them was Bruno.

I hadn't realized how big he was. His shirt

sleeves were rolled up, baring arms like muscled tree trunks. He looked up and saw me and his heavy brows drew together in a scowl. He went on rubbing the fender of the car with a sponge.

"If Bruno was what you were looking for, I don't admire your taste," said Smythe, taking my arm and turning me away.

"I was just confirming a theory."

"It can't be much of a theory. The count has a financial interest in the antique shop, as you may have surmised. When I had the good fortune to meet you, I was checking the books."

"And Bruno was helping you. I suppose he has a degree in accounting."

"He was in charge of the dog," Smythe said.

We had entered a kitchen garden, with neat rows of cabbages and feathery sprouts of carrots.

"That reminds me of a bone I have to pick with you," I said. "What have you done with Caesar?"

"I haven't done anything with him. I assure you, he is living off the fat of the land. We had to give up using him at the antique shop. He turned out to be rather a poor watchdog."

"Oh, really?"

"Yes. He's quite a remarkable animal,

though. He has learned to open tins, not with his teeth, but with a tin opener. He developed a regrettable passion for foie gras, and sulked when we offered him ordinary dog food."

"I'd like to see him."

"No, you wouldn't."

"Yes, I—" I stopped, before the discussion could degenerate into one of those childish exchanges Smythe seemed to enjoy. We were still in the service area, so, obeying a wild impulse of the sort that often seized me when I was with Smythe, I threw back my head and shouted, "Caesar? Caesar, where are you, old dog? *Cave canem*, Caesar."

There was a moment of silence, then a furious outburst of barking. Giving Smythe a triumphant glance, I followed the sound through the kitchen garden, into a courtyard filled with trash cans and empty crates, under an archway. Caesar never let up barking, and I encouraged him with an occasional hail. When he saw me he reared up on his haunches and his barks rose to a pitch of ecstasy. His lunges dragged the dog house to which he was tied a good six feet.

I squatted down beside him. He looked better than he had when I first saw him. His ribs weren't so prominent. The dog house was not elegant, but it was adequate, and his chain gave him ample room to roam. His water dish was full.

"What a touching sight," said Smythe, looking down his nose at the pair of us.

"I always say you can't trust a man who doesn't like dogs," I remarked, pulling Caesar's ears.

"I prefer cats myself."

"You're trying to mislead me. Cat people have a lot of good qualities, usually."

Caesar settled down with his head on my lap and his mouth hanging open in canine rapture. I scratched his neck and looked around.

Caesar's yard was a grassy plot, roughly mowed and enclosed by high brick walls. Against the far wall was a small building. It hadn't been painted in fifty years, but I observed that the structure was quite solid. The door was heavy and the windows were tightly shuttered.

Was this one of Smythe's tricks? To anchor Caesar in front of a mysterious-looking building might suggest that that building held something he didn't want me to see. Or it might be that he wanted me to waste a lot of time investigating a red herring. Or it might be that he would want me to think it was a red herring because it really did contain something. . . .

I decided I would investigate the building. Obviously I couldn't do it then. So I stood up—not an easy job, since neither Caesar nor Smythe assisted me. Caesar started to howl when I walked away. After I had closed the gate, I could hear the dog house being dragged along the ground, inch by scraping inch.

"He's bored," I said indignantly. "He needs exercise. Why don't you let him run? The field is fenced."

"You can come round twice a day and exercise him," Smythe said. "Good for both of you."

"Go away," I said.

"I shall. You'd better come along and have a bath. You smell like Caesar."

"If I thought the smell would keep you away, I'd bottle it," I said rudely.

Smythe grinned and walked off.

I might have gone back to the house to shower if Smythe hadn't suggested it. Instead I went toward the garage. Two men were polishing the Rolls, but Bruno was no longer one of them.

I sought the rose garden next, thinking that scent might overpower the smell of Caesar— an assumption which proved to be erroneous. I wondered why Smythe had chosen to leave when he did. And where was Bruno? What did it all mean? I threw up my hands, figuratively speaking.

The roses weren't doing me any good, so I proceeded into a part of the gardens I hadn't seen before. It contained one of the larger fountains, a spray of shining crystal water that dampened the marble contours of a complex sculptural group of nymphs and water gods. Beyond an oleander hedge I could make out the walls of a building. Once I got a good look at the place I knew what it was. I had found Luigi's studio.

It was a singularly unimpressive establishment for the heir to all the grandeur I had beheld—a low brick building that had once been a shed. Part of the roof had been knocked out and replaced by the skylight that is indispensable to a painter, but that was the only improvement that had been made.

The door was open. It had to be. With the sun beating down through that glass roof, the interior of the room had the approximate temperature of a pizza oven. Luigi was stripped to the waist. His paint-stained jeans hung low on my lean hips, giving me a view of a tanned back as smoothly muscled as that of Lysippus' athlete. I couldn't imagine how he kept his paints from running in the heat. Then I caught a glimpse of the canvas he was working on, and I realized that it didn't matter. No one would have known the difference.

I coughed and shuffled my feet. Luigi turned. He had a brush between his teeth and his face was stippled with red and aquamarine dots. Those, I regret to say, were the major colors of his canvas. I don't know what else I can say about it. It conveyed nothing in particular to me except "red, aquamarine." And particularly horrible shades of both, I might add.

Luigi was a lot nicer to look at. He was beautifully tanned, every exposed inch of him; the sheen of perspiration made his skin glow like bronze. He took the brush out of his mouth and looked at me soberly.

"You came. I thought you had forgotten your promise."

"I didn't know whether I should come without being invited," I said. "It can be annoying to have one's creative process disturbed."

Luigi's sulky face broke into a smile.

"I had reached an impasse," he said, with a

comical attempt at dignity. "That does occur at times, you know."

"So I understand. I'll leave, if you—"

"No, no." He caught my arm in his hard young fingers. "You must stay. Tell me, what do you think of this?"

I know the routine. I stepped back a few feet, put my head on one side, and squinted. I looked through my fingers. I moved to the right and squinted, to the left and squinted. Then I advanced on the painting and squinted at close range.

"Fascinating," I said finally. Luigi let out his breath. "Yes, it's a very interesting conception. Suggestive technique."

"Yes, yes," Luigi said eagerly. "You understand."

We discussed the painting. I pointed out several places where the tonal values weren't quite as sound as they might have been. Luigi told me what he planned to do about that. He had a very nice time. Once he caught me off guard when he asked me point-blank what the painting suggested to me, but I talked fast and got out of that one. The only thing it suggested was sheer chaos.

After ten minutes in that heat I felt as if I must smell like a goat. Luigi didn't seem to

197

notice, and I couldn't walk out on him, he was so pleased to have an audience. He showed me several other canvases. They were different colors. Mostly yellow and purple, I think.

"Have you tried other media besides oils?" I asked.

It was a silly question. I should have asked if there was anything he hadn't tried. Pen and ink, watercolor, pastels; silk screen, engraving, woodcuts. . . . He kept hauling out portfolios. I was so hot the perspiration ran down my face in streams, getting into my eyes and blurring my vision, and in desperation I finally gasped.

"I can't assimilate any more, Luigi. I must let the things I have seen sink into my subconscious and become part of me."

Luigi agreed. He would have agreed with me if I had told him it was brillig and the slithy toves were on the wabe. I escaped into the comparative coolness of the garden, leaving Luigi busy at work on his tonal values.

It wasn't funny, though. The frustrations of youth never are. Although I don't claim to know much about any form of art after 1600 A.D., I didn't think Luigi had much to offer. He would find that out sooner or later, and it would hurt like hell. In the meantime, let him enjoy himself; I certainly had no intention of telling him what I really thought.

I went into the villa by one of the innumerable side doors, planning to go straight to my room and some soap and water. As luck would have it, the first person I saw was the principessa. Things always work that way for me.

She was standing in the hall drawing off her immaculate white gloves while an obsequious butler waited to receive them and the jacket of her pale-yellow linen suit. She must have stood up in the car; there wasn't a crease in her skirt. Her shoes were as spotless as her gloves, and every hair on her shining dark head looked as if it followed a detailed masterplan.

She inspected me, smiling her faint antique smile, and I was conscious of every spot on my unkempt person. Grass stains from the field, damp spots where Caesar had drooled on me, dirt, paint, perspiration. . . . I pushed the limp hair off my forehead and saw her wrinkle her patrician nose, ever so slightly.

"Hi, there," I said.

"How nice to see you, Vicky." She handed the butler her gloves and came toward me, arms outstretched. I stepped back.

"Don't touch me, Bianca," I said. "I've been playing with the dog."

"Dog? Oh, that great beast of Pietro's. What peculiar taste, my dear."

"I must shower," I mumbled, retreating toward the stairs.

"I'll go up with you. I must freshen up before lunch."

"I can't imagine how you could look any fresher."

"How sweet of you to say so. Seriously, Vicky, I want to have a private word with you before we join the others. The matter you spoke of the other day . . . I promised you I would look over my collection."

She looked so serious that I stopped short, halfway up the stairs.

"You don't mean you found something!"

She shook her head.

"I didn't check every piece, of course. But I selected examples I thought would be most attractive to your hypothetical criminals. The Kurfürstenpokal cup, the Sigismund emeralds, a few others. They passed every test."

"Well, that's good news," I said, after a moment. "I'm not mean enough to hope you were robbed simply to justify my theories."

"That doesn't mean your theories are wrong."

She was trying to be nice, but she still didn't believe it, and I found myself unreasonably annoyed by the hint of patronage in her manner.

"My theories aren't wrong. I can't prove them yet, but I will."

"Have you discovered anything new?"

"No, not really. But I think I'm on the right track. That Englishman I told you about—the one who was in the antique shop. He's Pietro's secretary."

"So I learned," she said calmly. "You seem suspicious of him, but I can't think why. His credentials are excellent."

"Did you see them?" I asked bluntly.

She smiled her faintly sinister archaic smile.

"I have met the man himself. I find him attractive. Don't you?"

"His looks have nothing to do with his morals," I said.

"You sound like Queen Victoria," said Bianca, her smile widening. "Do relax, child, and enjoy life. I wonder if I was ever so deadly serious, even when I was your age. . . ."

And she sauntered off down the hall, leaving me standing in front of my door feeling more than a little foolish.

Compared to the other meals I had eaten with the Caravaggios, this one positively sparkled. The principessa was the catalyst. She controlled the conversation like an experienced hostess, drawing even Helena into it, heading off at least two quarrels between Pietro and his son, and managing simultaneously to flirt elegantly with Smythe, whose silly head was completely turned by the attention. He babbled and made jokes as if he were being paid for it.

The only thing that didn't glow was the weather. Clouds began to gather as we lingered over our coffee, and the dowager looked anxiously at her grandson.

"Luigi, promise you will not go back to that studio of yours while it is raining."

Luigi, who was in excellent spirits, grinned at me.

"She thinks I will be hit by lightning," he explained, patting the old lady's hand.

"My grandmother wouldn't let me play the piano during a thunderstorm," I said.

"Very sensible," said the dowager firmly. "Electricity is a strange substance. Who can understand it? Luigi, promise. Come and read to me. You know how I love to hear you."

"I must make a few telephone calls first," the boy said. "Then I will come, Grandmother."

"Telephone calls indeed," Pietro muttered. "He talks all day. No telephoning to that friend in Switzerland, Luigi, the last bill was absolutely outrageous."

Luigi's smile faded, but he said nothing. I wondered what perverse quality makes people so unfailingly rude to their nearest and dearest. Many of Pietro's remarks to the boy were quite uncalled for; he couldn't seem to resist needling him.

After lunch I went with the principessa and Pietro to look at his collection of rare china. She was preparing a publication on a certain type in private European collections, and she was trying to decide which of Pietro's possessions to include. China happens to be a subject I know virtually nothing about, and I have no desire to know more than I do. It was fun looking at some of the lovely dishes Pietro displayed, but I couldn't understand half of what they were talking about. So I made my excuses and went to my room. It was raining steadily, and the soft sound made me sleepy. I lay down on my bed and soon dropped off.

I don't believe that dreams are vehicles for messages from the supernatural world, but I do think they can serve as a means of dragging certain subconscious worries out into the open. I had a very peculiar dream that afternoon. It was all about art—Raphael's erotic drawings, the "Pietà" of Michelangelo, the Greek statues in Pietro's *salone*—all of them spattered and streaked with vermilion and aquamarine, like Luigi's awful painting. When I woke up, the rain was still drizzling drearily on the balcony outside my window, and I lay blinking into the gray twilight for a while, trying to think what it was that bothered me.

It had something to do with Luigi and his studio. Those portfolios of drawings, sketches, watercolors. . . . The boy had experimented with many artistic techniques. Why hadn't he tried sculpture or modeling in clay?

There were a number of reasonable explanations. Maybe he didn't work well in three dimensions. Yet some of the sketches I had seen through a haze of heat and perspiration had a certain something. . . .

It wasn't a theory, it was just a nebulous, incredible suspicion. But I knew I had to check it out, right away. I grabbed my raincoat and was almost at the door when I caught sight of the clock on the dresser. It was four thirty. So I went back to the telephone.

Schmidt's secretary, Gerda, answered the phone, and I had to gossip with her for a few minutes before she put me through. She is the worst talker I have ever met, but she's a good kid. Yet I found it hard to chat; a mounting sense of urgency made me as twitchy as a dog with ticks. Finally Schmidt came on the line.

"I think I may be on to something," I said. "No, I can't tell you yet, it's too amorphous. But I'll call you later if my hunch works out. If you don't hear from me tonight, forget it— but expect the usual call tomorrow."

He was full of questions, but I cut him short. I didn't have much time. If I did not show up in the drawing room for cocktails, someone might go looking for me. But I was wild to check out my crazy hunch, and with the rain keeping everyone indoors, I might never have a better chance.

The door of Luigi's studio was closed, but not locked. It yielded to the pressure of my hand. Once inside, I wiped the raindrops off my face and looked for a light switch.

In the bluish glare of fluorescent bulbs the studio looked cold and depressing. It certainly was a good imitation of a starving art student's garret. The velvet draping the model's throne was worn and dusty, and the chairs looked as if they had been chewed by a large dog. The rain pounded on the skylight like the drums of a regiment marching into battle.

I pulled out some of the canvases that had been placed in racks along the wall. Luigi had gone through several "periods." Like Picasso, he had enjoyed a blue period. Like his namesake Caravaggio, he had experimented with chiaroscuro. He had tried pointillism, and cubism, and imitations of Van Gogh, with an overloaded palette knife. The dreary collection proved that the boy couldn't paint in any style known to man, but it also proved that he was dedicated. Why hadn't he ever tried sculpting?

A long table under the windows held a miscellaneous assortment of paint tubes, turpentine, stained rags . . . and the portfolios of sketches. A bolt of lightning splashed across the skylight, but I hardly noticed it. Those sketches. . . .

They were bad; there was no question about that. But they had a certain quality. I looked at a dozen of them—amateur renditions of heads and animals and parts of bodies—before I realized what they did have.

His anatomy was terrible, and he had no

feeling for design or form. But there was one pen-and-ink drawing of a female head that was so good I thought for a minute it must be a print. I knew I had seen the original somewhere. Then I recognized it. I *had* seen the original, in the Bargello in Florence. It was a sculptured bust by Mino da Fiesole. Luigi had no creative talent, but as a copyist he was absolutely first rate. I put the drawings carefully back in the portfolio and started to search the room.

The trapdoor was under the model's throne, which slid on rollers. There must have been some way of anchoring the throne when it was in use, or Luigi's models would have gone gliding around the room like the Flying Manzinis; if so, he had forgotten to take care of that little detail. Why should he? If I was any judge, the trapdoor was used a hell of a lot more than the model's throne.

The light of the subterranean room at the bottom of the stairs went on automatically when the trapdoor was raised. There was a very complete little workshop down there. I couldn't identify all the objects, but many of the tools of the trade have not changed over the centuries. Gravers, punches, hammers, a soldering iron . . .

I got a little excited. I went running around the room grabbing things and dropping them, pulling out drawers, shuffling through papers. The tools of the trade might not be enthralling, but the materials certainly were. Gold wires and sheets of thin gold, silver nuggets; tiny compartments filled with imitation pearls and emeralds, rubies and opals; chunks of lapis lazuli and turquoise and orange-red carnelian— for the Egyptian crown and other objects of that period; stones of every color of the rainbow, from pale-yellow citrine to garnets like drops of blood; sheets of ivory, malachite, porphyry, jade. All fakes, no doubt, but the general effect was dazzling.

A file on one of the workbenches held detailed sketches of a number of pieces. They weren't all jewelry. Some were plates, reliquaries, goblets. The piece Luigi was working on had been covered with a cloth. I lifted it gently.

Only a few surviving pieces have been definitely attributed to Benvenuto Cellini. I had seen one of them, the Rospigliosi cup in the Metropolitan Museum. The bowl itself is shell-shaped, exquisitely curved; it stands on a base consisting of an enameled serpent mounted on a golden tortoise. Luigi had not ventured to copy any of the known pieces. Even that gang of arrogant swindlers wouldn't dare claim they had burgled the Met. But this could have passed for one of Cellini's works; the various elements of which it was composed were all based on parts of other pieces. It was a golden chalice, with the same elegant curves as the Metropolitan's bowl. The handles were jeweled serpents, and the whole thing was supported by a voluptuous nymph modeled on the lady on the saltcellar in Vienna. Luigi was branching out, no longer imitating known works of art. I wondered what a hitherto undiscovered Cellini would fetch in the market. I couldn't even guess. Worth the effort, certainly.

The thunder outside was making quite a racket. The noise itself didn't make me nervous. What made me nervous was the fact that I couldn't hear anything else over the thunder—like, for instance, the sound of someone upstairs. I had to get out of there fast, and I had to come back—with a camera.

I started up the stairs. My nerve ends were twitching, but when I cautiously put my head up out of the hole the studio was still deserted. I closed the trapdoor and shoved the throne back into position. I felt a little more secure then, but not much; no one would believe I had been overcome by an irresistible urge to see more of Luigi's work during a rainstorm. I wished I had not turned on the studio lights. They would be visible for quite a distance, thanks to that skylight.

The studio was perilous ground, but I would have to risk coming back, at least once more. I needed photographs of the shop, the tools, the sketches, the unfinished chalice. The photographs wouldn't be proof of a swindle. There is no copyright on antique art. But if I could find out what jewels had been sold, the photographs would be damning evidence of forgery.

I was awfully pleased with myself, and I guess conceit made me careless. I opened the door and stepped out into the rain, and a fist that hit me on the jaw.

Eight

I WOKE UP IN THE CELLARS. THERE WAS NO question about it. I had seen those rough-hewn limestone walls before, though I did not recall this particular room. There were actually three rooms, as I discovered when I got my aching body off the floor. Open archways, doorless, led from one chamber to the next. The only exit from the suite, if I may call it that, was in the room where I had awakened. The door was of wood so old it was practically petrified. When I pounded on it experimentally, I hurt my knuckles.

The rooms were windowless, but there was light in the first one from a single bare bulb hanging from the ceiling. I appreciated that light, though there was little to be seen: only a pile of blankets and comforters, upon which I had been lying, and a low wooden table. The air was cool and dank. The farthest room of the three, dirt-floored, had sprouted a fine crop of mushrooms. This room also boasted a primitive sanitary arrangement. I must admit I was relieved to see this. I had always wondered how prisoners managed that little detail; my favorite mysteries and thrillers ignored the point with prissy delicacy, but let's face it, the problem is important to the prisoner.

Exploring my prison did not take long. I lay down on the pile of blankets and nursed my aching jaw. I had been hit on the same place twice in a week, and it hurt. Maybe I would have to go on a liquid diet. Of course that might not be a problem. My captors might decide not to feed me at all.

I don't usually wear a wristwatch, so I had no idea of the time, not even the time of day. But I fancied it must be later the same evening. My next telephone call to Professor Schmidt wasn't due until five o'clock the following day. They had all night and most of the next day to decide what to do with me.

Schmidt would go to the police if I failed to report on time. I knew him well enough to be sure of that. I also knew him well enough to suspect that the police would not be impressed by what he told them. They would call the villa, and Pietro would have a plausible story to account for my failure to telephone. A young, healthy female has to be missing for much longer than twenty-four hours these days before any police department in the world is going to get worried. Pietro's social position would disarm suspicion, and even if they suspected something, they would be unable to prove it unless they could find me. My daily telephone calls had been a bluff, nothing more; and the gang had called my bluff.

Pietro must be a member of the gang after all. That workshop could not have been equipped without his being aware of it. I wondered how deeply involved Luigi was. Some famous forgers have claimed they were used by unscrupulous people; they had no idea their pretty little replicas were being sold as genuine art objects! Well—it was possible, if implausible; people can be pretty naïve. Luigi might be innocent, but his father was guilty as hell. As a detective, I was batting about .200. I hadn't figured Pietro for the mastermind.

I was lying there staring up at the stained ceiling and trying to decide whether the biggest patch of mold looked like a map of South America or George Washington's profile, when someone came to the door.

They had that place locked up like Fort Knox. Chains rattled, bolts squeaked, bars slid back, rusty keys turned in rusty locks. I lay still. There was nothing else I could do. I might have hidden behind the door and tried to hit the newcomer over the head, if (*a*) I knew which way the door opened, in or out; and (*b*) there had been anything in the room to hit him with.

The door opened inward. That wasn't much help, since point *b* was still negative. I closed my eyes and pretended to be unconscious. I felt sick. The man outside the door might be my executioner.

I was not reassured to recognize Bruno. However, the fact that he was carrying a tray cheered me somewhat. The cups and silver covers on the tray looked outré in that dank underground hole, but they obviously contained food, and if they were going to feed me, they couldn't intend to kill me right away.

Bruno stood in the doorway eyeing me suspiciously through squinted eyes, and I lay still, watching him through my lashes. Finally he put the tray on the floor, shoved it into the cell with his foot, and closed the door. I waited till the jangle of bolts and chains had stopped, and then got to my feet.

My appetite was not too good, but I took the covers off the plates to see what they were giving me. The food had undoubtedly come from Pietro's dinner menu; there was a veal Marsala with mushrooms, a dish of pasta, salad, bread, and even a carafe of red wine. I was reminded of the old tradition of feeding the condemned man a hearty meal just before the hanging.

However, I told myself I ought to keep my strength up and began to nibble on the salad. Then my appetite revived and I started on the veal. I had eaten most of the food before it occurred to me that it might have been drugged or poisoned. When it did occur to me, I shrugged mentally. There was no need for them to drug me, they could walk in and knock me out cold anytime they wanted to. Conscious or unconscious, I was no match for Bruno.

The food revived me, and I set out on another tour of my prison. It would have been a waste of time if I had had anything better to do, which I didn't. I found a pile of rotting wood, the remains of shelves, perhaps, and a couple of pieces of metal so rusted they broke in my hands. There was nothing that could possibly be used as a weapon, even supposing I got up enough nerve to try and ambush Bruno.

I thought about digging myself out, like the Count of Monte Cristo. How long had it taken him and his buddy, the old abbé, to get out of the Château d'If? Years. And if I remembered the story correctly, the tunnel hadn't worked anyway. The floor of the third room was of dirt, to be sure, but the only implement I had to dig with was the spoon that had been on the tray. Figure a teaspoonful of dirt every two seconds, one hundred teaspoons to a cup, four cups to a peck, five billion pecks of dirt between me and the open air. . . . I went back to the pile of blankets and lay down.

I should have been plotting and scheming and thinking up ways to escape. Instead I fell asleep. I don't know how long I slept, but I woke with a start when the chorus of chains and bolts began again. This time I was able to rise before the door opened.

It was good old Bruno again. He had brought me another present. It hung over his left shoulder, feet dangling. When Bruno saw me on my feet, he put his hand in his pocket and took out a long, shiny knife.

"Stand still," he muttered. "Do not move."

"Oh, no," I said. "I wouldn't dream of it."

He gave his shoulder a casual twitch. Smythe's body slid to the floor and lay still. His

head happened to land on the edge of the pile
of blankets, which probably saved him from a
concussion, since the floor was of stone, and
quite hard. I say "happened" because I don't
think Bruno really cared where or how he
landed. Bruno didn't need the knife; he would
have looked quite at home in Madame Tus-
saud's Chamber of Murderers without any
deadly implement except his hands.

He went out and closed the door. I stood
pressed against the wall, staring at Smythe's
recumbent body.

I hope I will not be accused of being para-
noid if I admit I suspected a trick. What trick,
I didn't know, but Smythe was not precisely
the most straightforward individual I had ever
met.

He was unconscious, though. Limp as a
stuffed snake. He had fallen on his back, and
his upturned face was an ugly shade of gray.
The blood trickling down his cheek was still
flowing, so I surmised that he had been hit on
the head not long before.

I sat down next to him and took a closer
look. It wouldn't have surprised me to smell
catsup. But the blood came from an actual
wound. It wasn't very deep, although the area
surrounding it was beginning to swell and

would soon be a nice rich purple color. If Smythe was up to something, he had gone to considerable lengths to ensure authenticity.

He was out for quite a while. I was beginning to get worried—the damned cellar was gruesome enough without having a corpse for company—when his eyelids popped open. He looked at me, then closed his eyes. An expression of acute agony contorted his face.

"Where does it hurt?" I cooed. "Tell Vicky and she'll kiss it and make it well."

As I had surmised, the expression of pain was not caused by physical discomfort. Without opening his eyes, Smythe let out a string of expletives remarkable for their originality and vigor.

"Serves you right," I said. "People who poke their noses into other people's business deserve—"

"Shut up," Smythe said.

I shut up. He really did look bad. After a moment, overcome by an uncharacteristic and, in his case, undeserved streak of kindness, I poured some wine into a glass and held it to his lips.

"Try this," I said. "A modest little wine, but I think you'll be amused at its presumption."

Smythe looked at me over the rim of the

glass, and a faint spark warmed his blue eyes.

"Thurber," he said. "Thanks . . . I needed that."

He sat up slowly and took the glass from my hand. I leaned back and crossed my legs.

"Have you dined?" I asked courteously. "There's some veal left, and quite a bit of bread."

"Thank you, I have dined. At least . . ." Smythe twirled the empty wineglass in his fingers and frowned. "Yes, that's right; it's coming back to me. You weren't at dinner."

"No," I said. "I was here."

"The principessa asked about you," Smythe went on slowly. "Pietro said you had gone to Rome for the evening—you had a date."

"I had a date, all right. With Bruno."

"In Luigi's studio? Pietro told me, later. He put on a good act at dinner, but as soon as it was over he called me into the study and told me what had happened. He was quite upset. You forced his hand, you know. He had to act at once, to prevent you from telling anyone about the workshop; but he is a rotten criminal. He hates violence."

"You aren't trying to tell me it was Pietro who hit me and put me here?"

"No, no, he wouldn't sully his hands with

that sort of thing," Smythe said contemptuously. "But you must have suspected that you have been watched whenever you left the villa. Bruno was the man in charge of you today. He had sense enough to snatch you as soon as you came out of the studio."

"And after ordering Bruno to lock me up in this den, Pietro contributed nice soft blankets and veal Marsala. He's a little inconsistent, isn't he?"

"Not really. If it were up to Pietro, you wouldn't have a thing to worry about."

Silence fell—a pregnant, unpleasant silence.

"You mean Pietro is not the one who is going to decide what happens to me?" I suggested.

"You've got it."

"Then who is? You?"

"That's why I'm here," Smythe said, with ineffable contempt. "Despite my pleasing facade, I am in my heart of hearts a sadist of the worst sort. I like to strangle my victims personally. I haven't quite decided whether to do it that way, or inflict some other, even more ghastly torture on you first, but—"

"All right; enough!" I interrupted. "Of all the things I loathe about you, I think I loathe your nasty sarcastic tongue the most. You aren't trying to imply that you are here because you quarreled with the mastermind on my behalf?"

Smythe didn't answer. He wriggled slowly back until he could lean against the wall; and there he sat, his legs stiffly extended, the wineglass poised in his hand, his face a mask of cold fury. If he had been six years old, I would have called it a bad case of the sulks.

"My hero," I said. "I have misjudged you. I am abject. I grovel. And of course my girlish heart is palpitating with rapture because you risked your life—"

The wineglass splashed against the wall with a musical tinkle, and Smythe, turning, threw his arms around me and yanked me up against his chest with a force that drove the wind out of my lungs.

"Will he kiss her or kill her?" I gasped. "Tune in tomorrow and hear the next—"

Smythe's face broke up. He began to laugh. He didn't release me, but his grasp relaxed, so that I was able to find a more comfortable position. We sat there side by side till he finished laughing. Then he said, "Suppose we declare a truce. I find your sense of humor as dreadful as you find mine; and I really don't think this is the time or the place for banal jokes."

"Have you got a plan?" I asked.

"I was hoping you had one," was the discouraging reply.

"I can't plan till I know more. If you would care to confide in me—"

"In return for immunity?" He cocked an inquisitive blue eye at me. What he saw in my face seemed to discourage him. He shook his head morosely. "All right, we'll skip that question for now. Unless we get out of here, the problem remains academic. I'll tell you as much as I can safely do."

"Safely for you?"

"Of course."

"All right, then. Who is the mastermind?"

"I don't know. Honestly! Whoever he is, he is too smart to let his identity he known to the rank and file. I'm something of a commuting courier, as you might say, so I know a number of the people involved, but I have never seen or spoken to the boss. He writes little messages. Here in Rome the only people I know are Pietro and Bruno and Antonio, and a few of the old family retainers who act as hatchet men."

"And Luigi."

"Luigi is outside the structure of the organization," Smythe said. "You might say he *is* the organization. Without his talent, this business would never have begun."

"I'm sorry about him. I had hoped he was unwitting."

"Well, really, he'd have to be pretty stupid not to suspect what was going on," Smythe pointed out. "Luigi is not stupid. But in a peculiar way he is innocent. He doesn't think of what he is doing as wrong. It's a gigantic joke—"

"Luigi was the ghost," I exclaimed.

"Obviously. Who did you think it was?"

"You."

"I am incapable of such childish tricks," Smythe said, insulted. "Luigi has a child's resentment of adults. Any trick perpetrated on a grown-up is fair in his book."

"It's not surprising, when you see how his father treats him."

"I gather you have fallen for his pretty face," Smythe said nastily. "The maternal instinct springs up in the most unexpected places. . . . He hates his father and finds poor old Pietro's amours disgusting. According to his ethical code, fornication is only acceptable for the young."

223

"Then why is he cooperating?"

"You figure it out. Perhaps because in this game he and the old man are equals. Actually, Luigi is more important than Pietro, and he is well aware of it, though he is so accustomed to being bullied by his father that he doesn't take advantage of his position as much as he might."

"And what precisely is this game you speak of? I have an idea, but—"

"That is all you are going to have," Smythe said calmly. "I have no intention of telling you anything except what you need to know to help me get out of this place."

"You surely can't imagine I'm going to keep quiet about—"

"You may talk all you like to whomsoever you like, darling. I will have taken my departure by then, to parts unknown, but if Pietro has an iota of common sense, he will have removed the evidence."

"Now, see here, Smythe—"

"That isn't my name."

"What is your name?"

"Never mind. You may call me John. That really is my name, believe it or not."

"I don't care if it's Rumpelstiltskin Damn it, you can't hope to walk away clean from this mess. It is a criminal conspiracy—"

"Oh, yes, but the law is so dull, isn't it? I'm afraid you have a very medieval idea of right and wrong. Many people do. They still tend to punish crimes against property more severely than crimes against people. Now I support the old Robin Hood ideal," Smythe said, warming to his subject. "I honestly do not feel that anything I have done is reprehensible. Dishonest, no doubt, but not immoral. A simple redistribution of wealth, no more. No widows and orphans have been deprived, no struggling old couples have been robbed of their sole means of support, no one has been injured—"

"I don't know about that," I said, interrupting this speech, which seemed to be developing into a lecture. "What about us?"

John's face fell.

"Nothing has happened *yet*," he said.

"What about kidnapping me?"

"That was Bruno. He's the overseer of the servants—the muscle, as we say—and like all noncoms, he has an exaggerated idea of his intelligence. He is dedicated to the family and sometimes acts on his own initiative."

"What about the man in Munich?"

"That really was an accident," John said,

brightening. "He had a weak heart. We think a thief held him up, probably scared him to death, literally. He was a gentle soul. . . ."

"Kind to his aging mother, good to his parakeet," I said sarcastically. "I don't really care about him except as a portent of things to come. You can't avoid the question, John. Pietro, or someone else through Pietro, presented a scheme for dealing with me that met with your vehement disapproval—if I am to believe your story of why you are here with me. What was the proposal?"

"He didn't mean it," Smythe said.

"You fail to convince me."

"He really didn't. He was sweating and wringing his hands and uttering agitated little screams in Italian at the very idea."

"What idea?"

Suddenly the situation was too exasperating to endure; the two of us sitting cozily side by side, with Smythe's arm draped casually over my shoulder as we talked about murder—my murder. I put my hands on his chest and shoved. I only meant to get away from him, stand up, pace, get some of my frustration out through physical action. I shoved too hard. His head banged against the wall and the second blow, on top of the first, was too much.

He didn't pass out, but his eyeballs rolled up till only the whites were showing, and he started to slide slowly sideways.

I caught his head before it hit the floor and eased him down till he was lying across my lap. After a while his eyes rolled back into place.

"Remind me," he said feebly, "to throttle you when I get my strength back."

"I imagine that little matter will be taken care of for you," I said, absentmindedly running my fingers through his hair. "Wasn't that the suggestion—to silence me permanently?"

He sighed and turned his head slightly, so that my hand was against his cheek.

"Perhaps I had better tell you exactly what happened."

"That would be nice," I said, trying to free my hand.

"Don't do that, it hurts my head. . . . That's better. You see, when Pietro told me he had received orders to deal with you, I remonstrated. No, don't thank me; my motives were purely selfish. I signed up for a spot of larceny, not for murder. I had, and have, no intention of being caught in the act, but if something should go wrong, there is quite a difference

between ten years with time off for good behavior, and the gallows."

"Do they hang people in Italy?" I asked.

"I have no idea. I carefully refrained from
looking it up. But they have reinstituted the
death penalty in dear old England, under certain conditions. I prefer not to meet those conditions. Don't interrupt, it's difficult enough
for me to think coherently with my head aching as it is. . . . Where was I?"

"You remonstrated."

"Oh, yes. Well, Pietro agreed with my rea-
soning, but he is in abject terror of his boss.
That's what he calls him, by the way. The
Boss. Curious, isn't it?"

"Maybe The Boss is American. Or English."

"Don't start getting ideas. I am not the master criminal. So, after an inconclusive argument, I went banging out of the library,
leaving Pietro gibbering. I went into the gardens. I wanted to walk, think what I ought to
do. He must have telephoned the big cheese
as soon as I left, and received further instruc-
tions. I hadn't been outside for more than a
quarter of an hour before Bruno and one of his
friends caught up with me."

"I see. Well, it's all terribly interesting, but,
I'm afraid, not very helpful. Er . . . was any

specific method of extermination mentioned? I mean, it makes a difference whether they are going to flood the cellar and drown me, or pump in poisonous gas, or put something in the food, or—"

"Good Lord, you have a lurid imagination," Smythe said, grimacing. "I don't really see that it matters, since there is nothing we can do to prevent any method from being carried out, including the ones you have mentioned."

"Do you have any idea what part of the cellar we are in?"

"No." John closed his eyes.

"You aren't being much help."

"I'm thinking."

"No, you aren't. You're getting ready to go to sleep. Not on me, if you please."

"I *am* thinking."

"Prove it."

"Have you explored this unwholesome den?"

"Yes. There are two other rooms, more or less like this one, but even less comfortable. No visible door or window. Stone wall, stone floors, except in the third room, which has a dirt floor."

"You seem to have done a very thorough

229

job," John said agreeably. "No point in my going over the same ground."

"I doubt if you would see anything I missed," I said. "What I want you to do is stand up and start exercising. Get yourself limbered up."

"Why, for God's sake?"

"So you will be in condition to jump Bruno the next time he comes in."

That roused him. He opened his eyes as far as they would go without actually popping out of his head.

"That is the most idiotic suggestion I've ever heard."

"It's our only hope of getting out of here. You can hit him with the tray."

"Why don't *you* hit him with the tray?"

I would hate to tell you how long this sort of thing went on. That man will debate with the devil when he comes to carry him away. (If he hasn't sold his soul, it is only because Old Nick isn't ready to meet his price.) Eventually I got John on his feet, not because he was convinced by my arguments, but because my shouting in his ear made him uncomfortable. The exercise did him good. After a few artistic stumbles and staggers he gave up trying to convince me that he was wounded unto death, and he regained his normal strength quite quickly. He even went so far as to investigate the other two rooms. He had to agree that there was no more practical method of escape than the one I had proposed.

It was not really all that practical, for we had no weapon. The tray and utensils were of silver, and although the tray was heavy enough to raise a bump on a normal skull, it was large and unwieldy. Besides, as John was quick to point out, Bruno's skull was a good deal thicker than normal.

"I might only irritate the fellow," he said. "And I would hate to do that."

"What's wrong with your fists?" I inquired.

"I might break a bone in my hand. Would you ask Rubinstein to hit a villain?"

"No. He's ninety years old."

"That is irrelevant."

"Besides, he plays better than you."

"In another sixty years or so, assuming I live that long, I expect to improve."

Ah, well. As John said, it passed the time. We had nothing else to do. But we had not prepared ourselves for action of any kind, and the now-familiar rattle at the door caught us off guard. I jumped up and gestured frantically.

"Get behind the door!"

"I'm not ready," said John, shifting uneasily from one foot to the other. "I'm still giddy. By morning I'll be in better shape. Let's wait till the next time."

"There may not be a next time. How long do you think—oh, damn!"

By then it was too late. The door was swinging open.

When I saw Bruno, I had a dizzying sensation of déjà vu. Once again he was carrying a limp body. The contours of this one were quite different from John's; I recognized the plump haunches and Gucci shoes.

Bruno didn't heave this body carelessly on the floor. He started into the room and then stopped and looked warily from me to John. There was nothing alarming about John's appearance, he was flattened up against the wall like a timid damsel expecting to be assaulted. Bruno jerked his head to the side.

"Come here," he grunted. "No, not you, signorina, you stay where you are. You, Smythe. Take him."

John advanced slowly. Bruno snarled.

"*Avanti, avanti!* Come, little coward, I will not hurt you. Take the master. Be careful. Do not drop him."

John received Pietro's limp form with all the ardor of a man embracing a large sack of fertilizer. His knees buckled as the weight dropped into his embrace, but Bruno's growl encouraged him to keep his feet.

"I said, do not drop him! Put him down, *cretino*; why are you standing there like a fool? Put him on the blankets—gently, gently. Do not hurt him."

With an eloquent glance at me, John obeyed.

"*Bene*," said Bruno. "Take care of him. If he comes to harm . . ."

"Don't you worry, Bruno, old chap. I'll tend him as if he were my own."

Bruno grunted and withdrew. John put his ear to Pietro's chest, flipped up his eyelid, took his pulse. Then he sat back on his heels.

"Drugged."

"Is he going to be all right?"

"Oh, yes. Just look at him."

Pietro looked like a sleeping baby, or a small pink piglet with a mustache. His lips were curved in a sweet smile. John loosened his silk cravat, tucked a blanket over him, and got to his feet.

"Nothing we can do for him. He'll have to sleep it off."

"Do you suppose he objected to The Boss's plans for us?"

"Possibly. A lot of good it did him."

"John, he must know who The Boss is. We've got to wake him up and talk to him."

"No chance. He'll be out for hours. Besides, what makes you suppose he would tell us? He's in no danger. The Boss probably tossed him in here to cool off. He tends to become hysterical in a crisis, but when he wakes up and looks at the situation sensibly, he will realize that he has to go along with whatever The Boss decides to do."

John leaned up against the wall, his hands in his pockets, but he no longer appeared lazy and helpless. Even his voice had changed. It was quick and crisp, with no trace of irritating drawl.

"Look at it this way," he went on, in the same incisive voice. "Pietro can't risk going to the police. He's in this scheme up to his fat little neck. He can't run away and establish a new identity; he'd have to give up everything he possesses, and somehow I can't see him making a successful career as an honest tradesman. He's not vicious, but he is weak. He had been drinking heavily tonight, and I expect he lost his nerve and started talking wildly. But tomorrow . . . He'll simply turn his back, Vicky. We will be handed over to another arm of the organization, and Pietro will never know what happened to us. He won't ask."

"Well, you are a cheery soul," I said glumly. "I think I preferred you in your giddy mood."

"So did I," said John, with a sigh. "You have no idea how I dislike coming to grips with cruel reality. But when my precious skin is at stake. . . . I think we had better make our move immediately. They may decide to deal with us while Pietro is unconscious—present him with a *fait accompli*. That would relieve his miserable little conscience. Yes, I think that's quite probable."

"Move?" I gaped at him. This new personality had me baffled. "What move?"

John was bending over Pietro, removing the blanket, arranging the lax body into a twisted position.

"You saw how concerned Bruno was about his master. Unless I miss my guess, he's hanging about somewhere outside. I'm going to bang on the door and scream. When he comes in, you start flipping Pietro around. Make it appear as if he's having a convulsion."

He looked up, saw my stupefied expression,

and said irritably, "Come on, girl, get with it. Something along these lines." And he began to shake Pietro's arms and legs, the way you might pretend to animate a large stuffed doll. It did look convincing. If you didn't know what he was doing, you would think he was trying to restrain the thrashing limbs of a man in an epileptic seizure.

Pietro's round head rolled back and forth, but his fixed smile never altered.

"Make sure your body hides his head," John added, with a disgusted look at poor Pietro. "I can't do anything about his silly face."

He stood up, dusting the knees of his trousers, and I took his place.

"I thought you were too weak to tackle Bruno," I said, practicing. The game had a bizarre fascination. Pietro was so nice and plump and roly-poly.

"I am. But at least this gives me a fighting chance, while he is off guard and thinking of other things. Don't be afraid to pitch in, darling, if you see me getting the worst of it."

He didn't give me time to reply, but went at once to the door and started kicking and pounding.

"Help, help!" he bellowed. *"Aiuto! Avanti!* Catastrophe, murder, sudden death. The master is dying. The count is dead. Help, help, help. . . ."

Bruno must have been right outside the door. Bolts and chains jangled in an agitated fashion. I started shaking Pietro, keeping a wary eye on the door. So far the scheme seemed to be working.

It almost failed in its inception, however. Bruno was so upset he threw himself against the door, and John let out a yell of pain as the heavy panels smashed him against the wall.

After that, things got confused. I slid out of Bruno's way as he came rushing toward me like a mother buffalo protecting her calf. He flung himself down on his knees and reached for Pietro. I stood up and clasped my hands together. If John was out of action, it was up to me. I planned to hit Bruno on the back of the neck, the way detectives do on TV, but I wasn't awfully optimistic about what would happen. The back of his neck looked like a chunk of granite.

Then John came staggering out from behind the door. His hand hid the lower part of his face and his eyes were swimming with tears. I don't know whether Bruno heard him, or whether he realized that his master was no worse off than before; something alerted him, at any rate, and he looked up at me with a scowl darkening his ugly face. Still on his knees, he reached out for me. I skipped back. Rumbling like an earthquake, Bruno began the monumental task of heaving himself to his feet. He was halfway up, still off balance, when John lowered his head and ran straight at him.

I have never seen—or heard—anything like it. Every bit of breath in Bruno's lungs went out of them, in a single explosive sound like a singing teakettle under full steam. His arms flew out, his head jerked forward. He hit the wall and slid down to a sitting position. His eyes were still half open.

John straightened up and rubbed his head. His other hand covered his nose.

"I think I fractured my skull," he said in a muffled voice.

"At least your precious hands are intact," I said callously. "Let's get out of here."

"Tie him up," John said, indicating Bruno.

I looked dubiously at Bruno. I would just as soon have approached a semiconscious grizzly bear.

"Cover me," I said.

"What with?" John took the tip of his nose between his thumb and forefinger and wriggled it gently. "I guess it isn't broken. It just feels like it. Come on, don't stand around arguing, we've got to get moving."

We tied Bruno up with strips of blanket, using his own knife to cut the fabric, and gagged him with another sizable scrap. He was beginning to stir and mutter by the time we finished. Pietro had not so much as wriggled. He must have been having lovely dreams, though. His smile had become positively seraphic.

In addition to the knife, we found another useful item in Bruno's pockets—a box of matches. It was the only light we had, once we had closed the cell door. The corridor was black as pitch. I lighted one of the matches while John restored the bars and chains to their position.

"Which way?" I whispered.

"Don't know. Try right."

His hand groped out. If he was reaching for my hand, he missed by a mile. I slapped his fingers.

"Naughty, naughty," I said softly.

"Pure accident." His voice was equally soft, but he sounded as jaunty as I felt.

Success had gone to our heads, but the euphoria didn't last long. We stumbled along the dark passageway, hands clasped, our free hands trailing along the wall on either side, dragging our feet for fear of stumbling. I wouldn't have been surprised to find a gaping hole in the floor, or a mantrap; it was that kind of a place. I suggested lighting another match, but John vetoed the idea. We only had a few of them, and we might find ourselves in a situation where we would have greater need of them.

Finally we came to a dead end. There was a door at the end of the passageway, but it was locked. There was nothing to do but retrace our steps and try the other direction. We went faster now, not only because we knew the way, but because we were both conscious of the passage of time. Even if Bruno managed to free himself, his shouts wouldn't be heard upstairs, but John's theory had impressed me as being only too plausible. There was no reason why the gang should wait until morning to dispose of us. They might come at any moment.

We got back to the cell—I felt the door as we passed—and went on more slowly. Despite my care I tripped over a chair—the one where Bruno had been sitting, I suppose. No reason why he shouldn't be comfortable.

This end of the passageway opened into another corridor. Here for the first time I saw a glimmer of light. We moved in that direction and discovered that it came from a barred window high in the wall. My eyes were adjusted to total darkness, so this radiance seemed almost brilliant, though it was only moonlight diffused by three-foot-thick walls and a screen of shrubs. We were in a room lined with shelves holding a miscellaneous assortment of objects, a storeroom, obviously. A dark opening on the other side of the room marked the exit. A flight of stairs led up to a door. John pushed it ajar and peered through the crack.

"Another storeroom," he said, after a moment. "All clear."

This room, on a slightly higher level, had several windows, and rows and rows of bins.

"Wine cellar," I whispered. "I know where we are now. I didn't realize this door was here. I never reached the part of the cellars where we were."

"Never mind the travelogue, just lead the way," John muttered.

It was easier said than done. The room was like a maze, with one row of bins looking just like the next. We had traversed one row without finding the door, and had started on the next, when John's hand clenched painfully over mine.

I heard the sound almost as soon as he did. They weren't bothering to move quietly. Why should they? One of them was whistling. There was at least one other man, from the sound of the footsteps. A few seconds ticked past, while we stood frozen. Then we saw a light, broken into grotesque shadows by the surrounding wine racks, but growing steadily brighter.

John dropped to the floor, dragging me with him. They passed not five feet from us. If they had looked to one side, they would have seen us. There were two of them. I recognized two of the men I had seen working near the garage. The light from the electric torch was so bright I hid my eyes.

Oh, well, I may as well be honest. I hid my eyes in the style of an ostrich, hoping they wouldn't see me if I couldn't see them. I have never felt more exposed and helpless.

But they went by without breaking stride, and turned into the next aisle. The light receded along with the sound of their footsteps.

John yanked me to my feet. He didn't need to tell me to hurry. We had about a minute and a half before the alarm would be raised.

I was ready to run, I didn't care where to. As soon as we got out of the wine cellar, John pulled me to a stop.

"Wait, let's not go riding off in all directions. Give me some idea of our options from here."

"The main stairs are that way," I said, pointing. "They come up in the service wing, near the butler's pantry."

"That's the way our friends came, most probably. They will be returning that way. There must be some other exit. Preferably out into the great out-of-doors."

I tried to remember. It was hard; my heart was making so much noise I couldn't hear myself think.

"Wait. Yes, there is another door. This way."

You never realize that time is subjective until you are in a spot like the one we were in. At every second I expected to hear howls and shouts and the sounds of pursuit, but actually we had covered quite a bit of ground before my ears caught the echo of thundering footsteps. They were muffled by distance and by the walls we had put between ourselves and our pursuers, but I heard them. I was listening for them.

I went even faster after that. It was a wonder we didn't brain ourselves against a wall, but there was some light, from windows, since we were now on the upper level of the cellars. It is even more of a wonder that I remembered the way. However, I have an excellent sense of direction, and one's senses work amazingly well when the alternative to failure is imminent execution. We ended up right where I hoped we would, at the bottom of a flight of rough stone stairs that ended in a heavy door.

We had to risk lighting a match or we would never have gotten that door open. The old lock wasn't very formidable, but it was reinforced by the usual bars, bolts, and chains. When we had disengaged the extra impediments, the door still refused to budge.

I could have picked the lock if I had had time, steady hands, and the necessary tools. I had none of the above. So I lighted another match and looked around; and sure enough, there was the key hanging on a nail. My grandmother always did that with her keys. It was an unexpectedly homey touch.

The door creaked hideously, but fortunately there was nobody around to hear. It opened onto a weedy patch of ground enclosed by plastered walls. There was a gate in the wall directly opposite.

John closed the door behind us.

"Not that it matters," he muttered. "They will know we came this way if they see the chains unfastened. Where are we?"

"Damned if I know."

The courtyard was about ten feet by fifteen. John walked out into the middle of it, put his hands on his hips, threw his head back, and contemplated the heavens. The moonlight silvered his hair and cast dramatic shadows across his body; he looked like one of the younger, more ineffectual saints addressing the Almighty. I stayed in the shelter of the house. I felt safer there.

"Well?" I said, after a while.

"Sssh." He came back to me. "We're behind the villa—"

"I could have told you that."

"It faces west," John went on imperturbably. "We want the road to Rome, which is that way." He pointed.

"That may be what we want, but what we need is to put some distance between us and the villa. There can't be many ways out of those cellars, and it won't take long to check them. Bruno could come bursting through that door any second. Let's get out of here."

"You have a point. Excelsior!"

The gate led into another courtyard. Every

acre of ground seemed to be walled, and I began to get an acute sense of claustrophobia. Finally, however, we came upon a familiar building—the garage.

"Hey," I said, catching John's arm. "What about—"

He wasn't actually reading my mind; we were both thinking the obvious things at the same time.

"No use. I don't have the keys to any of the cars. Antonio sleeps upstairs; by the time I could get one of them started he'd hear me. Besides, if we steal a car, all they have to do is call the local constable in Tivoli and tell him—"

"One reason is enough," I snapped. "*Avanti*, then."

Another gate and another courtyard brought us to the shelter of a stone wall, where we collapsed to catch our breath.

"The gardens begin here," I said softly. "Plenty of cover in all that fancy landscaping. We should be all right now."

Squatting on all fours like a nervous rabbit, John suddenly stiffened and lifted his head.

"Look."

Atop the hill the villa loomed up against the stars. It should have been a dark and shapely silhouette. But as we watched, lights sprang up in window after window, like a fireworks display. I was still staring in dismay at this lovely but ominous spectacle when a light went on right next to me, as if one of the trees had sprouted light bulbs instead of leaves. I transferred my horrified glance to John. I could even see the drops of sweat on his forehead, and the dark pupils of his dilated eyes. The pupils started to shrink.

"We should be all right now," John repeated bitterly. "Damn it! Some bright soul has turned on the garden illumination."

Nine

PIETRO HAD BOASTED THAT THE NIGHT lights of the garden made them as bright as day. He hadn't exaggerated by much. There were patches of shadow, but the lights made our job of getting out of the gardens about a thousand percent harder.

A cute little dangling lantern was practically on top of us. We moved away from it into the concealment of a giant rhododendron, and sat there musing aloud.

"How many of them are there?" I asked. "The bad guys, I mean."

"I know what you mean. Not many of the servants are in on the plot, but that doesn't matter. They will all be looking for us, you can bank on that. The Boss will have concocted some plausible story to explain why we must be apprehended. And," he added, "don't get your hopes up. Some of them will be armed. We won't know which ones until they shoot at us. What's the quickest way out of here? I haven't explored the grounds as thoroughly as you have."

I closed my eyes and tried to remember. I think better with my eyes closed. The plan of the gardens was fairly clear in my mind.

"The quickest way isn't the safest," I said, after a while. "But if we cross the English garden and pass the Fountain of the Turtles, we'll be in the rose garden. After that it isn't far to the wall. . . ."

My voice trailed off in dismay as I remembered that wall. It was twelve feet high, with barbed wire on top.

"We'll worry about the wall when we come to it," John said. "The way my adrenaline is pumping, I could probably get over it in a standing jump."

I really hated to leave that rhododendron. It had gorgeous purple flowers and lots of nice thick foliage. We went scuttling along behind the wall, which ended in an open, trellised summerhouse. We skirted this and struck out across the grounds. I was thankful it was spring, when the grass was lush and soft, and there were no fallen leaves underfoot to crackle.

The English garden was enclosed by a high

hedge of boxwood. This particular plant gets very thick and high when it is old. It is sometimes used for mazes because it is so difficult to break through. Keeping in its shadow, we found a place where the hedge was a little thinner, and peered through.

The garden was one of Pietro's favorites. He had not stinted on the lights. One look and I knew it would be impossible to cut directly across. It would be like walking onto a lighted stage.

We didn't cross the English garden. We circumnavigated it, crawling on our stomachs next to the roots of the boxwood. I do not recommend that means of locomotion. But we saw no one, and when we reached the entrance to the long avenue, I thought we had it made. Tall, pointed cypresses lined the way like living pillars. There was plenty of shade under the trees, and the low lights lining the path did not reach far into the shadows. The avenue sloped down, following the contours of the hillside. We made good time. We were almost at the end of it, near the rose garden, when I heard a sound that startled me so much I tripped over a petunia. It was a dog barking.

"Bloodhounds!" I gasped.

"Don't be an idiot." John had stopped to listen. "It's worse than bloodhounds. It's Caesar."

"Oh, no!"

"Oh, yes. He's the only dog on the premises. You would have to be an animal lover, wouldn't you? Hurry."

We plunged down the hillside, abandoning caution in the need for haste. Caesar could mean big trouble for us. Bloodhounds would follow a trail out of a sense of duty, but good old Caesar would be anxious to find his buddy who had fed him the pâté and the smoked oysters, and rolled around on the grass with him. Dogs have long memories for things like that, bless their hearts. They also have excellent senses of smell.

When we reached the bottom of the avenue, I veered left, toward the rose garden. John's hand closed on my arm and yanked me around.

"What the hell," I began.

"Forget the rose garden, we need water. Running water . . . Get that damn dog off the trail . . ." He was panting, and I didn't blame him.

There was plenty of water. However, the fountains were magnificently illuminated. We splashed recklessly through one of the largest of them, tripping over nymphs and water gods. John slipped on the wet stone and clutched at one of the nymphs to keep his balance. The affectionate tableau was so funny I started to laugh. A spray of water hit me in the mouth, and the laugh turned to a gargle, which won me a hateful look from John as he untangled himself from the outstretched marble arms. He was too out of breath to comment, which was probably just as well.

We climbed over the parapet of the fountain and rushed on. I had completely lost my sense of direction, but John seemed to know where he was going, so I followed him, spurred on by the sound of joyful barking somewhere in the distance. But when I saw what he had in mind, I stopped dead.

One of the showpieces of the Villa d'Este is the Avenue of a Hundred Fountains. Each "fountain" is a simple jet of water, but en masse they look impressive, lined up as they are in a long basin. Not to be outdone, Pietro's ancestor had constructed an avenue of *two* hundred fountains. From where we stood at the bottom of the slope, looking up, the fine spray seemed to mount straight up into the sky. John took a long running jump, landed flat, and made swimming motions.

I don't know what was the matter with me. Hysteria, perhaps. I laughed so hard I had to hang on to a carved dolphin to keep from falling.

John pulled himself to his feet, clutched another dolphin—the fountain was lined with them, all the way up—and glared at me.

"The salmon do it," I gurgled. "Upstream. To spawn."

He was streaming with water, from his soaked hair to the bottoms of his pants. He flung out his arm, his forefinger extended.

"Swim, damn it!" he shouted, and started to climb.

The rush of falling water almost drowned out his voice, but I got the idea. I climbed into the basin.

We didn't swim. It would have been impossible, the fountain was only three or four feet deep and about six wide, and the water poured down like a flood. It would have been hard enough to climb without the current dragging at our feet, but we did it, thanks to the dolphins. The two hundred fountains of water poured from their mouths, and there was one of them every three or four feet, so we were able to pull ourselves along by means of them. I wish I had a movie of that performance. Even then I was occasionally convulsed with laughter at the sight of John's drenched figure doggedly dragging itself forward just ahead of me.

We got about halfway up without being seen. I had gotten into my stride by then—step, slip, grab the next dolphin, step, slip, grab—and was fully prepared to keep on doing the same thing till we reached the top. We were still some distance away from that goal when John took a giant step up onto the head of one of the dolphins, caught the top of the wall, and pulled himself up. Squatting there like a dank frog, he extended a hand toward me.

"I was just beginning to enjoy myself," I said mildly, as he yanked me up beside him. "Where now?"

He shoved me off the wall.

I landed in a clump of azaleas. If you think azaleas aren't prickly, try falling into one. Before I could start swearing, he landed next to me and slapped his hand over my mouth.

Then I heard Caesar. He was hot on the trail, too close for comfort. The first fountain hadn't confused him at all. We could only hope that he would lose our scent at the bottom of the

Two Hundred Fountains complex, and that, if the men who guided him were smart enough to realize we had taken to the water, they would try casting about at the top of the slope.

In the meantime, it behooved us to make tracks. We did so, back down the hill we had climbed with such effort. It was not until we had gone some distance, and Caesar's excited barks had taken on a frantic note, that I realized where we were going. Our best route now was through the garden of the monsters. To avoid it would double the distance to the outer wall and would necessitate passing through some of the most open areas of the grounds.

In the smoky green and purple lights the monster garden was straight out of Lovecraft. The great hollow head was lighted from within by a powerful red lamp; its slitted eyes glowed like those of a demon out of hell, and the fangs looked as if they had been dipped in blood. John took my hand. His was wet, but it felt warm and hard and comforting. I don't think he was trying to comfort me, though. He was just as scared as I was. I heard his teeth chattering. We were soaking wet, but it was a nice warm night.

Some of the smaller monsters weren't illumined, and I would have fallen over a baby dragon if John hadn't been holding on to me. The adult dragon, which had come so close to running me down, was ahead of us, looking unpleasantly lifelike in a rippling lavender searchlight. Then I heard a sound behind us, near the great guardian head.

A flashlight beam sprayed out. Its white light seemed sane and normal compared to the ghastly tints of the other lights, but I could have done without it. Simultaneously, without discussing it aloud, we both dropped to the ground. Then something really unpleasant happened. From the opposite end of the garden, near the exit, another flashlight appeared.

I invoked my Maker in a one-word whisper, and was promptly shushed by John. My whisper could not have been heard; someone spoke at that precise moment. His voice was soft, but I could hear him quite clearly. He was that close.

"Alberto *qui*."

The other man identified himself.

"Bassano. Have you seen them?"

"No. I have just come from the back gates."

Bassano let out a string of lurid curses.

"Get back there, fool. The gates must be guarded."

"What about this garden?"

"I'll have a look around. Quickly, now."

I crouched there trying to compress myself into a smaller piece of air as the flashlight moved in closer. The second man had left. . . . And so had John. He had let go of my hand when we fell flat; he must have slipped away during the conversation between the two men.

I had just enough time to think bitter thoughts about him when the stone dragon began to move. I jumped a good three inches. So did Bassano; I saw the flashlight beam shoot skyward before he got it under control. He swore again—sheer bravado, his voice was tremulous. I understood his feelings. The moving statues had looked ghastly enough in broad daylight. Bathed in a lurid glow, with shadows slipping over their stony hides like muscles twitching, they were like creatures out of a feverish nightmare.

They were all moving, now, the rusty mechanisms grating and groaning. I was debating which way to go when I saw John hugging the massive flank of the dragon, which was swinging on a curving course in my general direction. As it rolled out of the glow of the purple searchlight, its rear end was deeply shadowed. I wouldn't have seen John if he hadn't beckoned urgently.

Bassano and his flashlight were no longer visible. I think he ran. So did we, as soon as the dragon's ponderous path took it near the rear gate. There was only one more garden, and then came a flight of stairs, with an artificial waterfall flowing down them, before we reached the lower terrace and the wall. But we had to hurry. As soon as Bassano got his wits back, he would know who had started the monsters moving.

I thought of mentioning this to John, but decided I had better save my breath for more important matters, such as running away. He was splashing merrily down the middle of the stairway, through the waterfall, like Gene Kelly in "Singing in the Rain." He was built like a dancer, slim and wiry, but at that moment his excellent physique was only too visible in the amber lights that flooded the fountain. He had abandoned secrecy for speed, which made sense; if our pursuers didn't know exactly where we were, they knew where we had just been.

John was well ahead of me when we got to the bottom of the stairs and raced across the terrace. The wall loomed up ahead, the tangle of barbed wire on top looking like delicate black lace against the moonlit sky. There were trees to right and left, but not directly ahead. John decided to go right. He made a quick turn. His wet shoes slipped on the flagstones, his feet went out from under him, and he fell forward with a splat like a large flounder being landed. At the same moment I heard voices raised in excited comment at the top of the stairs.

I skidded to a stop beside John and hauled him to his feet.

"The heroine is the one who is supposed to fall over her clumsy feet," I said sweetly.

I'm sure he would have had a snappy answer if the fall had not knocked the wind out of him. He hung on to me for a few moments, whooping for breath. Then he headed for the nearest tree and started climbing, without waiting to see whether I was following.

They were flowering trees of some kind, in full blossom, and the scent was sweet as perfume. Velvety petals brushed my face and arms as I climbed.

John was above me, agile as a monkey. I had to admire his well-developed sense of self-preservation, which was uncluttered by any taint of old-fashioned chivalry. He was heavier than I was, though, and he was stuck, about six feet from the top of the wall. The branches were getting too fragile to support him.

"Get out of the way," I hissed. "I'm lighter; maybe I can—"

He didn't say anything, but I stopped talking, because the voices and the flashlights were coming down the stairs. When they reached the bottom, they would fan out to right and left, and if they had the elementary intelligence to shine their lights up into the trees, we were sitting ducks—stuck, like ripe fruit in the skinny branches.

A fragrant cascade of satiny petals showered down on my upturned face. John seemed to be having a slight fit up there. Then I realized he was struggling out of his jacket—no mean task, wet as it was. He stood upright, swaying perilously, and threw first the jacket and then himself onto the top of the wall.

I climbed up to the limb he had vacated and caught his hand. He let out a smothered yelp.

"What's the matter?" I asked. I didn't bother to lower my voice. The boys in the background were making considerable noise.

"You just pulled me down onto the barbed wire," said John. It had to be John, because he was the only one up there, but I would never have recognized his voice, he was gritting his teeth so hard. "Damn it, use your feet! Haven't you ever done any climbing? I can't possibly drag your not inconsiderable weight—"

I got my elbows over the edge of the wall, where his jacket had padded the spikes on the wire, and hauled myself up. The pursuers were on the terrace, baying like a pack of wolves or a bunch of middle-aged male congressmen debating ERA.

"All right," John said, as I balanced precariously on the edge of the wall. His voice was almost calm now.

"Take it slowly. The wire doesn't quite cover the entire surface; there is a good two inches free on either side. Step over. No, not there, a little to your left. Good. It's about eight feet down. The ground is higher on the other side. Lower yourself by your hands and drop."

His hand on my elbow steadied me as I stepped high over the barrier of wire. I was concentrating so hard on avoiding the barbs that I was only dimly aware of the brouhaha going on in the background, not ten yards away. The searchers had gathered in a gesticulating group on the terrace. Several of them had flashlights, but at that moment they had succumbed to one of the weaknesses to which the engaging Latin temperament is susceptible. They were arguing about what to do next. Some of them wanted to go right, some left; one cool-headed character suggested they split up, but he was shouted down by the others, who were enjoying the argument too much to settle it sensibly. They were waving their flashlights around as they talked—no real Italian can converse without using his hands— and the beams reminded me of old World War II movies, with the antiaircraft beacons crisscrossing the dark sky.

Sooner or later one of those beams was bound to find us. It was pure bad luck that it happened about sixty seconds too soon.

I was hanging by my hands, but my toes were dug into a crack in the outer surface of the wall. I couldn't quite bring myself to let go. John said it was eight feet down, but what did he know? There might be a bottomless abyss under my feet. It was dark down there.

John was bending over me. My right hand still clutched his wrist. He must have been squatting on the barbed wire, because his admonitions to me were interspersed with profane comments. All of a sudden his ruffled hair lit up like a pop-art halo, and light focused on his face. His eyes widened and his lips parted, but I didn't hear what he said. It was drowned out by the sound of the shot.

I let go of the wall, but I did not let go of John. I dragged him with me as I fell, and if he yelled when the barbed wire raked across his body I didn't hear it; the crowd on the terrace was shooting up a storm. If I hadn't known better, I could have sworn they had an automatic rifle or a machine gun.

It was about nine feet down, as a matter of fact—three feet below the soles of my shoes. I landed with scarcely a jar, then John fell on top of me. We went down in a confused tangle and continued to roll. The slope must have been almost 45 degrees, and every rock on it left a bruise on my aching body. There was a stream at the bottom of the hill. Naturally, we rolled into it. If there was a natural obstacle on that hillside that we missed, I would be surprised.

I had been holding on to John, probably out of some vicious urge to use him as a buffer, so we ended up in the same place. In the stream. I don't mean to disparage the stream. It was a nice stream. Shallow, with a soft, muddy bed, and quite warm. I lay there with the water rippling gently across my bruised body till I got my breath back. Off in the distance there were lights, and people yelling. Somebody's head was pressing down on my diaphragm.

"John?" I said.

No answer.

"I hope it's you down there," I said. "Because if it isn't, who is it?"

The head moved feebly. Then a disembodied voice said, "Water. More water. It must have some deeper meaning. In Freudian terms—"

"Freud be damned. It's a stream. We're in it. John, we made it; we escaped from the estate."

"That's nice." The weight on my diaphragm increased.

"We got out, but we're still in danger. I think we had better move on."

We had come a long way down. The moving lights at the top of the hill looked far away, the voices sounded like insects buzzing. But I was not deceived.

"John," I said. "Some of those men have guns."

"Too true." John sat up. "You weren't joking, were you? We really are in a stream. I have never seen such a damp country. The English climate is considered wet, but this—"

"It was the dog," I said. "We could have avoided some of the water if it hadn't been for the dog. John, I am worried about Caesar. That Bruno is no fit keeper. Once we get out of this—"

"Thanks for reminding me." John got slowly to his feet. "So long as we're in the stream we may as well stick to it, in case they fetch Caesar."

"We couldn't be much wetter," I said.

John made no reply to this cheerful speech except for a grunt.

We went downhill, walking in the stream. Gradually the banks rose on either side until we were splashing through a miniature ravine, with trees leaning down from above and roots reaching out of the muddy sides like gnarled arms. To judge from the cries of inquiry and alarm behind us, the search had not been abandoned, but I began to relax. The dog couldn't track us through the water, and the human pursuers couldn't see us unless they shone lights straight down on us. In some places the banks were severely concave; the stream must run high and fast at certain seasons in order to have cut out so much dirt. The only difficulty was that it was hard to see where we were going. The steepness of the sides and the branches overhead cut out most of the moonlight. I reached out and caught John's sleeve. It was very wet—soggy, in fact. He stopped when I touched him, and his breath came out in a sharp gasp.

"Don't be such a scaredy-cat," I hissed. "I can't see. I just wanted to—"

The truth began to dawn on me then; not all at once, but a little bit at a time. The first thing to strike me was the strange feel of the fabric I was touching. It was wet, all right—wet and sticky. Before my feeble brain could go on to the next step, John collapsed into the water with a splash that sent water sloshing up my shins.

The water was only three or four inches deep, but that's deep enough if you are face down in it, which he was. I don't suppose it took me more than a few seconds to turn him over, but it seemed a lot longer. He didn't help any. For the second time in a few hours he was out cold, and I must admit that I didn't draw a deep breath until his breath came out with a watery gurgle, and I knew he was alive.

The water was trickling up around his face, so I dragged him out onto the bank, which was deeply undercut at that point. He was so wet I had a hard time figuring out where he was hurt. I couldn't see anything except the faintest glimmer of fair hair, since even his shirt was muddied and dark. But I finally decided that the major damage was a bullet hole in his arm. He must have lost quite a bit of blood; it was still flowing freely.

It never rains but it pours. I was plucking frantically at my scanty attire, trying to figure out what I could spare for a tourniquet and bandage, and wondering how I was going to do the job in absolute darkness, when something above my head snapped and dirt dribbled down into the water. One of the searchers must have heard the splash and decided to investigate. He had been walking in darkness; now he switched on his light and shone it down into the ravine.

Luckily for us he was on the same side of the stream. I had pulled John completely out of the water, so I could check him over, and we were pressed up against the undercut side of the bank. The flashlight beam illumined the opposite bank, and a good part of the stream itself.

If the searcher had been as smart as he thought he was, he would have noticed that a miniature tide had gone in and out over that far bank in the last few minutes, and he might have drawn some interesting conclusions. It was so obvious to me that I held my breath, expecting a shout that would summon the others.

We were saved by an animal. I don't know what kind of animal, because I never got a good look at it; it was only a sleek, shining blur as it slid through the shallow water and popped into a hole in the opposite bank. A water rat, maybe. Anyhow, the man up above must have assumed that it was responsible for the splash he had heard. He muttered something and threw a stone at the animal—which shows you what kind of person he was. It missed by a mile. The searcher turned back; I heard him crunching through the weeds, no longer trying to move quietly.

His light had served one useful purpose. In its reflected glow I had gotten a good look at John's arm. With an inaudible sigh I started squirming out of my blouse. It was as clean as any other garment we owned—not very clean, in other words. But it would have to serve temporarily. I was going to feel a little peculiar, trying to hitch a ride without a blouse, but the moments of illumination had told me something else—if I looked as disreputable as my companion, a blouse more or less wouldn't matter.

Ten

I AM BY NATURE AN OPTIMISTIC PERSON. BUT during those minutes in the mud and the dark, alone with a man who was quietly bleeding to death on my lap, with a mob of murderous brutes scouring the fields to find us ... I was depressed. I got so discouraged I even considered giving ourselves up, in order to get medical attention for John. However, I dismissed the thought as soon as it surfaced. Slight as our chances of escape were, they were better than no chance at all, and that was what we would have if we surrendered. No chance.

My father, who knows more corny old aphorisms, mottoes, and adages than any man alive, would have found encouragement in his collection of truisms. "Never say die." "Don't give up the ship." "Don't let the bastards get you down." And he would have been right.

Four hours after I had been almost ready to give up the ship, we were sitting in the back

271

of a pickup truck that was speeding through the suburbs of Rome.

The sky to the east was brightening and the stars were fading. The truck was an antique, held together by wire and prayer, and I was not really awfully comfortable, because I was squeezed into a space not quite adequate for a lady of my size. The bed of the truck was filled with vegetables. The corner of a crate of tomatoes dug into my back, and I was holding a sack of carrots on my lap. John was half lying, half sitting on a bag of potatoes. They must have been as lumpy and as hard as rocks, but he didn't complain.

The way in which we had attained these positions is a saga in itself.

John came to while I was fumbling around trying to bandage his arm, and made several heated comments on my clumsiness before I shut him up. When I asked him if he could walk, he replied that he would be willing to consider any reasonable alternative, if I could think of one. There weren't many, and none of them were reasonable. I couldn't carry him. We couldn't wait till morning gilded the skies and made us visible to anyone who might be looking for us.

So we walked. The clothes were partly luck,

but I must claim some of the credit. I looked for them. We had to go into the outskirts of Tivoli before we found a housewife who had been too slovenly to take her wash in at nightfall. John complained bitterly about those clothes. True, his pants were six inches too short and considerably too big in every other direction, but the coarse blue shirt was nice and large. He needed a lot of material to cover bandages and battle scars.

I had a choice: a rusty black shapeless garment that belonged to the mother of the house, or the cheap rayon skirt and blouse that were her daughter's. John accused me of vanity when I took the latter. They were a little short and a lot too tight, but it was not vanity that prompted my selection, as I proved when the first truck I hailed on the highway came to a screeching stop as soon as the headlights caught me.

The drivers weren't as enthusiastic about John, who had kept out of sight while I waved my thumb, but they accepted the pair of us with a grin and a shrug. (One grinned, the other shrugged.) There were two of them, and they were brothers, on their way to a market in Rome.

So we ended up among the vegetables. I

273

don't know what our newfound friends thought of us. I don't suppose they cared. We could have been penniless students, many of whom wander the roads of Europe during the summer, sleeping in haystacks and less-reputable places, scrounging for food and transportation.

John dropped off to sleep shortly after we climbed aboard. I should have been tired too; it had been an active night. But I was too keyed up to sleep. I sat clutching the carrots and watched the sun come up over Rome.

The mists that hung over the city turned the exquisite pearly pink of a shell as the light struck them. Then they burned away as the sky deepened from rose to blue. High above the angled roofs, Michelangelo's great cupola dominated the skyline. As we neared the city, other landmarks, high on the seven hills, took shape out of the haze; the pointed bell tower of Santa Maria Maggiore, on the Esquiline; the dome of the Gesù; the twisted Baroque towers of Trinita dei Monti, atop the Spanish Steps.

We came into the city by way of the Porta Pia, between the old walls of the Empire, and went roaring along the Via Venti Settembre at a speed that seemed excessive even for that early hour. There was not a great deal of traffic, and the one policeman we passed simply waved. I guess the boys were a familiar sight, covering the same route six mornings a week.

When we crossed the Piazza Venezia, I began to wonder where we were going. We were in the heart of the city now; Mussolini had addressed the Romans from the balcony on the Palazzo Venezia, and the square was dominated by the huge white marble structure of the Victor Emmanuel Monument. I would have exchanged all this guidebook knowledge for a quick trip to the prefecture of police. I didn't dare ask the boys from Tivoli to take us there; people are leery about picking up strangers who demand the cops.

When we passed the basilica of San Andrea delle Valle, I began to get premonitions. I shook John. He opened one eye.

"Wake up, we're almost there," I said.

The narrow street where the truck finally stopped was only a couple of blocks from the Via delle Cinque Lune. With a discouraged feeling that I was right back where I started from, I climbed over the vegetables and jumped down.

It couldn't have been later than 6 A.M., but the vendors had already set up their stalls. These booths ran along both sides of the street, which was one of the medieval alleyways with no sidewalks or yards, only tall dark fronts of stores and houses walling in the narrow pavement. The stalls were rickety affairs of rough wood; some were brightened by striped canopies, but artificial adornment was unnecessary. The wares on sale made marvelous compositions of shape and color, brighter than any bunting. Soft, crumpled chartreuse leaves of lettuce, symmetrical heaps of oranges and tangerines, tomatoes red as sunrise, bins of green beans, black-red cherries, peaches and strawberries in little wooden boxes. All these and more were being unloaded from the trucks that blocked the street. The noise was deafening—engines were roaring, crates and boxes clattering, people yelling. A good deal of argument seemed to be going on, most of it more or less good-natured bickering over the quality of the goods and the prices.

Our driver jumped down from the cab and came toward me, smiling pleasantly. He was young and rather good-looking, and he knew it; his shirt was open to the waist and a gold crucifix shone against his brown chest.

"*Va bene, signorina?*" he asked.

"*Molto bene, grazie.* Thanks for the ride."

"Niente, niente." He waved my thanks away. *"Dov'è vostro amico?"*

Yes, indeed, where was he? I looked up. All I could see of John was a foot sticking out from among the cabbages. I shook it gently, out of deference for his status as wounded hero. I was worried about him. He had kept up the pace without complaint or visible faltering, but I meant to find a doctor for him first thing.

"John, wake up. We're here."

The driver lowered the tailgate and began unloading, assisted by his sober-faced companion. The proprietress of the nearest stall, a short, fat woman with three gold teeth, came stumping over, ostensibly to ask the price of the carrots. She let out a howl of pretended outrage when my friend told her how much he was asking. I could see that her eyes were on me, though, and after the first feint she gave up all pretense of being interested in anything else.

"Who's this?" she demanded, jerking a calloused thumb at me. "Another of the foreign tarts you pick up, Battista?"

Battista, who knew I spoke Italian, made deprecatory noises. I smiled sweetly at the old busybody and handed her the sack of carrots.

"They are very cheap, signora, good, sweet

carrots. A bargain. My friend is there in the truck. He fell and hurt himself yesterday, when we were hiking in the hills. Signor Battista was kind enough to give us a ride."

I thought I had better mention that John was hurt in case he had passed out again. It was just as well I had done so. He came crawling out from among the cabbages and he looked awful. He must have scraped the scab off the cut on his head, because there was blood running down his cheek.

The old lady gave a cry of distress and sympathy. Women of all ages and all nationalities are suckers for a boyish face and a little blood.

"Ah, *poverino*—poor child, how did you hurt yourself?"

Squatting on the tailgate, John gave her a long look out of his melting baby-blue eyes, and smiled wanly.

"I fell, signora. Thank you . . . you are very kind . . ."

She put out a plump arm to steady him as he slid down. He had gone a sickly gray under his tan, and he looked as if he would have fallen but for her support. If it had been anybody but John, I would have melted with sympathy too. Seeing as it was John, I reserved judgment.

"I will take him to a doctor," I said.

"No, I'm all right. Just need to rest awhile."

"Where?" I demanded. "We can't go to a hotel looking the way we do. Especially when we haven't any money."

The old lady must have picked up some English from the tourists.

"My daughter has rooms for rent," she said. "Just around the corner is her apartment."

She didn't finish the offer; it was clear from her expression that her native caution was at war with her maternal instinct.

John looked like Saint Sebastian minus the arrows—all noble suffering.

"We have money, signora," he murmured. "Not much, but we could not accept charity. Take this, please—I think I can walk a little. . . ."

He held out a handful of crumpled hundred-lira notes.

Everything I owned was in my purse and my suitcases back at the villa. Fool that I was, I had forgotten men carry their junk in their pockets. Not that I had planned to go to a hotel anyway. I intended to head straight for the police station. When I had mentioned this during our wanderings the night before, John had not been overly enthusiastic, but he hadn't objected. Now I began to suspect he had something else in mind.

There was nothing I could do about it. We had attracted quite a crowd by this time. Romans are cynical, big-city types, but in any city—yes, even in New York—you will collect a certain number of willing helpers if you are young and beautiful and in trouble. Helpful arms gathered John up and propelled his tottering footsteps in the direction the old lady had indicated. I could only trail along, thinking nasty suspicious thoughts.

The apartment was old and poorly furnished, but it was reasonably clean. The room had an iron bed, a pine dresser, two straight chairs, a washbasin, and a picture of Saint Catherine accepting a ring from the baby Jesus. Once again I mentioned a doctor, and was shouted down by my assistants, who now felt that we were all one big happy family. They wouldn't call the doctor until the patient was just about ready for the last rites. A little wine, a little soup, a little pasta, and the poor young man would be just fine. The bump on the head had hurt him, but there was nothing seriously wrong. A little wine, a little soup, a little pasta . . .

Finally I got rid of them and closed the door.

Then I turned to John, who was lying on the bed staring blandly at the cracked ceiling.

"I'll send a doctor," I said. "On my way to the prefecture."

"Wait." He sat up with an alacrity that confirmed my worst suspicions, and caught at my arm. "Let's discuss this first."

"There is nothing to discuss. I told you what I meant to do. The longer we wait, the more opportunity Pietro will have to clear out that workshop."

"Sit down." He gave my arm a shrewd twist. I sat down.

"Did I hurt you?"

"Didn't you mean to?"

"No. I'm sorry. But you are so damned impetuous. . . ." He swung his legs off the bed, so that we were sitting side by side. The sudden movement made him go a shade grayer. He might have been putting on some of his weakness, but not all of it was pretense.

"Are you really going to turn me in?" he asked, with a faint sideways smile. "After all we've been through together?"

"You stuck with me," I said grudgingly. "You would have had a better chance of escape alone, I suppose. Damn it, John, I don't like to be a fink, but what choice do I have? I refuse to let that gang of swindlers get away with this. Why are you so considerate of them? They tried to kill you."

"I don't think there was anything personal in that," John said.

"Personal, impersonal, who cares? How can I agree to let you off when I don't even know what you've done?" I demanded, my mounting anger compounded with a certain degree of shame. "If you would tell me about the plot—give me some alternative . . ."

"That does seem reasonable."

"I mean, if you won't even . . . Oh. You will tell me?"

"Yes."

"Good. Lie down," I added. "You look like hell."

He obeyed. I turned so that I could see him. It was amazing how innocent that man could look when he wanted to. His eyes were very blue. The shadows under them were like bruises. Then he grinned, and his fine-boned face was transformed—from Saint Sebastian to Mercutio.

"I was born of poor but honest parents," he began.

"Be serious."

"I am. My parents were extremely poor.

They were also of the gentry—not the landed gentry, unfortunately. Only a few paltry acres around the family mansion, which has approximately five years more to go before the termites devour it. Do you have any idea what a handicap that combination is—poverty and gentility? I couldn't get a position—"

"Horsefeathers," I said rudely, fighting the melting effect of those cornflower-blue eyes. "The class barriers went down with a crash in World War Two, even in England. When the Duke of Bedford is selling souvenirs to tourists who visit his stately mansion, anybody can work."

"Ah, well, it was worth a try," John said, without rancor. "You sense the truth, of course; I am personally disinclined to engage in vulgar labor. It's a psychological handicap. If you knew my mother—"

"Scratch excuse number two," I said. "I don't buy the theory that perverts and criminals are the guiltless products of a corrupt society. And as a woman I'm sick and tired of the attempts to blame Mom for every crime that has been committed since Cain and Abel."

"Eve was probably overprotective," John said speculatively. "She always liked Abel best. Naturally this upset his brother . . . My mother's name is Guinevere."

I stared at him for a minute and then started to laugh.

"You are hopeless," I said. "Is that really her name?"

"Yes."

"You may have an excuse after all."

"We're an old Cornish family," John explained. "Old and decadent. However, I cannot honestly blame my sins on Mum. She's a good old girl, even if she does look like Judith Anderson playing a demented housekeeper. No, my sins are my own. I simply cannot settle down to an honest spot of work. It's so boring."

"And swindling isn't boring?"

"Well, this particular scheme isn't as ingenious as some I have engaged in. There was one stunt. . . . But perhaps we had better not recall that. It was brilliant, though. Almost worked, too. It failed only because I was too innocent to understand the depravity that lurks in the hearts of men. One man in particular—my partner."

"It appears to me that you haven't overcome that weakness," I suggested politely.

"Too true. I simply must become more cynical. At any rate, this plan seemed quite fool-proof. I was approached by an acquaintance of mine in London—and, pardon me. I simply will not mention names. I don't mind about some of the others, but he's a good chap, and a friend."

"Never mind the noblesse oblige. What was the plan?"

"Don't rush me," John said, savoring the syllables. "I must think how to explain it convincingly."

"I think I see another of your troubles," I said maliciously. "You talk too much. You are so enamored of the sound of your own voice that you babble on and on when you ought to be doing something."

"That is unkind, but probably correct. Very well, I'll get on with it.

"My friend, whom I shall refer to as 'Jones'—to go with 'Smythe,' you know—is the sole heir of a wealthy old aunt. At least she was wealthy; at the rate she is using up her resources there won't be much left for poor old Jones—which is one of the reasons why she is living so well, since she doesn't care much for Jones. She thinks he is a lazy ne'er-do-well, and she is absolutely right. The only asset she possesses that she won't pawn or sell is her antique-jewelry collection. She plans to leave that to the British Museum, in order to spite Jones.

"So, when Jones was contacted by a strange little man who proposed a deal, he listened. The deal was simple enough. The old lady doesn't trust banks. She keeps her jewels in a safe in her flat. (The family mansion went on the block years ago.) The jewels are amply protected, not only by the safe, but by a dozen nervous dogs. The old witch adores the creatures.

"Now Jones admits that he had thought of—er—borrowing a few small diamonds, but he gave up the idea because he would be the first one to be suspected. His newfound friend's scheme disposed of this difficulty. He would supply Jones with imitations good enough to deceive even the old lady's sharp eye.

"Jones jeered at this—until he was shown a sample. It was the Charlemagne talisman, which I gather you've already seen. Good, isn't it?"

"Superb," I said honestly. "It ought to have relieved Jones's scruples—though he doesn't appear to have had many."

"I must confess he was ready to be persuaded," John said demurely. "The deal went off quite neatly. Jones supplied photographs and measurements, and the switch was made one night while Auntie was at the opera. Wagner.

"The gang split the proceeds with Jones, who is now living comfortably on the Riviera. When they asked him to recommend a friend who might assist them in finding other—er—"

"Victims," I suggested.

"Victims," John agreed, without batting an eye. "He thought of me. I was happy to oblige. I have a fairly wide acquaintance among the undeserving rich."

"But how do they sell the things?" I demanded. "If the jewels are so well known, no fence—"

"That's the beauty of the scheme. There are no middlemen. The gems are sold directly to collectors. There is a lot of money floating around the world these days, my dear. In the Near East, South America, the States. . . . People are buying jewels as investments, and antique jewelry is increasingly popular with collectors. The buyer knows, of course, that there is something shady about the transactions. He doesn't care. He is willing to keep quiet about his acquisitions."

"That's crazy."

"I quite agree. But there are a lot of crazy people in the world too. It happens all the time, Vicky. There is a large underground movement in forgeries of all kinds. Antique furniture, Chinese ceramics, famous paintings. Read some of the literature. The list of detected forgeries is enormous. And the objects on the list are the *unsuccessful* fakes. God knows how many imitation Rembrandts and Vermeers there are still in the museums. Where have the genuine pieces gone? Into private collections. The only thing that makes this scheme better than others is that the imitations are virtually undetectable. I doubt that even the great British Museum will notice the difference when Auntie finally passes her jewels on to them."

"And Pietro is one of the people who are allowing their collections to be copied?"

"Right."

"But why? The man is rich as Croesus. Villas and palaces stuffed with antiques, fancy cars, servants. . . . Why should he participate in a crummy deal like this?"

"Vicky, Vicky! It is clear that you, like my parents, come from the poor but honest class. I suppose you don't buy things unless you can pay for them."

"I *can't* buy things unless I can pay for them," I said, remembering my ivory loden cloak with the silver buttons and the swollen price tab.

"That's because you are one of the deserving poor. The Conte Caravaggio—who is one of the undeserving rich—can walk into a shop and walk out with a new Rolls, and the vulgar subject of money is never mentioned. Eventually he has to put a bit on account, but you'd be surprised how long this economic ruin can be juggled before it collapses. Pietro has already sold many of his treasures; half those paintings at the palace are copies. You didn't examine them because you were concentrating on jewelry. The property is mortgaged to the hilt and the servants haven't been paid for years. He needs money, darling, and so do many other people in his position. If he weren't of noble blood he'd stop buying Beluga caviar and handmade leather shoes, and declare bankruptcy; but the Caravaggio honor won't allow him to be an honest pauper."

"Very eloquent," I said. "Very convincing. . . . You don't have a high opinion of my intelligence, do you?"

"My dear girl, what do you mean?"

"My dear boy, the scheme you have outlined isn't larceny—except for the initial transaction. I suppose you thought I'd concentrate on that and overlook the fact that there is no law to prevent a man like Pietro from selling his possessions if he wants to. And no law to keep him from having copies made for himself."

"It was worth a try," John said coolly.

"So what is the plot? No, don't tell me, it's quite obvious, really. Pietro doesn't sell his jewels, he sells the copies. Not once, but several times! He and the others who are cooperating in this scheme never appear—that's your job, to peddle the merchandise. The collectors who buy from you think they are buying stolen property, so they don't compare notes or publicize their purchases. Luigi's copies will pass any test they can devise. And if they see references in the press to the original jewels—the Gräfin von Hochstein at the opera wearing the Hochstein emeralds—they think she is wearing the fakes! That's it, isn't it?"

"Essentially, yes. That's it."

"It's incredible," I muttered.

" 'Brilliant' is the word I would choose," John said complacently. He sat up and moved in close to me, but he didn't touch me. "Well,

Vicki, what do you say? Wasn't I right when I claimed no one has been hurt? Most of these jewels will end up in museums eventually, like the Hope diamond and other famous gems. The museums will get the copies—quite adequate for their purpose, which is to display objects of unusual beauty or historic interest. Luigi's copies are as good as the originals, which are, after all, only chunks of raw material. Honestly, only a stuffy pedant could claim that this is an immoral trade."

"You can't get at me that way," I said severely. "I am too old to wince at unkind names. I may be a stuffy pedant, but there are flaws in your argument. For one thing, I don't like the idea of stealing from museums."

"But we don't actually steal from the museums," John said. "The Charlemagne piece was only a sample. Museums are too dangerous. They have quite up-to-date security systems, and my crowd is an amateur lot; nothing like the people who robbed Topkapi. We don't *rob* anyone; and we only steal from people who can well afford it. They are just as dishonest as we are, or they wouldn't accept what they believe to be stolen property."

"No," I said stubbornly. "I still don't buy it."

"Why not?"

I felt my cheeks getting warm. My generation is sometimes accused of having no verbal inhibitions, and God knows I use words in ordinary conversation that would have sent Granny Andersen running for the soap, so she could wash my mouth out. But here I was, all embarrassed, blushing, at the prospect of explaining my moral standards.

"It's a question of—of integrity," I stuttered. "Honesty. Everybody lies these days, from politicians and statesmen to the people who repair my car and my radio. Everybody has a specious excuse for chiseling the other guy. It's got to stop somewhere. I know the arguments, I've heard them. 'If these people weren't basically dishonest, we wouldn't be able to cheat them; and besides, the ignorant cruds don't deserve to own beautiful things, they can't even tell the difference between the real and the fake.' The critics have been rooked too, plenty of times, but that is beside the point. The point is that if you have a skill, or a talent, or a body of knowledge, you are obliged to use it honestly. Obliged to yourself! There is no difference between a man who robs a little old lady who is living on social security and a swindler who cheats a nasty, greedy oil millionaire. He is still a crook. And I'm sick and tired of crooks."

My cheeks were flaming by the time I finished. I expected him to laugh—or put his arms around me. Men always think they can overcome a woman's scruples by fondling her.

Instead he sat quite still, his head bowed.

"If you feel that way," he said, "then I couldn't talk you out of it even if I wanted to. Shall we go to the police?"

"No," I said, with a gusty sigh. "I'm going to break this racket wide open, Moriarty. But I'll give you twenty-four hours to get lost. I owe you."

He looked up, his eyes twinkling with amusement.

"Don't think I won't take you up on it. I'm not as honorable as you are."

"But you'll have to help me. I may need a statement from you."

"I'll do better than that. I've got documentary evidence."

"What?"

"I am not quite as naïve as I appear," said John, trying, without conspicuous success, to look naïve. "I have learned to take precautions. The things I have aren't conclusive, mind you; but I have a list of names and copies of Luigi's drawings. You may need them if Pietro destroys his files and dismantles the workshop."

"They would help, certainly. I'm well aware of the fact that it is going to take some time to get the ponderous machinery of the law moving. It's a wild tale, this one."

"All right, it's a deal. Suppose I get my papers. They are in a bank on the Corso, along with some cash I had the good sense to stash away. The problem is going to be a passport."

"Good Lord, yes. You can't get out of the country without one."

"Oh, I can get out of the country, all right. But I can't get back into England unless I take risks that far outweigh the risks involved in retrieving the thing."

"Why do you want to go back to England? I would have thought you would head for the Sahara, or a South Sea island."

"No, that's stupid. The best place to lose oneself is among one's own kind. A foreigner stands out like the Eiffel Tower in another country. I've got friends at home."

"Your future movements are a matter of indifference to me," I said. "How do you propose to get your passport? I suppose it is back at the villa."

"Never mind where it is. I'll deal with it."

"If I were in your shoes," I said ominously, "I would prefer someone to know where I was at all times."

"In case I don't come out?" He grinned feebly. "What would you do, rush in with your six-guns blazing?"

"I would call the cops."

"Hmm." John considered this. "Yes, I can visualize situations in which I might find that prospect consoling. All right. I have a little pied-à-terre here in Rome. . . ."

"With half a dozen extra passports? No, never mind, don't tell me. I don't want to know about your criminal activities."

"Much better for you if you don't." He dropped his head into his hands. "Damn, my brain seems to be petrified. I could do with a few hours' sleep, after our wild night."

"That might not be such a bad idea." The nape of his neck looked thin and defenseless, like a young boy's. I wondered cynically if he was aware of the effect it had on women.

"It might not be a good idea either. We ought to move out of here." He didn't move, though; he just sat there, all hunched over, exuding stoic control and suppressed pain. "They must know the only way we could get out of the area was by car. The buses don't run that late. There isn't much through traffic in the wee small hours. . . ."

"So it might occur to Pietro to inquire about us in Tivoli," I finished the train of thought. "Yes, you're right. But we've got several hours. Our drivers won't get back to Tivoli till midmorning. What about your pied-à-terre? You didn't tell anyone where it is, I hope?"

John looked up at me. There was the funniest expression on his face for a moment. Then he shook his head.

"We needn't hurry, then," I said. "You lie down and sleep for a while. Give me some money."

"What for?" He looked at me suspiciously.

"I'm going to the *farmacia*, if I can find one that's open. And to a grocery store. A little bread, a little wine. . . . And a little penicillin."

They sell all sorts of drugs in Italy that you would need a prescription for back in the States. I told the clerk my boyfriend had fallen off his bike and hurt himself. He was very sympathetic.

I half expected John would be gone when I returned, but he was flat on his back, sleeping heavily. My first aid woke him with a vengeance. The bullet wound looked nasty in the bright light of day. He played the tight-lipped hero, stifling his groans, until I finished the bandaging and took out the hypodermic needle.

"Oh, no," he said energetically. "Where the hell did you get that?"

"They sell them over the counter," I explained, squinting professionally at the tip of the needle. "Roll over."

"Not on your life."

"I didn't think you were so modest."

"Modest, hell. If you think I'm going to let an amateur jab that thing into my defenseless backside—"

"Look, you've probably got enough germs in your bloodstream to kill a whole village. You don't want to get sick while you're on the run, do you?"

John stuck out his lower lip and pressed his body firmly into the mattress.

"Come on, don't be such a baby. I know how to do it. The clerk at the *farmacia* showed me. It's easy." I could see that my rational arguments weren't having any effect, so I tried threats. "If you don't, I am going straight out of here to the police."

If I do say so, I made quite a neat job of it.

But he carried on more about the needle than he had about being shot.

"There, now, that wasn't so bad, was it?" I said soothingly.

"I think I would prefer gangrene."

"Don't be silly. There are some pills, too. You're supposed to take one every four hours."

With a martyred groan, John hoisted himself up off the bed.

"It's late. We had better get moving."

We went to the bank first. I waited outside till John came out with a thick manila envelope.

"You got the papers?"

"Yes. Here you are. And I got some money."

"Give me some."

"The age-old feminine cry," John said disagreeably. "What do you need money for?"

"Clothes. I had three propositions while I was standing here. This skirt is too tight."

"Too tight for what? All right, perhaps that's a good idea. The honest householder whose clothesline we robbed may have reported his loss. Get something inconspicuous, please. And a hat. All that blond hair is horribly noticeable."

"What about yours?" We retreated into a

corner behind one of the marble pillars of the bank. John peeled off some bills from a roll the size of a loaf of bread, and handed them to me.

"I'll buy a hat too. Or perhaps a cassock. How do you think I would look as a Franciscan friar?"

"Unconvincing."

John glanced at his wristwatch. It must have been a good one, because it had survived water, shock, and other destructive activities.

"I'll meet you in an hour by the Ponte Milvio, this side of the river. Then we'll go have a spot of lunch."

"Good idea," I said gratefully.

"I am not thinking of your appetite, my dear. Haven't you put on a few pounds since I met you? I told you Pietro's cuisine would be disastrous for your figure. . . . My little place is in Trastevere, and there is a very inquisitive *portiere* on duty. He takes a nap after lunch, like all good Italians, so we can probably sneak in without being seen if we wait until then."

Under most circumstances I would have hooted with laughter at the idea of taking only an hour to buy a whole new outfit. That morning I did it in fifteen minutes—a green cotton skirt, a white blouse, a scarf to tie over my hair, and a shoulder purse large enough to hold John's papers. The salesgirl gave me a paper bag for my old clothes, and I dropped them into the first trash can, reminding myself that I owed a family in Tivoli a couple of new outfits as soon as I got the rest of my affairs straightened out.

I walked along the river toward the Ponte Milvio. The view was dazzling. I wondered how it could look so bright and picture-postcard pretty when I was so nervous. I was beginning to hate the dome of St. Peter's, hung up there in the sky like a swollen blimp. Upriver, the faded brownish-red cylinder of the Castel San Angelo no longer looked quaint and medieval; it reminded me of its original function—a tomb.

Now that I had time to think, away from the distracting influence of John's silver tongue, the stupidity of what I was doing over-whelmed me. I should have gone straight to the police. At least I would feel safe in a nice dirty cell. However, I was not looking forward to talking to the cops. They would think I was nuts. I was accusing one of Rome's most re-spected citizens of grand larceny; and al-though the papers John had given me were evidence of a sort, they would not appear convincing until the rest of the story I had to tell was accepted. And to explain how I had obtained possession of them, I would have to admit that I had let one of the gang make his escape. The more I thought about it, the more depressed I got.

When I reached the bridge I propped myself against the parapet, turned my back on St. Peter's, and tried to think what I ought to do. No, that isn't accurate. I knew what I ought to do. I ought to go to the telegraph-telephone office and place a call to Munich. Schmidt would believe my wild story; he would believe anything I told him, bless his heart. If the Munich police contacted their counterparts in Rome, I would be received as a young woman of some professional standing, instead of having to talk my way through fourteen layers of bureaucratic disbelief. Yes, that was the sensible thing to do. So why didn't I do it?

I didn't recognize John at first. He was wearing a hideous print sport shirt and pants that bagged around his ankles, and his nose was buried in a guidebook. The guidebook was in German, and John was the very picture of an earnest student—thick glasses, a blank, solemn expression—except for his hat. It was a straw hat, the kind Sicilian farmers put on their mules, with holes cut in the crown for the ears. He stood next to me, peering near-sightedly at the guidebook.

"If that is your idea of inconspicuous attire," I began.

"Let us eschew sarcasm for the rest of the day, shall we?" John shifted his shoulders uneasily. "I'm suffering from premonitions."

"What happened?"

"Nothing. I don't know why I'm so edgy. I have a delicate, sensitive nature, and this sort of thing is not good for me."

"Let's go eat."

"All right." He closed the book and squinted at me through his glasses. *"Fräulein, du bist sehr schön. Hast du auch Freundschaft für eine arme Studenten?"*

I took the arm he extended.

"I don't know which is more deplorable, your German or your technique."

"I do better in English."

"I've noticed that."

Trastevere is a favorite tourist area. There are a lot of charming little trattorias and res-taurants, most of them overpriced and crowded. I get hungry when I'm nervous, and I was very nervous, so I ate *tagliatelli alla bol-*

ognese, and *cotoletta alla milanese*, and something *alla romana*, and a few other odds and ends, while John sat there poking at his food with his fork.

"You had better eat," I said, through a mouthful of *insalata verde*. "Keep your strength up. Do you feel all right?"

"No, I do not. Spare me the motherly concern, will you?"

We had had to wait for a table. By the time we finished eating, it was late enough to go to John's apartment. It was on one of those quaint little side streets in Trastevere, with a fountain on the corner and a wall shrine just above. The garish statue of the Madonna had flowers at her feet. The entrance to the apartment was marked by an iron grille that opened into a courtyard. There weren't many people on the street. It was siesta time, and the shops were closed.

The courtyard was empty except for a fat black cat sleeping in a patch of sunlight. On the left of the gateway a door stood open; from it came the sound of gargantuan snores. John put his fingers to his lips and we tiptoed past. The cat opened one eye, looked at us with the ineffable contempt only cats can express with one eye, and closed it again.

There was a stairway on each of the four sides of the court, leading up to the apartments. It sounds more pretentious than it was. Everything about the place, except the cat, was weedy and shabby. The staircase smelled of garlic. We went up on tiptoe, meeting no one. On the top floor John produced his key and opened the door.

I was so on edge I half expected Bruno to come bounding out at us. But the apartment was empty. It had the dusty, unoccupied smell of a place that had been uninhabited for many days. Yet my nostrils seemed to catch another, more elusive scent, though it was almost buried under the aroma of garlic from the hall. John noticed it too. His nostrils quivered. Then he shrugged.

"My things are in the bedroom," he said softly. "Wait here."

He closed the door. It had an automatic spring lock that snapped into place. As John crossed the room I looked the place over. A cubicle at the end of the living room had a tiny refrigerator and a two burner stove. Apparently that was all there was to the place—living room and bedroom and, presumably, a bathroom.

John opened the bedroom door.

He stopped in midstride as if he had run into a wall of hard, invisible glass. I ran to him. He lifted one arm to keep me out. His muscles were as rigid as steel. I couldn't get past him, but I could see; and after the first glance I had no desire to proceed any farther.

The room had a single window and two doors, probably those of bathroom and closet. It was a small room. The bed almost filled it.

She was lying on the bed. She wore a pale-blue negligee of thin silk, all wrinkled and crushed under her, as if she had struggled. Her body was beautiful—a little too plump, but exquisitely curved. I recognized the curves, and the silky pale hair that fanned out across the pillow; but I would never have recognized her face.

Eleven

I TURNED ASIDE AND LEANED AGAINST THE doorframe, my hands over my eyes. Through the roaring in my ears I heard John's footsteps, then a series of rustling, rubbing noises, unpleasantly suggestive. Finally he spoke, in a voice I never would have recognized as his.

"It's all right. I've covered her."

I looked out of the corner of one eye. The thing on the bed was anonymous now—a long, low mound of white cotton sheeting. But it would be a long time before I could forget that hideous, bloated face. John was standing by the bed. His features were under control, but a tiny muscle in his cheek quivered like a beating pulse.

"Why?" I whispered. "Why would anybody want to kill her?"

"I don't know. She was so harmless. Stupid and vain and silly, but utterly harmless. . . . And so proud of her pretty face."

There was a note in his voice as he said that, a look on his face.... It reminded me of the way he had looked earlier that day when I had asked him whether anyone knew about his apartment.

"She knew," I said. "That's how the gang found out. You brought her here. You and she were—"

"For God's sake, do you think I'm that stupid? She was Pietro's mistress, and utterly without guile. I wouldn't risk telling her, or bringing her here."

"But you and she—"

"That makes no difference," John said. "Except, possibly, to me."

"You've got to get out of here," I exclaimed. "They put her here so that you would be blamed for her death."

"That was a mistake," John said, in the same quiet voice.

"I can give you an alibi."

He shook his head.

"She's been dead at least twelve hours, possibly longer. They will claim I killed her last evening, before they locked me in the cellar."

I understood then why he looked so sick. It could not have been easy for him to handle the cold flesh he had once caressed.

"I'm sorry," I said haltingly. "I rather liked her."

The faintest ghost of his old smile touched the corners of his pale mouth.

"So did I.... This changes the situation, Vicky. I'm too confused to think clearly, but I don't believe I can walk away from this."

"You must. I can't seem to think either.... When do you suppose they brought her here? John, you must have told her about this place. How else would they know about it?"

He started to speak. Then his jaw dropped, and the most extraordinary expression transformed his face.

Knowing what I know now, I'm not sure he would have told me the truth about the revelation that had just struck him, but I am sure that things would have worked out much more neatly for us if he had had time to think it over. But at that moment someone started knocking at the door of the apartment.

This final shock, on top of all the others, was almost too much for my bewildered brain. I can't say I was surprised—only infuriated that I had not anticipated this. If the gang wanted to incriminate John, what better way to ensure that he would be caught than by making an anonymous phone call to the police? They had laid a neat little ambush, and now we were trapped.

John slammed the bedroom door shut and—after a moment's hesitation—shoved the bed up against it.

"There's no way out," I gasped. "Maybe we should give ourselves up. John, I'll tell them—"

"Shut up." He crossed the room in a single bound and flung up the window.

The wall went straight down, three stories, to a narrow alley paved with stone.

"I am not a human fly," I said. The pounding at the outer door was now decidedly peremptory.

"Up," John said. He had his head and shoulder out of the window. I looked out.

This building wasn't one of your palatial high-ceilinged old mansions. The eaves of the roof were less than six feet above the windowsill. It still didn't strike me as such a great idea, and I was about to say so when John grabbed me around the waist.

"I hope you aren't afraid of heights," he said, and helped me out the window.

I am not afraid of heights. As I stood there, my fingers curved over the eaves, and John's arms clasping my thighs, I heard the outer door give with a crash. The pounding re-commenced, on the bedroom door.

"Get to a phone," John snapped. "Call Schmidt. Tell him everything."

I started to say something, but before I could speak he transferred his grip to my knees and heaved me up. I saw his face go dead white as his arms took my full weight. Then my elbows were over the edge of the roof. From then on it was a piece of cake. John's hands on the soles of my shoes gave one last push that took me onto the flat roof.

He had time to close the window and move away from it before the bedroom door gave way. When I peered down, I saw the window was closed, and I heard the sounds from inside the room. He put up quite a fight.

He could never have climbed onto the roof. I kept telling myself that as I scuttled across the steaming, tarred surface. Without his pushing me from below I couldn't have made it myself, and he only had one good arm. I also kept telling myself that he was safe now, in the hands of the police, and that as soon as I could reach Schmidt he would be all right. At least he wouldn't be charged with murder. I wondered if the Italian police used the third degree on suspects.

I knew he hadn't killed Helena. I couldn't think of a reason why anyone would want to kill her. Pietro wasn't the type to fly into a jealous passion, even if he had discovered she was unfaithful to him; he would just curse and shrug and dump her. There was, of course, the possibility that she had stumbled on some information that made her dangerous to the gang. But what? She wasn't awfully bright, poor girl, and I doubted that she could have learned more than John and I knew. The gang had imprisoned us when they decided we were dangerous. Perhaps they had meant to kill us. But why kill her? A handful of diamonds would have shut her mouth quite effectively—and they needn't have been real diamonds. One of Luigi's pretty copies would have fooled her nicely. No, there was no need to commit murder—unless the streak of hidden violence I had already sensed beneath the seeming harmlessness of the original plot had finally surfaced.

These ideas were swimming around in my mind, not quite as coherently as I have expressed them, as I went loping across the roofs of Trastevere like Zorro or the Scarlet Pimpernel or somebody of that ilk. Those fictitious heroes weren't as foolhardy as they appeared;

they always had a stooge down below, with a wagon filled with hay or with a snorting white stallion, so that they could drop dramatically onto the animal's back and go riding off into the sunset shouting "Vengeance," or "I will return."

I stopped and took a look around. Nobody had climbed the wall after me. Either John had convinced the policemen that he was alone, or they had concluded I had made my getaway. I felt horribly conspicuous up there, though. The apartment building was of moderate height; some of the neighboring structures were higher, some were lower, and there were balconies and windows all around. I sat down in the shade of the parapet that ran around the roof and tried to catch my breath.

I wasn't going to have any problem getting down from the roof. The old buildings of Trastevere don't boast modern luxuries like fire escapes, but they have other features that would make cat burglary a cinch. There are no yards or gardens in that crowded quarter, so the people use the roofs for out-of-doors living. Some of them were prettily arranged, with furniture and awnings and potted palm trees. Obviously there was access to the roofs from the lower floors. All I had to do was select a building at a safe distance from the one where I was sitting, and descend.

I was about to rise and go on my way when I heard noises from the street below. A car stopped with a faint squeak of tires and someone called out. I stood up and peeked over the parapet.

The car was big enough to fill the street from side to side. It was parked in front of John's apartment building, and as I watched I saw three men emerge from the courtyard. All I could see from up there were the tops of their heads and odd, foreshortened views of shoulders, but it wasn't hard to identify John. He had lost his hat, and his head flopped forward as the other two pulled him along between them. They looked like big men, but that may have been because John wasn't standing up straight. His feet dragged helplessly along the pavement as they threw him into the car. They got in after him and drove off.

I will not repeat the thoughts that passed through my mind. They were irrelevant and immaterial and sloppily sentimental.

I climbed up onto the roof of the adjoining building, pushed through a pretty little hedge of evergreens, and found myself face to face with a well-rounded Italian matron who was enjoying the sunshine. She let out a squeal when she saw me and clutched her towel to her bosom.

"Buon giorno," I said politely. *"Dovè l'uscita, per favore?"*

She just sat there with her mouth open, so I had to find the exit myself. The stairs went straight on down—and so did I, as fast as I could, expecting to hear shrieks from the roof. But she didn't yell. I guess she decided I was harmless, if eccentric.

I knew that making a call to Munich wasn't going to be easy. The intricacies of the Italian telephone system are incomprehensible to anyone who is used to the high-priced but efficient manipulations of Ma Bell. For instance— how do you make a long-distance call from a pay phone when the small change of Italy consists of dirty crumpled little paper bills? But money talks, and I had some left from what John had given me. After a long, agitated exchange with the operator, the proprietor of the tobacconist's shop finally consented to take every cent I had and let me make the call. It was about three times what a call to Alaska would have cost, but I was in a hurry.

The greedy little so-and-so hovered over me, ready to snatch the phone from my hand if I talked more than three minutes. Finally, after a series of buzzes and shrieks in three different languages, and a misconnection with a garage in downtown Frankfurt, I heard the familiar voice of Schmidt's secretary.

"Gerda," I shouted. "It's Vicky. Give me Herr—"

"Ah, Vicky. Where are you?"

"Still in Rome. Let me talk to—"

"You lucky girl." Gerda sighed, a long, expensive sigh. "How is Rome? I'll bet you have found a nice Italian friend, haven't you? Tell me what—"

"Gerda, I can't talk," I shrieked, glaring at the proprietor, who was breathing garlic over my shoulder. "Quick, let me talk to Schmidt."

"He isn't here."

"What?"

"Signorina, it is already two minutes—"

"Shut up! No, not you, Gerda."

"What did you say, Vicky?"

"Signorina, you have told me you would only speak—"

I turned away from the fat, hairy hand that was trying to grab the phone from me.

"Gerda—where is the Professor?"

"He had to go out. Tell me about the night clubs."

"Signorina!"

"When will he be back?"

"Oh, soon. Was he expecting a call from you?"

"Yes," I screamed, spinning around as the proprietor made another grab at the phone. The cord wound around my neck.

"Signorina, you cheat me! I call the police—"

"You blood-sucking leech, I paid you twice what this call will cost!"

"Vicky, who are you talking to?"

"You, unfortunately! I was supposed to call Professor Schmidt at five, Gerda. It's vital—an emergency."

"Your voice sounds funny," said Gerda interestedly.

"That's because I am being strangled by a telephone cord," I said, jabbing my elbow into the tobacconist's stomach.

Gerda giggled.

"You are so funny, Vicky. Always we say here, Vicky is the one who makes us laugh."

"*Polizia! Polizia!*"

"Who is calling the police?" Gerda asked. "Oh—oh, is it a robbery, your emergency? Vicky, you should not be calling Herr Professor Schmidt; you should telephone the police."

"Gerda," I said, between my teeth, "tell me when Professor Schmidt will be back. Tell me now, this instant, or I will send you a bomb in the mail."

"But at five, of course," said Gerda. "He said you would be calling then. Vicky, have you bought any clothes? The boutiques of Rome are famous."

I glanced over my shoulder. The tobacconist had never had any intention of calling the police, his cries had only been an attempt to scare me off. He had summoned more effective assistance. From the rear of the shop came a huge woman brandishing a frying pan. I dropped the phone and ran.

I ran all the way down the Viale Trastevere till I reached the river, not because I feared pursuit from the angry spouse of the tobacconist, but because my frustration demanded rapid movement. It was unreasonable of me to be angry with Schmidt; I couldn't expect him to sit in his office all day waiting for me to call, when I told him I would telephone at a specific hour. But now I didn't know what to do. I couldn't telephone Munich police because I had no money.

I collapsed onto one of the benches along the boulevard by the Tiber. People looked at me oddly as I sprawled there, streaming with perspiration and gasping for breath, but I didn't care. What bothered me was the fact that I wasn't thinking clearly. The situation wasn't all that bad; there was no reason for me to get in a state just because I couldn't find Schmidt. I had no watch, but I knew it must be late in the afternoon, and Schmidt would be sitting in his office like a good little spy in a couple of hours at the latest. In the meantime, I could go to the Rome police and get things started. I could call Schmidt from the station. It was the only sensible thing to do. So why did I have the feeling that time was running out—that every second now was a matter of life and death?

I respect hunches. Sometimes they are the product of irrational, neurotic fears, but I am no more neurotic than the next person, and a good many of my "premonitions" have been caused by subconscious but perfectly rational thinking. As I sat there with the cool breeze from the river fanning my hot face, I knew there was something I hadn't taken into account—some fact, observed but not yet consciously catalogued, that was responsible for my present state of uneasy tension. I put my head down into my hands, pressed my knuckles into my skull, and tried to think.

Bright against the black background of my closed eyes, in full living color, came Helena's face, black and swollen, framed by the swirling masses of her silvery hair.

I opened my eyes in a hurry. The sun was halfway down the sky, its mellow rays gilding the golden domes and spires of Rome. The shadows were lovely soft colors, not gray, but shades of blue and lavender and mauve.

Go back to Helena's death, I told myself. Never mind why she was killed; just take the fact itself and go on from there.

Once she was dead, some smart guy—The Boss, perhaps—got the idea of killing two birds with one stone. It is very difficult to pass off death by strangulation as an accident. By putting Helena's body in John's apartment they provided the police with a murderer, and discredited anything John might say about them.

John was their big problem. Not me; I couldn't prove anything. Give them a few hours in which to dismantle the workshop and hide any other incriminating evidence, and I would have a very hard time nailing them. The kidnapping, the hours of imprisonment in the cellars, the homicidal chase across the gardens—all my word against theirs. By this time the little room under Luigi's studio might be full of extra canvases, or bales of hay. Thanks to the lists John had given me, I knew the names of the collectors he had sold things to, and eventually I would be able to track down the fake jewels. But the gang didn't know I had that information. They couldn't be greatly worried about me.

John was a horse of a different color. He knew names and details, and he would talk, to clear himself of a murder charge. . . .

Alarm bells began ringing in my brain. Something didn't make sense. A murder charge might discredit John's testimony, but the police were bound to check up on the things he told them, and that wouldn't be too good for the gang. They could count on his silence if he was not provoked; he couldn't accuse them of fraud without incriminating himself. But murder . . .

They knew where his apartment was located. (Another alarm bell jangled; I ignored it, that was a side issue, and I was nose down on another trail, hoping against hope that I wouldn't arrive at the conclusion I was already anticipating.) They had taken Helena's body to the apartment, and then. . . . No. No, of course they wouldn't call the police. They could call later, if the concierge didn't discover the body, but not right away. Because there was a good chance that John would return to the apartment before he left the country. He had to have that passport. And when he returned . . .

Then I remembered. I knew what it was that had been nagging at my subconscious, the unnoticed fact that had started those alarm bells ringing. It was such a little thing—just a small metal insignia on the hood of a car. I don't care much about cars, and my attention had been focused on more important details in that scene, as John was heaved into the waiting vehicle, but the emblem had registered, all the same. The car had been a Mercedes. Romans are great believers in making a *bella figura*, but I doubted they would go so far as to buy a Mercedes for their policemen to drive around in.

I started up off that bench as if I had been stabbed, then forced myself to sit down again. I had already committed one catastrophic error of logic. From now on I had to consider all the angles.

John had never been under any illusions as to who our pursuers were, I realized that now.

I was developing a deplorable tendency to think of him as surrounded by a rosy halo of heroism, but helping me to get away hadn't been noble, it had just been common sense. Together we could never have made it. He was counting on me to come to his rescue. Why he thought he could count on it I couldn't imagine—but of course he was right. Only I didn't know how to go about it.

John had told me to call Schmidt. With my boss to back me up I could convince the Roman authorities of my bona fides much more quickly, but even assuming I could enlist police assistance, where was I supposed to look for John? They wouldn't take him to the palace or the villa. Maybe they would just kill him immediately.

Again I forced my brain away from a series of nasty technicolor images—all the possible methods of mayhem and torture John might be experiencing at this moment—and tried to think positively. They wouldn't kill him, not if he got a chance to talk first. John had a few heroic qualities—more than he liked to admit— but he also had a very devious mind. I knew the way that mind worked, and I could make a good guess as to the type of story he would tell. Incriminating documents, photographs, statements—all in my hot little hands. Yes, he would tell them that, damn his eyes, with no qualms about endangering me. As he would have said, he wasn't that noble.

I wondered why they hadn't chased after me, onto the roof. They must have known I was with John. Hell, they must have seen us go in together. Several answers suggested themselves. For one thing, they wouldn't be anxious to be seen galloping around the roofs of Rome. They had made quite a bit of noise breaking into the apartment, and it behooved them to get out in a hurry before someone called the real police.

I had it figured out now, clever me. I almost wished I hadn't. John was in the hands of Pietro and his friends, who were probably calling the police now, if they hadn't already done so, to inform them that there was a dead woman in an apartment just off the Viale Trastevere—an apartment rented by a blond Englishman. When Helena was identified, Pietro would be prepared with a convincing story. Alas, the murderous foreigner was his missing secretary, who had seduced and then murdered his mistress. The police would look for John—and they would find him. But not alive.

I couldn't sit still any longer. I started across

the bridge, weaving in and out of the traffic at top speed. No local police station for me; I was going straight to the center, on the Piazza San Vitale. It was a long walk, but I didn't have money for a taxi.

I was about halfway across the bridge when another idea hit me. It was such a brilliant idea I wondered why I hadn't thought of it before. I kept on walking, and as I went I fumbled around in the bottom of my purse. I always have odds and ends at the bottoms of my purses, even when I have owned the purse for only a few hours. I almost cheered when my fingers found a crumpled, limp scrap of paper. It was a battered hundred-lira note, which had somehow escaped my notice when the bloodsucking tobacconist was relieving me of my worldly wealth. I had just enough money for one local phone call.

I bought a *gettone* from the clerk behind the counter of the first café I came to, and dashed to the phone. There was no telephone book, of course, but the operator gave me the number. I identified myself, and was put through to the secretary.

The principessa wasn't in her office. With a little pressure I got her home address from the secretary. I don't know what I would have done if she had lived out in one of the suburbs. I didn't even have bus fare. Fortunately her house was on the Gianicolo, not far away.

I could call Schmidt on her telephone. And even if she didn't believe my story, she could vouch for me to the police. I wondered why it had taken me so long to remember that I had a prominent reference, right here in Rome.

Europeans like privacy. They don't put up cute little picket fences, they build walls. The principessa's house was a fairly modest modern structure, but the walls were very high. The gate stood invitingly open, however, and I walked along the graveled path between beds of flowers up to the front door.

Before I could search for a bell or a knocker, the door was opened by the principessa herself.

The rays of the declining sun cut straight across the garden, so that she stood pilloried against the darkness of the hall as if by a searchlight. She was wearing a long silky robe of brilliant scarlet. It was belted tightly at the waist and clung to her hips and breasts like plastic wrap. The light was not flattering to her face. I saw sagging muscles and wrinkles I had not noticed before.

"Oh," I said startled. "Did—I guess your

secretary must have told you I was coming."

"Yes."

"I'm sorry to bother you. I wouldn't have come if it hadn't been an emergency."

"That is quite all right. Do come in."

She stepped back, with a welcoming gesture. The hall inside was dusky, all the shades drawn against the heat of the day. Suddenly I was so tired my knees buckled. I caught at the door frame.

"Poor child," she said warmly. "Something has happened. Come in and tell me about it."

She put out her hand to help me. It closed over my arm with a strength I would not have suspected, and drew me in. The door closed, and we were in semi-darkness.

"This way," she said, and preceded me along the hall, past several doors that were closed or slightly ajar. She opened a door at the end of the hall. Sunlight flooded into the dark.

The *salone* was a long room with a fireplace on one wall and a series of windows looking out upon a green garden. I collapsed into the nearest chair, and Bianca went to a table. Ice tinkled.

"You need a stimulant," she said, handing me a glass.

"Thank you." I took the glass, but I was literally too bushed to raise it to my lips.

"Now tell me."

"I don't know where to start," I mumbled. "There's so much to tell you. . . . And I've got to tell it right, you have to believe me. They have him. They'll kill him, if we don't stop them."

"Him?" Her arched brows lifted. "Ah, yes. Your lover."

"He's not my lover," I said stupidly. "We never—I mean, there wasn't time!"

"No? What a pity. I assure you, you have missed a unique experience."

Her lips tilted up at the corners. . . . The Dragon Lady, the primitive goddess smiling her strange archaic smile.

All at once my exhaustion and confusion vanished. I was wide awake, enjoying a kind of mental second wind. It was a pity it hadn't happened just a few minutes earlier.

She was a canny lady. She saw my face change, and her smile stiffened.

"Ah, so you know. How, I wonder?"

"I should have known a long time ago," I said disgustedly. "I kept telling myself to sit still, stop rushing around, think. . . . I did figure most of it out. But I ignored one signal. I should have stopped to think it through all the way." I raised the glass to my lips, then did a silly double take and put it carefully down on the table. She found my caution amusing.

"I haven't tried to drug you." She smiled. "Tell me how you knew."

"It was the apartment," I explained. "John said he had never taken Helena there, and there was no reason for him to lie about it. He made no bones about the fact that . . . But somebody knew about the place. If he didn't take Helena there, he might have taken some other—let's say 'lady,' shall we, just for laughs?"

"But why me?" she asked, smiling. "I don't imagine I am the only—do let us say 'lady'— whom Sir John has distinguished with his attentions."

"Oh, for heaven's sake," I said irritably. "He may be the greatest lover since Casanova, but there are only twenty-four hours in a day. He's been in Rome for less than a week, and he has had other things to do. You and Helena—how many others could he work into his schedule? Besides, you fill a great gap in my speculations, Bianca. I wondered who the mastermind could be; you are the only person I know who is smart enough and selfish enough to organize this swindle. It had to be someone in Rome, someone close enough to the Caravaggios to know about Luigi's talent. Besides, it isn't fair to have a villain whom the reader doesn't meet till the very end. What have you done with John?"

"He is here." The amusement had left her face. She studied me curiously. "We had thought of using him as a hostage to ensure your silence. Who would have supposed you would be foolish enough to come of your own free will? Why in God's name *did* you come?"

I thought I knew the answer to that one, but it was too complicated to explain. My good old useful unconscious mind had been working again, supplying the missing answers, but working as it was against a superstructure of solid stupidity, it had only succeeded in conveying a partial message. I had thought of Bianca, but didn't realize why her name came to my mind. In the future I might do better to stop thinking altogether, and operate on sheer blind instinct. If I had a future . . .

"You don't suppose I came here like a lamb to the slaughter without taking precautions," I said, hoping I sounded more confident than I felt. "Ha, ha. Nobody would be that stupid, my dear principessa. If I don't walk out of here in five minutes, with John, you will be in trouble."

She didn't seem to be listening to me. She was sitting straight and rigid in her chair, her head slightly tilted, as if she heard sounds I couldn't hear.

"I said, you had better let us go," I repeated. "We'll give you time to make your escape. I bet you have a tidy sum stashed away. You can get halfway around the world in a few hours. You're a sensible woman, Bianca; you must realize you can't keep strewing the landscape with dead bodies."

"That is true," she murmured.

"Then . . ."

"I am sorry." She shook her head. "But I am afraid you don't understand. You have committed one serious error, my dear."

"What do you mean?"

"I mean that I am not the one who decides your fate." She leaned forward, flinging out her thin hands in a gesture that was oddly convincing in spite of its theatrical quality. "Oh, yes, I began the scheme. It was mine from the start. Can you believe that a mind of such subtlety, such—forgive my immodesty— such intelligence could commit the unforgivable blunder of destroying that poor little fool of a prostitute? That was stupid, brutal, unnecessary. You must suspect—"

"That is enough, Bianca," said a voice.

The sea-green draperies near the fireplace billowed and parted. There was a door behind them. Out he stepped, beautiful as a Michelangelo sculpture, holding his little gun. Luigi.

Twelve

◖○◗

HE LOOKED SO YOUNG. THE SULKY FROWN on his face made him appear like an unhappy child, several years younger than his real age. I couldn't believe what I had heard. If it hadn't been for the gun, I wouldn't have believed what I was seeing.

"You had better stop calling me stupid," he said, glowering at Bianca. "That was how she spoke to me. Stupid child, infant, innocent . . . me, the most important of all! Without me you could not have done it. The rest of you can be replaced; but without me, there was no plan! It took me too long to realize that. But now I am in control, I take my rightful place. And none of you will laugh at me again, do you understand?"

She was no coward, I'll say that for her. She was in greater danger than I was at that moment; he was as unstable as a two-legged table, his adolescent ego smarting and hurting.

But she didn't cower or cringe or try to apologize. She gave me a twisted smile.

"Like other tyrants, I have been supplanted, you see. A palace coup. Behold the new ruler."

"He's right, of course," I said smoothly. "Without him, you couldn't have done it. He's a genius. You know, Luigi, you could be the greatest jeweler the world has ever seen."

He liked the first part of that disingenuous speech. His scowl smoothed out as he turned toward me. But at the last sentence he shook his head.

"Jewelers are artisans, craftsmen. I am an artist. If my father had not tried to crush my talent, this would not have been necessary. I am no stupid craftsman!"

"Cellini was a maker of jewelry," I said. "Holbein designed jewels for Henry the Eighth."

"That is true," he said thoughtfully.

It was like trying to cross rotten ice; a false move, a single wrong word could break through the flimsy rapport that lay between us. He was thinking, too. He wasn't stupid, that boy, even if he was crazy.

"What was it you said to her just now?" he demanded. "About letting you go away from here? You have laid a trap. What is it?"

I hesitated. His eyes narrowed and his finger tightened on the trigger of the gun.

"I didn't understand," I said quickly. "I didn't realize you were involved, Luigi—not like this. I don't want to get you in trouble."

"Wait," he said, as if to himself. "Let me think a moment. You have some scheme. . . . Ah! The telephone calls you made. My father told me, it was to some man in Munich. That is your plan, is it not? If you don't telephone this person, he will send the police. You see, I am more clever than you thought!"

His young face beamed with pleasure. My brain knew this handsome, charming boy was a killer, but my emotions just wouldn't take it in.

"You are clever," I said. "Yes; that was my idea. But I won't—"

"Make your call." The gun dipped toward a low table that held a telephone. "Go on, make it. You will be very careful. You will say all is well. And to be sure you are careful—" He turned. "Bruno! Bring him here."

I looked at the principessa. She raised slim shoulders in that ineffable Italian shrug.

"Fat lot of help you are," I said bitterly.

The door through which Luigi had come was still open, the draperies flung back. I heard footsteps, very slow and dragging. Then John appeared, supported by Bruno. His face was bruised, and he had the makings of a magnificent black eye.

"I was questioning him," Luigi explained simply. "I wanted to know where you were hiding, with the information he had given you."

John and I contemplated one another across the length of the room. He was leaning heavily on his captor. I couldn't read his expression, his face was too battered, but his first words left me in no doubt as to his state of mind.

"You've really mucked it up this time, haven't you?"

"You might have warned me," I said, stung to the quick. "You knew—damn it, that's why you looked so funny, in the apartment, when I said—"

"Warned you! I didn't have time to take a deep breath with those gorillas battering at the door. I have heard of stupid heroines in my time, but you are the prize. I risk my life and limb to save you from violent death, and you turn right around and walk back into—"

Luigi, who had been listening with a disapproving frown, put an end to John's tirade—

which I had to admit had some justice behind it—by pointing the gun at him.

"Enough," he snapped. "That is no way to talk to a lady, especially when she has risked herself to save you. You should be ashamed."

I thought for a minute John was going to laugh, and I made a horrible grimace at him. Luigi seemed to be very sensitive about being ridiculed.

"You are right," John said, after a moment of struggle. "I apologize. Maybe we ought to try something more in keeping with this hideous farce we seem to be involved in. How about this? Oh, darling, how brave and how foolish of you! Don't you know I would rather die a thousand deaths than see a single hair of your silly little head in jeopardy?"

"But, sweetheart," I said. "I couldn't go on living if your unfortunate habit of reticence had cost you your life. I had to come, if only to die with you."

John had that effect on me anyway, but there was some method in our madness—at least, there was in mine. Maybe if we stalled long enough, Luigi would forget about the telephone call. It was an awfully dim chance. Even if Schmidt called the police promptly at five, it would take them a long time to get rolling, and even longer to extract an admission from Pietro that the principessa was one of the conspirators. In fact, the chance was so dim as to be nonexistent. If I could have thought of any sensible alternative, I would have tried it.

John had launched into another speech. I turned my wandering wits back to him in time to catch the last part of it.

". . . . the memory of your courage and unthinking devotion. Fear not, my dearest, we will not die in vain. The minions of the law will avenge us, and as my last request I would like to compose a suitable epitaph, which I feel sure our gallant adversaries will have carved on our tombstone. 'They were lovely and beautiful in their lives, and in their deaths—' "

I might have known he would get carried away and go too far. Luigi finally caught on that he was being kidded. His face darkened ominously.

"You mock me!" he exclaimed.

"Impossible," said John. "I mean, I wouldn't dream of it, Luigi."

"The telephone," said Luigi. "Call. Bruno—"

Bruno let go of John, who promptly collapsed onto the floor. Luigi snapped out an order; Bruno picked John up and dumped him into a chair. Luigi pressed the gun to John's forehead.

"Do watch your words, love," said John.

There was nothing for it but to place the call. With the perversity of things in general, this one went through as smoothly as silk. I didn't even have to penetrate the impenetrable wall of Gerda's chitchat. Schmidt answered the phone himself.

"Ah," he squeaked, as soon as I had identified myself. "There you are, Vicky. Gerda told me you had called. I am sorry I was not here. What is the emergency?"

"Oh, it's still here," I said heartily, wishing Schmidt's voice wasn't quite so shrill and penetrating. I wondered whether Luigi knew any German. The principessa probably spoke it quite well.

"You don't understand me," Schmidt said. "I hear you quite well; can you not hear me?"

"Oh, yes," I said, laughing hysterically. "I can hear you just fine. But I'm afraid you can't understand me."

"But it is an excellent connection."

"Oh, no, it isn't," I said.

"How is the case proceeding?"

"Not too well. You might even say disastrously. At the moment, that is."

"I am so sorry," Schmidt exclaimed. "But I have great faith in you, Vicky. You will solve it; I know you will."

I felt like biting the telephone. I had been as direct as I dared. I thought of referring obliquely to Herr Feder of the Munich police, but I was afraid to risk it; the principessa might know who he was, and Luigi was already uneasy; he was mouthing suggestions at me from across the room, and the muzzle of the gun was pressed so hard against John's head that it dented the skin. John didn't dare move, not even his lips, but his eyes were eloquent.

"It's all right," I said feebly. "I—good-bye, poopsie. Auf Wiedersehen. I hope."

The phone clattered as I put it back onto the stand. My hands were shaking.

"Poopsie?" Luigi repeated incredulously.

The principessa stirred.

"It is the name given him by his intimates," she said.

It took me a minute to realize what she had said, and what it meant. She met my surprised stare with a slight shake of her head. Her back was to Luigi. Her lips silently shaped a word.

I put a hand to my forehead.

"Oh," I said weakly. "I feel so strange. I think I'm going to faint."

It wasn't all an act. My knees were getting very shaky. I couldn't see what good this was going to do, but at least Bianca was on our side. Maybe she had something in mind. Mine was an absolute blank.

I fluttered lithesomely onto the sofa, and Bianca bent over me.

"She is ill," she exclaimed. "My smelling salts, Luigi—in my bathroom cabinet. And fetch a blanket from the closet, she is in shock, I think."

"Bruno—" Luigi began uncertainly.

"No, I will not have that ape touching my things! Give him your gun, if you don't trust me."

I didn't dare open my eyes, but my ears were tuned to their highest pitch. After a suspenseful moment Luigi trotted out of the room; his light, athletic footsteps could not be mistaken for anyone else's. As soon as he was gone, the principessa began to speak soothingly, as if she were trying to bring me out of my faint. But she spoke German.

"There is only one hope. We must fetch the count here. He is at the palazzo, in Rome. Think."

I groaned artistically, and muttered in the same language,

"The boy hates his father. What good—"

"These thugs—there is another man, in the hall—they will obey their master. All this happened last night after I had drugged Pietro. It was a mistake, I admit it; but they were willing to take orders from me until the boy defied me. It is a feudal feeling, you understand. He is the heir. If we can reach Pietro, he will not—"

In her distress she slipped, and mentioned a name. "Pietro" sounds the same in any language. Bruno cleared his throat.

"Why do you speak of the master? Do not speak. I do not trust you."

"She is delirious," Bianca said. "She asked for the count; she could not believe he would let this happen. You know, Bruno—"

"I obey the young master," Bruno said sullenly.

"But he has not told you to injure the signorina," John said suddenly. "He has gone to get medicine to help her. Hark—I think she calls me!"

"John," I moaned obediently. "Oh, John—"

"There, you see? Don't shoot, Bruno, old chap, I'm just going to hold her hand." He dropped to one knee beside the couch. At close range his face looked even worse. "The *Fernsprecher*, you bloody idiot," he said tenderly. *"Mio tesoro, mein Liebchen . . ."*

He broke off abruptly as Luigi came trotting back.

"What is going on?" he demanded. "Bruno, you let them speak, you let them—"

"You did not tell me they could not speak together," Bruno exclaimed.

"Never mind. You, Smythe, back to your chair. Here are the smelling salts. Is she—"

"I'm better now," I murmured. The incredible young creature was bending over me, looking genuinely worried. I smiled at him. "Thank you, Luigi. You are kind."

He helped me to sit up and hovered anxiously while Bianca waved the smelling salts under my nose. I sneezed.

"You are very good," I said, blinking at Luigi. "I know you don't want to hurt me, Luigi. I can't lie to you. I respect you too much. That call to Munich . . . it wasn't the important call. There is someone else I must reach. If I don't call him, he will open the envelope I left with him."

"Who? A lawyer?" Luigi asked. "The police?"

"A lawyer," I said.

"Then call him. Now. Quickly."

I dragged myself up off the couch and went with faltering steps toward the phone. Then a thought hit me, and I really did falter. I didn't know the number of the palazzo.

I turned a horrified face toward John, who had returned to his chair and was watching me intently.

It might not have been ESP, just plain common sense. But ever since that moment I've had a sneaking, half-shamed belief in thought transference. John folded his arms and began holding up fingers.

Thank God we're on the decimal system. I don't know how we would have managed with a system of twelves, like the Babylonians used. All eyes were on me, so nobody noticed John's contortions, which were done with considerable skill. The only number that gave him any trouble was nine.

The system worked fine, but I dialed slowly, because I needed time to think. There were so many obstacles to be overcome. The first one was the fact that Pietro probably wouldn't answer the phone himself.

He didn't. The voice was that of his butler, very smooth and impersonal. Obviously I couldn't ask for Pietro.

"This is Signorina Bliss speaking," I said slowly. "I am calling for Sir John."

Luigi, who had recovered his gun from Bruno, looked at me suspiciously. I smiled and nodded at him. After all, he couldn't know what arrangements I had made with the fictitious lawyer. It was not surprising that I should mention John's name.

The butler might or might not be in on the plot, but he certainly knew about John.

"Sir John?" he repeated, forgetting his dignity. "Is it Sir John Smythe that you speak of, signorina?"

"That's right."

"But then you will wish to speak to his Excellency."

"That's right too."

"I will call him. Please to wait, signorina."

"Thank you," I said, trying not to gasp with relief. I turned to Luigi. "The secretary is calling him to the phone."

"Be very quick," said Luigi suspiciously. "No tricks."

He pointed the gun at John, who folded his arms and tried to look inconspicuous.

Then the familiar high-pitched voice came on.

"Vicky? Vicky, is that you?"

"Yes, that's right; Signorina Bliss. I am with Sir John." Pietro started to splutter. I raised my voice and went on talking. This was the dangerous moment. There was a chance Luigi might recognize the familiar paternal shout. "No, everything is fine; we're having a drink with Bianca and some people she knows, having a nice time. . . . You must meet her some time, she's anxious to meet you. I can't talk now; my friends won't let me."

I hung up and smiled brightly at Luigi.

Perhaps he had half recognized Pietro's voice, or perhaps he was affected by the tension that gripped the rest of us. He scowled.

"That did not sound right," he said. "If you have tricked me, signorina . . ."

"I wouldn't do that," I said. "I admire you too much. Luigi, I wish you would tell me how you learned to do goldworking. You are such an all-around genius; just like Cellini, only better."

This time the flattery didn't work.

"There is no time to talk," Luigi said. "I must—I must act."

The trouble was, he didn't really know what to do. He didn't have Bianca's experience or intelligence, he had simply flipped his lid and flown into action, and a bizarre combination of circumstances had put him in temporary control of a situation he could not handle. He would be caught sooner or later, but by the time the police or his father stopped him, a lot of people would be dead—including me.

I'm sure the Freudians could glibly account for Luigi's breakdown. His father's dislike and contempt, his mother's death (I assumed she was dead, since nobody even mentioned her), the succession of cheap women who had replaced her in his father's life. . . . It doesn't matter; nobody really knows why some people crack and some don't.

"What are you going to do?" John asked, nervously eyeing the gun that was waving around six inches from his head.

"I suppose I will have to kill you," Luigi said uncertainly. "I regret, Signorina Bliss; you have been *simpatico*, but you understand—"

"There is an alternative," I said. "You've been so busy you probably haven't had time to think about it."

"What is that?" Luigi asked.

How long would it take Pietro to get from the palazzo to the Gianicolo? It was after five, rush hour in Rome; the traffic would be appalling.

"We could make a deal," I said, with my

most engaging smile. "Bianca is already involved; she doesn't want to go to the police. I'm sure she would be happy to continue in her present role—under your direction, of course. The same thing applies to—er—Sir John."

"And you, signorina?" Luigi asked. "You are a scholar, an honorable lady. You came here to stop us. My father told me so."

Here we were, back on the rotten ice. The wrong word, the false step . . . I couldn't be too obvious about my change of heart. Paradoxically, the boy's respect for me depended on that honorable facade I had presented to him.

"It is difficult for me," I said truthfully. "But there are circumstances where the ordinary rules of conduct do not apply. There are men who stand outside the conventions of society. You are such a man, Luigi. How can I presume to judge you?"

"You are right," said Luigi modestly.

He stood pondering. I risked a glance at John, and what I saw made my breath catch. He hadn't forgotten the gun, which was now dangling in perilous proximity to his body; but his eyes were narrowed with amusement. As I caught his eye it closed in a wink, and the corners of his no longer well-shaped mouth quivered.

"But the woman," Luigi said suddenly. "I killed her, you know. The filthy whore, she took my mother's jewels—lived in her room. . . . She had no right. And when she came to me, laughing at me, and yet touching me, stroking me, as if she wanted . . ." His lips curled in savage disgust. "I killed her and she deserved it. But . . . I didn't mean to, you know. I only meant to stop her, shut her dirty mouth. She was saying such things. . . ."

I forgot discretion in sheer pity.

"Luigi, I understand. You won't have to go to prison. There are doctors. You are sick, you can't help—"

"Foul," John said suddenly.

It was too late. I had seen my mistake too, but I couldn't take the words back.

"So that is what you think," Luigi whispered. "You think I am mad. You want to lock me up in a . . . They had my mother in one of those places. I remember. I remember how she wept when she came home for a visit, and my father forced her to go back. . . ."

Well, there it was. A nice facile textbook explanation. I had thought the dowager's concern for Luigi's health was only grandmotherly fussing. She had reason to worry. Whether his problem was congenital or not, having a mother who had to be confined in an institution hadn't done the boy's mental health any good.

Poor old Bruno was staring at the boy in bewilderment. Luigi's face was unrecognizable. He was crying, but the tears didn't dim his vision. The gun was pointed straight at me.

It wavered when we heard an automobile horn blare and the crunch of gravel as a heavy car screeched into the driveway. I had just time enough to damn Pietro—why hadn't he brought a couple of police cars, with sirens?—when John came up out of his chair like a jack-in-the-box. His shoulder knocked the boy's arm up, and the bullet whined over my head. Not for the first time, I regretted my inches.

The room exploded into chaos. I hit the floor, Bruno hit John, the principessa streaked toward the front door, and Luigi fumbled wildly for his gun, which he had dropped. I got to it before he did, but I needn't have worried. The boy slumped over in a sobbing heap before I plucked the weapon from under his fingers.

I pointed the gun at Bruno, who had John in a bear hug.

"Let him go," I gasped.

"Don't shoot," said Bruno and John in chorus.

The front door banged and an outraged miniature fury came stalking into the room. Pietro must have been changing when my call came. He was still in his dressing gown, a gorgeous heavy green silk affair; and I knew then why even the fatter, funnier-looking Caesars had been able to command an empire.

"Bruno," he thundered. "Drop him!"

So Bruno did. John hit the floor like a sack of wet cement. It had not been one of his better days. He was unconscious when I crawled over to him and lifted his head onto my lap.

"Where are those smelling salts?" I asked.

II

Thanks to his kindly disposition, and a five-thousand-lira bribe, the little man at the door of the terminal let me go out onto the field to make sure the crate was loaded properly. There was no mistaking which one it was; it was the biggest box on the truck, and as it passed me I heard a low grumbling sound coming from it. The vet had given Caesar a massive dose of tranquilizers, to prepare him for the flight, but even in a semiconscious state Caesar had his doubts about the whole thing.

Standing beside me, one hand in his jacket pocket and the other arm supported by a black silk sling, John looked dubiously at the crate.

"What the hell are you going to do with that monster?"

"Take long walks," I said dreamily. "Late at night. Through the slums of Munich. I can hardly wait."

"I'm glad you warned me. I shall try to limit my nocturnal activities to other cities."

"I don't suppose you would consider getting a job. An honest job."

"What, go straight? Me, the local successor to Raffles and the Saint and all those other debonair, gallant British adventurers?" John started to smile and then thought better of it; his lower lip was still a peculiar shape. "Anyhow, I can't very well quit now, with the police of at least three countries after me."

"I'm sorry," I said.

"Oh, that's quite all right. I'd hate to have your little conscience harassing you because you had failed in your duty. Are you at peace with yourself, my child?"

"Luigi is under treatment, so that's all right," I said, refusing to be baited. "My poor little conscience will be at rest once restitution is made to those stupid millionaires. But Pietro is going to weasel out of it, you watch. He'll say—"

"That he sold his jewels through an intermediary, in good faith, and had copies made because he was embarrassed to admit to the world that he had been forced to sell his family treasures. He had no idea his emissary would cheat his customers! He was quite candid about it," John said. "I was the intermediary, and I am therefore the logical scapegoat. I'd be in for it anyway, so why not take all the blame?"

"I suppose he sweetened his candor with a considerable bribe," I said.

"Oh, quite. You must admit he has behaved rather well."

"I guess I can't blame him for anything except being dishonest. Bianca was the one who wanted to have us put down."

"Oh, didn't she explain that? She never intended any such thing. Pietro misunderstood her."

"So she says. I can't think too fondly of dear Bianca. She helped us with Luigi, but only because he threatened her. I feel sorry for Pietro, though. He's awfully upset about Luigi. And with reason."

"I think the boy will be all right," John said gently.

"I wish I thought so. But everything possible will be done. Pietro really loves the kid. Too bad he didn't realize it until the damage was done."

"Didn't he offer you a little present?" John asked.

"Yes, he did. The most gorgeous necklace— emeralds and opals. Of course I couldn't take it."

"Why not?"

"It wouldn't have been ethical. Besides," I added, with a rueful laugh, "I'd never be sure whether it was real or fake."

"It was such a beautiful swindle," John murmured wistfully.

"And the only one who is going to suffer for it is you. Damn it, John, I really am sorry. I know you don't believe me, or understand, but—"

"I understand. I don't agree, but I understand. I had the same trouble myself, years ago. Only constant practice can overcome the disability. The day I forged my first check I really felt quite uncomfortable for a few hours. The second time—"

"Can't you ever stop joking?"

"No, why should I? Laughter is one of the two things that make life worthwhile. Aren't you going to ask me what the other one is?"

"That was totally meaningless," I said haughtily, lowering my eyes before his meaningful regard. "Merely an interlude. It would never have happened if you hadn't taken unfair advantage last night—flaunting your cuts and bruises and pretending to be helpless. That, and the fact that I was curious about . . ."

"About what? Don't be so mysterious."

"Never mind," I said, with my most mysterious smile. There was no sense in telling him what Bianca had said—or that I was inclined to agree with her evaluation. The man's ego was swollen to monumental proportions already.

"It was just one of those things," I repeated. "One of those crazy things . . ."

"Not for me, it wasn't. Never before in my life . . . Well, perhaps one other time, but she was Spanish, and you know how these Latin—"

"Ships that pass in the night," I said loudly. "Never to meet again . . ."

"Oh, we'll meet again," John said coolly. "I'll be in touch."

"How? One red rose, once a year?"

John forgot himself and started to laugh.

"Caught you," he said, dabbing tenderly at his lower lip. "I knew it; I knew that under that tough exterior you were a secret romantic. *The Prisoner of Zenda*, for God's sake."

"No, *Rupert of Hentzau*. And I'm not a romantic, I'm a compulsive reader. Mother has shelves of books like that—*Graustark, The Scarlet Pimpernel* . . . I read everything in the house, including old Sears, Roebuck catalogs."

"You protest too much."

The loudspeaker overhead burst into a babble of Italian, in which I caught the word "Monaco." That's Italian for "Munich."

"My flight," I said. "Good-bye."

"Time for one last passionate embrace," said John, and put his arm around me.

I braced myself; even with one arm he could literally sweep a lady off her feet, as I had good reason to know. But instead of pulling me close to him he just stood there looking into my eyes. His face was unmasked and vulnerable—and dangerously appealing. It was an unbelievably effective performance; my insides started to go soft, like melting jello. I had to remind myself that with John it was hard to tell what was real from . . . a forgery.

He brushed my lips gently with his, and stood back.

"I'll be in touch," he said again, and walked away.

"One red rose?" I called. He turned.

"Nothing so jejune. I won't tell you what the message will be. You'll know."

That was six months ago; but he was right. When the message came, I knew who it was from.

It arrived yesterday. There was no note, nothing in writing. Only a little box containing Marie Antoinette's engagement ring. Six rose-cut diamonds encircling a ten-carat sapphire.

It's in the Louvre. I think.

I have some leave time coming. Schmidt agreed I didn't have to count the Rome trip. Getting kidnapped, hit on the jaw, and threatened by a mixed-up kid with a gun is not anybody's idea of a vacation—not even Schmidt's. I've always wanted to go to Paris. They say if you stand on the Champs Élysées, sooner or later you will meet everyone you've ever known.

Here's a thrilling excerpt from the new
Amelia Peabody Mystery

HE SHALL THUNDER
IN THE SKY

Another three years have passed, and the
dark shadows of World War I loom over
the Peabody Emerson clan. As the family
gathers for a season of archaeology and
adventure, faithful readers can't help but
wonder:

RAMSES AND NEFRET—
WILL THEY, OR
WON'T THEY?

Read the Avon hardcover:
Available on May 2, 2000,
wherever books are sold

"LET US MAKE CERTAIN WE UNDERSTAND ONE another, Russell," Emerson said. "I agree to accompany you in order that I may speak with Mr. Wardani and attempt to convince him he ought to turn himself in—for his own good. I will make no promises and I will brook no interference from you. Is that clear?"

Russell looked him straight in the eye. "Yes, sir."

I had not anticipated this particular development, but I had thought something of interest might ensue, so I had come prepared. As I watched a bemused Assistant Commisioner of Police help Nefret on with her cloak, I realized she had done the same. Like my outer garment, hers was dark and plain, with no glitter of jet or crystal beads, but with a deep hood that covered her hair. I doubted she was armed, for the long knife she favored would

361

have been difficult to conceal on her person. Her skirt was straight and rather narrow, as layers of petticoats were no longer in fashion.

My own "arsenal," as Emerson terms it, was limited by the same consideration. However, my little pistol fit neatly into my bag and my parasol (crimson to match my frock) had a stout steel shaft. Not many ladies carried parasols to an evening party, but people had become accustomed to my having one always with me; it was considered an amusing eccentricity, I believe.

"I will drive us to our destination," Emerson announced, as we left the hotel. "Fortunately I brought the motorcar."

Unfortunately he had. Emerson drives like a madman and he will allow no one else to drive him. I did not express my misgivings, for I felt certain Mr. Russell would express his. After a long look at the vehicle, which was very large and very yellow, he shook his head.

"Everyone in Cairo knows that car, Professor. We want to be unobtrusive. I have a closed carriage waiting. But I wish the ladies would not—"

Nefret had already jumped into the cab. Russell sighed. He got up onto the box next to the driver and Emerson politely handed me in.

After circling the Ezbekieh Gardens the cab passed the Opera House and turned into the Muski. The hour was early for Cairo; the streets were brightly lighted and full of traffic, from camels to motorcars. The excitement that had filled me at the prospect of action began to fade. This section of Cairo was boringly bright and modern. We might have been in Bond Street or the Champs Elysée.

"We are heading toward the Khan el Khalil," I reported, peering out the window.

But we never reached it. The cab turned south, into a narrower street, and passed the Hotel du Nil before coming to a stop. Russell jumped down off the box and came to the door.

"We had best go on foot from here," he said softly. "It isn't far. Just down there."

I inspected the street he indicated. It appeared to be a cul-de-sac, only a few hundred yards long, but it was nothing like the enticingly foul areas of the Old City into which I had often ventured in search of criminals. The lighted windows of several good-sized houses shone through the dark.

"Your fugitive appears to be overly confident," I said disapprovingly. "If I hoped to elude the police I would go to earth in a less respectable neighborhood."

"On the other hand," said Emerson, taking my arm and leading me on, "they aren't as likely to look for him in a respectable neighborhood. Russell, are you sure your informant was correct?"

"No," the gentleman replied curtly. "That is why I asked you to come with me. It's the third house—that one. Ask the doorkeeper to announce you."

"And then what?" Emerson inquired. "Upon hearing our names Wardani will rush into the room and welcome us with open arms?"

"I'm sure you will think of something, Professor. If you don't, Mrs. Emerson will."

"Hmph," said Emerson.

Russell struck a match and examined his watch. "It is a quarter past ten. I'll give you half an hour."

"Hmph," Emerson repeated. "Nefret, take my other arm."

Russell withdrew into a patch of shadow and we proceeded toward the door he had indicated. The houses were fairly close together, surrounded by trees and flowering plants. "What is he going to do if we don't come out within thirty minutes?" Nefret asked in a low voice.

"Well, my dear, he would not have implied he would rush to our rescue if his men weren't already in position," Emerson replied placidly. "They are well-trained, aren't they? I've only spotted two of them."

Nefret would have stopped in her tracks if Emerson had not pulled her along. "It's a trap," she gasped. "He's using us—"

"To distract Wardani while the police break in. Certainly. What did you expect?"

Raising the heavy iron ring that served as a knocker, he beat a thunderous tattoo upon the door.

"He lied to us," Nefret muttered. "The bastard!"

"Language, Nefret," I said.

"I beg your pardon, Aunt Amelia. But he is!"

"Just a good policeman, my dear," said Emerson. He knocked again.

"What are you going to do, Professor?"

"I'll think of something. If I don't, your Aunt Amelia will."

The door swung open.

"Salaam aleikhum," said Emerson to the servant who stood on the threshold. "Announce us, if you please. Professor Emerson, Mrs. Emerson, and Miss Forth."

The whites of the man's eyes gleamed as he rolled them from Emerson to me, to Nefret. He was young, with a scanty beard and thick spectacles, and he appeared to be struck dumb and motionless by our appearance. With a muffled oath Emerson picked him up and carried him, his feet kicking feebly, into the hall.

"Close the door, Peabody," he ordered. "Be quick about it. We may not have much time."

Naturally I obeyed at once. The small room was lit by a hanging lamp. It was of copper, pierced in an intricate design, and gave little light. A carved chest against one wall and a handsome Oriental rug were the only furnishings. At the far end a flight of narrow uncarpeted stairs led up to a landing blocked by a wooden screen.

Emerson sat the servant down on the chest and went to the foot of the stairs. "Wardani!" he bellowed. "Emerson here! Come out of your hole, we must talk."

If the fugitive was anywhere within a fifty-yard radius, he must have heard. There was no immediate reaction from Wardani, if he was there, but the young servant sprang up, drew a knife from his robe, and flew at Emerson. Nefret lifted her skirts in a ladylike manner and kicked the knife from his hand.

The youth was certainly persistent; I had to whack him across the shins with my parasol before he fell down.

"Thank you, my dears," said Emerson, who had not looked round. "That settles that. He's here, all right. Upstairs?"

He had just set foot upon the first stair when two things happened. A police whistle sounded, shrill enough to penetrate even the closed door, and from behind the screen at the top of the stairs a man appeared. He wore European clothing except for low slippers of Egyptian style, and his black head was uncovered. I could not make out his features clearly; the light was poor and the dark blur of a beard covered the lower part of his face; but had I entertained any doubt as to his identity, it would have been dispelled when he vanished as suddenly as he had appeared.

Fists and feet beat on the door. Amid the shouts of the attackers I made out the voice of Thomas Russell, demanding that the door be opened at once. Emerson said, "Hell and damnation!" and thundered up the stairs, taking them three at a time. Skirts raised to her knees, Nefret bounded up after him. I followed her, hampered to some extent by the parasol, which prevented me from getting a firm grip on my skirts. As I reached the top of the stairs I heard the door give way. Whirling round, I brandished my parasol and shouted, "Stop where you are!"

Somewhat to my surprise, they did. Russell was in the lead. The small room seemed to be filled with uniforms, and I noted, more or less in passing, that the young man who had admitted us had had the good sense to make himself scarce.

"What the devil do you mean by this, Mrs. Emerson?" Russell demanded.

I did not reply, since the answer was obvious. I glanced over my shoulder.

Straight ahead a corridor lined with doors led to the back of the villa. There was an open window at the far end; before it stood the man we had followed, facing Nefret and Emerson, who had stopped halfway along the passage.

"Is that him?" Emerson demanded ungrammatically.

There was no answer from Nefret. Emerson said, "Must be. Sorry about this, Wardani. I had hoped to talk with you, but Russell had other ideas. Another time, eh? We'll hold them off while you get away. Watch out below, there may be others in the garden."

Wardani stood quite still for a moment, his

frame appearing abnormally tall and slender against the moonlit opening. Then he stepped onto the sill and swung himself out into the night.

Emerson hurried to the window. Putting out his head, he shouted, "Down there! He's gone that way!" Shouts and a loud thrashing in the shrubbery followed, and several shots rang out. One must have struck the wall near the window, for Emerson ducked back inside, swearing. After milling about in confusion, the policemen who were inside the house ran out of it, led by Russell.

I descended the stairs and went to the door, which they had left open. There appeared to be a great deal of activity going on at the back of the villa, but the street was dark and quiet. Cairenes were not inclined to interfere in other people's affairs now that the city was under virtual military occupation.

After a short interval I was joined by Emerson and Nefret.

"Where did he go?" I asked.

Emerson brushed plaster dust off his sleeve. "Onto the roof. He's an agile rascal. We may as well go back to the cab. I'll wager he's got well away by now."

Mr. Russell was quick to arrive at the same

conclusion. We had not been waiting long before he joined us.

"Eluded you, did he?" Emerson inquired. "Tsk, tsk."

"Thanks to you."

"I was of less assistance than I had hoped to be. Confound you, Russell, if you had given me five minutes more I might have been able to win his trust."

"Five minutes?" Russell repeated doubtfully.

"It would have taken Mrs. Emerson even less time. Oh, but what's the use? If you are coming with us, get in. I want to go home."

We spoke very little on the way back to the hotel. I was preoccupied with an odd idea. I had caught only a glimpse of the silhouetted figure, but for a moment I had had an eerie sense of déjà vu, as when one sees the unformed features of an infant take on a sudden and fleeting resemblance to a parent or grandparent.

Nefret had put the idea into my head. I told myself it was absurd, and yet . . . Had I not sworn that I would know Sethos at any time, in any disguise?

The carriage drew up in front of Shepheard's. Russell got down from the box and opened the door for us.

"It's still early," he said pleasantly. "Will you do me the honor of joining me in a liqueur or a glass of brandy, to prove there are no hard feelings?"

"Bah," said Emerson. But he said no more.

We made our way through the throng of flower vendors and beggars, dragomen and peddlers who surrounded the steps; and as we mounted those steps I beheld a familiar form advancing to meet us.

"Good evening, Mother," he said. "Good evening, Nefret. Good evening—"

"Ramses," I exclaimed. "What have you done now?"

It might have been more accurate to ask what someone had done to him. He had made an attempt to tidy himself, but the raised weal across his cheek was still oozing blood and the surrounding flesh was bruised and swollen.

Russell stepped back. "I must ask to be excused. Good night, Mrs. Emerson—Miss Forth—Professor."

"Snubbed again," said Ramses. "Nefret?" He offered her his arm.

"Your coat is torn," I exclaimed.

Ramses glanced at his shoulder, where a line of white showed against the black of his coat. "Damn. Excuse me, Mother. It's only a ripped seam, I believe. May we sit down before you continue your lecture?"

Nefret had not said a word. She put her hand on his arm and let him lead her to a table.

In the bright lights of the terrace I got a good look at my companions. Emerson's cravat was wildly askew—he always tugged at it when he was exasperated—and he had not got all the plaster dust off his coat. Nefret's hair was coming down, and there was a long rent in my skirt. I tucked the folds modestly about my limbs.

"Dear me," said Ramses, inspecting us. "Have you been fighting again?"

"I might reasonably ask the same of you," said his father.

"A slight accident. I've been waiting a good half hour or more," said Ramses accusingly. "The concierge informed me you had left the hotel, but since the motorcar was still here I assumed you would be back sooner or later. Might one inquire—"

"No, not yet," said Emerson. "Was it here at Shepheard's that you had your—er—accident?"

"No, sir. It was at the Club. I dined there before coming on to meet you." His lips closed tight, but Emerson continued to fix him with that cold blue stare, and after a moment he said reluctantly, "I got into a little argument."

"With whom?" his father inquired.

"Father—"

"With whom?"

"A chap named Simmons. I don't think you know him. And—well—Cartwright and Jenkins. Egyptian Army."

"Only three? Good Gad, Ramses, I had thought better of you."

"They didn't fight like gentlemen," Ramses said.

The corners of his mouth turned up a trifle. Ramses's sense of humor is decidedly odd; it is not always easy for me to ascertain whether he is attempting to be humorous.

"Are you attempting to be humorous?" I inquired.

"Yes, he is," Nefret said, before Ramses could reply. "But he is not succeeding."

Ramses caught the eye of the waiter, who hurried to him, ignoring the urgent demands of other patrons. Being snubbed by the Anglo-Egyptian community has only raised Ramses in the opinions of native Cairenes, most of whom admire him almost as much as they do his father.

"Would you like a whiskey and soda, Mother?" he asked.

"No, thank you."

"Nefret? Father? I will have one, if you don't mind."

I did mind, for I suspected he had already had more than was good for him. Catching Emerson's eye, I remained silent.

Nefret did not. "Were you drunk tonight?" she demanded.

"Not very. Where did you go with Russell?"

Emerson told him, in some detail.

"Ah," said Ramses. "So that was what he wanted. I suspected as much."

"He told us you had refused to help him find Wardani," Emerson said. "Ramses, I know you rather like the rascal—"

"My personal feelings are irrelevant." Ramses finished his whiskey. "I don't give a damn what Wardani does so long as David is not involved, and I won't use any influence I may have with Wardani to betray him to Russell."

"The Professor felt the same," Nefret said quietly. "He only wanted to talk to the man. We tried to warn him—"

"How kind. I wonder if he knows that." He

turned in his chair, looking for the waiter.

"It is time we went home," I said. "I am rather tired. Ramses? Please?"

"Yes, Mother, of course."

I let Emerson go ahead with Nefret, and asked Ramses to give me his arm. "When we get home I will rub some of Kadija's ointment onto your face," I said. "Is it very painful?"

"No. As you have so often remarked, the medicinal effects of good whiskey—"

"Ramses, what happened? That looks like the mark of a riding crop or whip."

"It was one of those fashionable little swagger sticks, I think," Ramses said. He opened the door and helped me into the tonneau.

"Three of them against one," I mused, for I now had a clear idea of what had occurred. "Contemptible! Perhaps they will be too ashamed of themselves to mention the incident."

"Everyone who was at the Club knows of it, I expect," Ramses said.

I sighed. "And everyone in Cairo will know of it tomorrow."

"No doubt," Ramses agreed, with—I could not help thinking—a certain relish.

I had never known Ramses to drink more

than he ought, or allow himself to be drawn into a vulgar brawl. Something was preying on his mind, but unless he chose to confide in me there was nothing I could do to help him.